MAUREEN CHILD

is a California native who loves to travel. Every chance they get, she and her husband are taking off on another research trip. The author of more than sixty books, Maureen loves a happy ending and still swears that she has the best job in the world. She lives in Southern California with her husband, two children and a golden retriever with delusions of grandeur. Visit Maureen's website at www.maureenchild.com.

USA TODAY Bestselling Author

Maureen Child

The Littlest Marine

The Oldest Living
Married Virgin

Harlequin®

TORONTO NEW YORK LONDON
AMSTERDAM PARIS SYDNEY HAMBURG
STOCKHOLM ATHENS TOKYO MILAN MADRID
PRAGUE WARSAW BUDAPEST AUCKLAND

Recycling programs
for this product may
not exist in your area.

ISBN-13: 978-0-373-68830-2

THE LITTLEST MARINE & THE OLDEST LIVING MARRIED VIRGIN

Copyright © 2011 by Harlequin Books S.A.

The publisher acknowledges the copyright holders
of the individual works as follows:

THE LITTLEST MARINE
Copyright © 1998 by Maureen Child

THE OLDEST LIVING MARRIED VIRGIN
Copyright © 1998 by Maureen Child

This edition published by arrangement with Harlequin Books S.A.

For questions and comments about the quality of this book
please contact us at Customer_eCare@Harlequin.ca.

® and TM are trademarks of the publisher. Trademarks indicated with ® are registered in the United States Patent and Trademark Office, the Canadian Trade Marks Office and in other countries.

www.Harlequin.com

Printed in U.S.A.

CONTENTS

THE LITTLEST MARINE

Maureen Child

To Amy J. Fetzer,
friend and fellow writer—
thanks for walking me through
life in the corps, and for a friendship
that means a lot to me.
Also, my thanks to Sergeant Major Robert Fetzer,
USMC, for allowing me to borrow his rank—and for
answering all of the questions I pestered
Amy with. Be happy in your new home, Amy.
You'll be missed.

One

The maid of honor and the best man were barely speaking. Other than that, the rehearsal of the rehearsal dinner seemed to be a success.

Still, Elizabeth Stone thought, nowhere was it written that as maid of honor she *had* to like the best man.

"So—" her sister, Terry, leaned in close to her and whispered beneath the hum of conversation around them "—what do you think of him? Wasn't I right? Isn't he perfect for you?"

The "he" being Harding Casey, best man, career Marine and the source of the jitters rattling around in the pit of Elizabeth's stomach.

She reached for her wineglass, took a slow sip of

white Zinfandel, then answered in as low pitched a voice as possible. "I'm trying *not* to think about him."

"Ooooh," the younger woman said as her eyebrows arched high on her forehead. "Sounds promising."

Frowning slightly, Elizabeth set her wineglass down and told herself that it was useless to argue with her sister over this. For almost a year, Terry had been trying to set her up with Harding Casey, her fiancé Mike's best friend. This little gathering was as close as she had come to succeeding.

"Look," Terry said quietly, "you two are going to be together practically every day for the next week. Wouldn't it make more sense if you at least *tried* to like him?"

"Now that you bring it up," Elizabeth said, half turning in her seat to face her sister squarely. "I still don't understand why I have to spend all week with the man. *You're* the one getting married."

"Yeah...." Terry's expression went soft and dreamy, and despite the fact that Elizabeth had no real desire of her own to get married, a small sliver of envy pierced her heart. What would it be like, she wondered, to feel what Terry so obviously felt for Mike?

In the next instant, though, she remembered that she wasn't interested in finding a man. She had her own life. A successful one, thanks very much, and she was already happy. Why should she go out looking for someone who would only require her to make all kinds of changes in what she considered a darn near perfect existence?

With that thought firmly in mind, she prodded her sister. "Terry, you know I'm delighted to be your maid of honor, but—"

"No *buts*," she interrupted. "You promised that you would help out, Lizzie."

"Sure, but why—"

"There's no way I can do all of the little things that have to be done this week." Terry leaned forward and clutched her sister's hand. "Come on, Lizzie. You can handle Harding for one little week, can't you?"

There was a challenge if ever she'd heard one. Grimly Elizabeth shot a covert glance at the man across from her. Black hair, cut into a military, "high and tight" haircut, strong jaw, straight nose, well-shaped mouth, and eyes blue enough to make Paul Newman's look a dingy gray. Standing up, he was six-feet-five inches of solid muscle, had a voice deep enough to cause earthquakes and made her stomach pitch with nerves and expectation with a single glance. Sure. She could handle him. No problem.

Lordy, she was in trouble. The only thing that kept her from having some serious fantasies about the man was the uniform he wore so proudly.

Muffling a sigh, she said softly, "Little sister, you should understand better than anyone else why I don't want anything to do with a military type."

Terry did nothing to hide her grumble of frustration. "Honestly, Lizzie, you would think you grew up manacled to a wall."

"Yeah. A wall that was reassigned every two or three years."

Elizabeth, known as "Lizzie" only to her family, had hated growing up as a Marine brat. Shifting from place to place, moving wherever their father's orders had taken them. Never really at home. Making new friends only to leave them behind. The one constant in her life...the one friend she had always been able to count on was Terry. Her sister. Who had grown up to fall in love with a Marine. But at least Terry's soon-to-be husband had left the Corps.

Harding Casey—Hard Case to his friends, looked like a lifer to her.

"You just hate the military."

"No, I don't," Elizabeth said. "I've just served my time, that's all. You've got to be relieved that Mike left the Corps. Admit it."

"I told him he didn't have to. It was his decision."

"A good one, too." Elizabeth reached for her wineglass, then rethought it and settled her hand in her lap. "At least you won't be stumping all around the world like Mom did, trying to make homes out of impersonal barracks buildings."

"Jeez, Lizzie—" Terry's voice dropped as she shot a quick look at the other diners to make sure no one could hear them "—you make it all sound so ugly. We had a great family. A terrific life. We've seen places most people only dream about."

True, Elizabeth thought. All true. But while they had been traveling around the world like modern-day gypsies, all Elizabeth had ever wanted was a home. A real home. One where she could stay put for more than three years. One where she could paint the walls any color she liked and not even consider who might be moving in after she'd gone.

Apparently, whatever gypsy gene Terry had inherited from their parents had bypassed Elizabeth altogether.

"Yeah," Elizabeth said quietly. "It was terrific."

Terry grinned, obviously not hearing the sarcasm. "Okay, now tell me how right I was about Harding. He *is* a babe, isn't he?"

Babe? Oh, he was more than a babe. But there was no way she would admit as much to Terry. She shot Harding Casey a covert glance only to find him watching her through those incredible eyes of his. Goose bumps raced up her arms. Her heartbeat quickened, and her palms were suddenly damp. This was no ordinary attraction to a handsome man. It was almost as if something inside her...*recognized* him. As if he was someone she had been waiting for.

Get a grip, she told herself as the ridiculous thought took root.

Grab her, Harding thought. Grab her, kiss her, caress her...he shook his head slightly in a vain attempt to rid himself of the almost-overpowering impulses throbbing inside him. Impulses that had been haunting him since meeting Elizabeth Stone three hours ago.

Her chin length, curly brown hair seemed to tempt him to spear his fingers through it. Those even darker brown eyes of hers mesmerized him, and he wanted to lose himself in their depths, discover her secrets. He called on years of strict military training to hide his reaction to her figure. A body made for lounging beside a fire and quiet, private picnics on moonlit beaches. His gaze slipped lower, and Harding felt something in his chest stagger. The deep vee neckline of her red silk blouse gaped a bit as she leaned in toward her sister. He caught a fleeting glimpse of pale ivory flesh and felt his mouth go dry.

He was in big trouble.

Harding shifted his gaze from Elizabeth's face to the bottle of beer in front of him. He *had* to quit staring at her. Curling his fingers around the still-cold bottle, he lifted it and took a long drink.

"So, you old Devil Dog," Mike Hall whispered as he leaned in close. "What do you think of our Lizzie?"

A brief smile touched Harding's lips, then faded. Devil Dog. The traditional greeting between Marines. Even though Mike had left the Corps a year ago, after meeting and falling in love with Terry, clearly the Corps hadn't left him.

But, *Lizzie?*

He risked another quick look at the woman opposite him, reminding himself not to eat her alive with his eyes. No, she was no *Lizzie*. Definitely an *Elizabeth*.

Perhaps, he mused, *Beth*.

"C'mon Hard Case," Mike prodded. "What's the verdict?"

He forced a casual shrug. "She seems…nice."

"Nice?" Mike looked at him, astonished. "A solid year I've been telling you about her, and all you can say when you finally meet her is that she seems *nice?*"

"Yeah, you told me about her." Harding snorted a smothered laugh. "You also told me about how she hated growing up in the Corps. And about all the grief she gave you when she was trying to get Terry to dump you."

Mike frowned. "She was trying to protect her sister."

"Sure, by taking shots at you and the Corps."

"She's changed. She likes me now." Mike shook his head slowly. "Finally figured out that I really do love Terry."

Fine. He could understand defending and protecting a sister. But Elizabeth Stone had made his friend miserable for almost six months. The fact that she was gorgeous didn't make up for that. He took a long swig of his beer. "Great, she likes you," he said slowly. "But she still hates the Corps."

Mike shrugged. "Terry says that Lizzie never liked all of the moving around their folks did while they were growing up. Even I don't think that's an easy way to raise kids…which is why I got out."

"I still can't believe you left."

"Twenty years was long enough for me."

"Not me," Harding said flatly. Why any man would give up the Corps for a woman was simply beyond him. The Marines had given him everything. A home. A family that included every Marine stationed anywhere in the world. A sense of belonging…of doing something for his country.

Nope. He would *never* give up all that to please a woman who would probably just end up leaving him, anyway.

"You and she would be great together."

Harding scowled. "Butt out, buddy."

"Hell, Hard Case." Mike sat back, shaking his head. "You're in worse shape than I thought."

He snapped his friend an irritated look.

Mike ignored it. "If you don't know a gorgeous, successful woman when you see her, the Corps ought to drum you out on the grounds of failing eyesight."

"Very funny."

"I'm serious."

"Will you let it go?"

"Probably not," Mike admitted.

"What is it with you and your kind?"

Mike laughed easily. He was still the only person Harding had ever known who was unimpressed with the patented Hard Case glare.

"What do you mean, my kind?"

Harding took another swallow of beer, deliberately kept his gaze from sliding toward Elizabeth and concentrated instead on getting his best friend off his back. "You Noah's Ark people."

Mike laughed again, but Harding went right on, warming to his theme.

"The minute you find somebody, you're just not happy until everyone around you is traveling in pairs." He kept his voice low so that only Mike would be able to hear him above the hum of other conversations taking place in the crowded, oceanfront restaurant. As he talked, he saw that Mike's smile faded. "You try every which way to drag the rest of us off, kicking and screaming toward some fairy-tale ending. Some of us are meant to be alone, you know. Not everybody finds happily ever after. Hell, not everyone is *looking* for it."

Leaning forward, resting his forearms on his thighs, Mike held his beer bottle cupped in both hands and stared at it thoughtfully before saying quietly, "You need more than the Corps, Hard Case."

He snorted. "Look who's talking. You joined up the same time I did. For twenty years, the Corps was enough for you."

"I retired when I found out different."

"Yeah." Harding shook his head. He still couldn't understand how a man walked away from his whole life without a backward glance. As for himself, he was in the Corps for the long haul. He already had twenty years in, and he planned on staying until they threw him out. Bodily.

How did Mike stand it, going from gunnery sergeant of a batallion to head of security for some civilian computer firm?

"There *is* life off the base," his friend commented as if reading his mind.

"Not so I've noticed."

"You know," Mike said, and this time his voice held a tinge of the old impatience, "they should have named you Hard *Head,* instead of Hard Case."

Harding swallowed a smile along with the last of his beer, then set the empty bottle down on the table.

"That's it for me," Mike said and stood up. "I know when to quit."

"Never have before," Harding pointed out.

"For tonight, Hard Case. Only for tonight." Mike grinned again and patted his friend's shoulder as he moved around the table. "But for right now, I think I'll steal a dance with your date. I'll even let you borrow my gorgeous, almost bride for a quick spin around the floor."

Mike took Elizabeth's hand and led her onto the shining wooden dance floor. And even when the rest of the wedding party left the table to join the dancers, Harding's gaze never left them.

Two

The recorded easy-rock music swelled softly, drowning conversation.

Harding looked at Terry and found her watching him with a knowing smile.

"Pretty, isn't she?"

Just what he needed—another prospective matchmaker. He shook his head and stood up. Walking to her side, he said, "Don't you start on me, too."

Terry was a good dancer, but short enough that Harding felt as though he was doubled over on the dance floor. He nodded as she talked, and hoped he wasn't agreeing to anything he would regret later. But dammit, he just couldn't seem to keep his mind on what she was saying. Instead, his gaze continued to dart around the floor, following Elizabeth and Mike's progress. She smiled at his friend, and Harding's insides tightened.

One song led into the next and he hardly noticed, until Mike and Elizabeth stopped alongside them.

"Okay, pal," Mike said. "You've had enough time with that gorgeous woman, and this one—" he jerked his head to indicate Elizabeth "—keeps begging me to get you to dance with her."

"Mike!"

Her future brother-in-law ignored her as he deftly pulled Terry into his arms and gently shoved Elizabeth at Harding. "Have fun!" he said as they danced away.

Someone bumped into her, nudging her closer to Harding.

"Nice music," she commented, and glanced around the floor at the dancing couples.

"Yes, ma'am," he said.

She winced and tilted her head back to meet his gaze. "If we're going to be together all week, Mr. Casey, I think you should know, I *hate* being called 'ma'am.'"

"Yes, ma'am," he said deliberately. "Probably as much as I hate being called, 'Mr. Casey.'"

"What should I call you," she asked, "Sergeant?"

"It's Sergeant Major, actually."

"I know."

"That's right," he said with a short nod. "Your father is a Marine."

"Was," she corrected, loudly enough to be heard over the music. "He's retired."

"Impossible," he retorted. "Once a Marine, always a Marine."

"Yeah," she admitted on a sigh. "I know."

He decided to ignore her obvious dislike for the military. "How about you call me Harding, and I'll call you Elizabeth?"

She pulled in a long, slow, deep breath, and he fought to keep his gaze from dropping to the swell of her breasts.

"Deal," she said. "'Harding.' It's an unusual name."

He shrugged. "Old English. It means 'son of the warrior.'"

She nodded. "Naturally."

An exuberant dancer bumped against her, sending her crashing into Harding's chest. She put her hands up to stop her fall, then backed away from him quickly, as if burned.

Silence again. Two people, standing in the middle of the dance floor, surrounded by whirling couples. Stupid for the two of them to simply stand there and get trampled.

He didn't have the slightest doubt that Mike and Terry were covertly watching...hoping for *something* to happen between the two of them. In fact, that was the main reason he hadn't already asked Elizabeth to dance. He knew it was just what his old pal wanted—no, expected. Mike probably figured at the same time, though, that Harding would refuse to dance just to spite him.

With that thought firmly in mind, Harding smiled to himself. He had always believed in keeping the enemy guessing.

"Would you like to dance?" They both said at the same time.

Harding looked at her, catching the amusement twinkling in her eyes, and found himself smiling in acknowledgment.

"There's no reason we shouldn't enjoy ourselves, is there?" Elizabeth asked.

"Not a single one," he agreed, and extended one hand toward her. As her palm brushed across his, that same sense of electricity shot up the length of his arm. He gritted his teeth and muttered, "Ooo-rah!"

"Oh, Lord," she groaned quietly.

He pulled her into his arms.

It felt as though she had been made just for him. Her head nestled beneath his chin, her breasts pressed to his chest, her hand resting lightly in his. Harding closed his eyes briefly and prayed for strength.

He felt solid, Elizabeth told herself. Right. Her left hand stole across his shoulder to the back of his neck. Miles of muscles, she thought, and briefly entertained the notion of seeing those muscles in their bare naked glory. Her breath caught in her throat, and her stomach did a series of somersaults. She stumbled slightly, then stepped quickly to get back into the rhythm of the dance.

Nope, she told herself firmly. She would *not* let him get to her. She had spent a whole year avoiding this man and, darn it, she wasn't about to cave in to hormones in one night.

Elizabeth's three-inch heels wobbled beneath her, and Harding's arm around her waist tightened in response. Glancing up at him, she met his smile with one of her own.

"Did I step on your toes?" he asked.

Good-looking, great body *and* polite, she thought. He knew very well he hadn't stepped on her toes. He was simply covering for her misstep.

"No," she said. "My mind must have drifted." Now that had to be the biggest understatement since Custer said, "I think I see an Indian." Of course, nowadays, it would be "Native American."

"It's been a while since I've been dancing," he said.

"Me, too." Brilliant, she thought. Nothing better than some scintillating after-dinner conversation.

"So," she said, trying to say *something* intelligent, "how long have you and Mike known each other?" She already knew the answer to that one. Hadn't she been hearing Mike sing this man's praises for the past year?

"We met in boot camp."

"Long time ago?"

"Twenty years."

Oh my, yes, this conversation was getting better and better.

He executed a smooth turn that lifted the hem of her skirt to swirl around her legs. "So what made you stay in the Marines?" she asked, needing to talk to keep her mind off other, more distracting thoughts.

"What made you decide to be a cook?"

She bristled slightly. "Chef," she said. "Pastry chef, to be specific."

His eyebrows lifted. "I stand corrected." He held her tightly to him, did a series of turns that left her breathless, then led her back into a standard waltz.

When she could speak again, she tilted her head back to look into those blue eyes of his. "I enjoy cooking. I'm good at it."

"Ditto."

"Huh?"

"I enjoy being a Marine," he explained further. "I'm good at it."

"Oh." Yep, she thought. Her father would *love* this guy. Two men cut from the same cloth, so to speak. "Where are you stationed?" she asked next.

"Camp Pendleton."

She bit her tongue to stop herself from admitting that she had already known that, too. Terry and Mike talked about him all the time. She would even be willing to bet that she knew what he had for breakfast every morning. The bridal couple had not been exactly subtle in their matchmaking efforts.

"Isn't that sort of a long drive from here?"

"With traffic, about an hour."

She nodded as his thighs moved against hers. Her brain slipped into neutral. They moved through the dancing couples with an almost magical ease. Gliding, swaying around the floor, it was as if they had been dancing together for years.

The song ended, giving way to another, and they went on, oblivious to anyone else in the room.

His legs brushed hers. He threaded his thick, callused fingers through hers, and their palms met. His hand on her waist dipped a bit, coming to rest on the curve of her behind. Everywhere he touched her, Elizabeth felt as though she was on fire.

Raw, primitive heat coursed through her body, making her heart pound and her blood race. Her breasts rubbed against his chest and her nipples tightened expectantly. A damp ache settled in her center, making her thighs tremble.

How was she supposed to ignore him if her own body was working against her?

"So," he asked suddenly, "what made you change your mind about Mike and Terry?"

She squeezed her eyes shut briefly before looking up at him. "They told you I was against their marriage?"

"Yes, ma'am."

"I was afraid of that."

"Don't worry about it," Harding told her. "Mike admired you for it even while he was complaining to me about you trying to split them up."

"He did?"

"Yeah. Said you were just trying to protect your sister." His gaze settled on her. "Loyalty's something we admire in the Corps."

She nodded, understanding completely. *"Semper fi,"* she whispered.

"You got it."

Elizabeth was a little ashamed now of the hard time she had given Mike when he and Terry had started dating. And she had to give her sister's fiancé points. He hadn't given up and he hadn't held her opposition against her. "He's a nice man."

"The best." His tone changed when he added, "I'm not so nice. You made Mike pretty miserable for a long time."

"I guess I'm not so nice, either." She stiffened in his arms. It was one thing for her to regret her own behavior privately, but she wasn't about to stand still for a lecture. "Terry's always been too romantic for her own good. I had to look out for her."

After a long moment he nodded, then asked, "And who looks out for you?"

Her stomach flip-flopped as she stared into his eyes. Ignoring it, she answered, "I do."

As another song ended, he looked down at her, his gaze clashing with hers in a silent tumult of emotion. Elizabeth drew one long, shuddering breath. What was it about this man? She wasn't a stranger to men in uniform, so that old cliché didn't hold true. Clearly then, it was something about Harding Casey himself that was getting to her. She wasn't willing to risk that. Desperately unsettled, she whispered, "I think I'd better get back home."

"Already?" That voice of his rumbled along her spine and sent every one of her nerve endings into overdrive.

Deliberately she took a step back, pulling her hand from his grasp. "Yeah. Terry wants me to run a couple of errands for her in the morning, and who knows what she and Mike will have planned for us later in the day."

"They are trying to keep us together, aren't they?"

"Terry's always been stubborn."

"Mike, too."

She nodded, telling herself to move. Get away.

Walk fast, no, *run* to a car. Any car that promised her a ride home. Why hadn't she driven herself?

Because she had listened to Terry, that's why.

"Anyway," she said, starting off the dance floor toward their table. "Thanks for the dances, and I guess I'll see you tomorrow."

"Just a minute," he said, and she glanced back to see him wind his way through the swaying couples to speak with Mike. In moments he was back again. Taking her elbow, he said, "All right, let's go."

"*Let's?* You're leaving, too?"

He shot her a quick look. "I'm taking you home."

"Oh, that's not necessary," she babbled. "I'll just grab a cab."

"Look," he said, "you came with Terry. You need a ride. I'm available. Why wait for a cab when you're ready to leave now?"

Terrific, she thought. Not just a Marine. The Sir Galahad of Marines.

"Really, Harding…" she started to say.

The sentence trailed off into silence as soon as she met his gaze. There was no way this man was going to put her in a cab.

Inhaling deeply, she blew the air out in a rush and accepted the inevitable. "Okay then, let's go."

Windows down, the cold, sea-kissed air rushed in at them as Harding steered his late-model Mustang north, up Pacific Coast Highway.

"Nice car," she said after several moments of tense silence.

"Rented," he muttered.

"Where's yours?" Elizabeth asked, more out of politeness than actual curiosity.

"Don't have one."

Conversation would be a lot simpler, she told herself, if she didn't have to practically use a bayonet to force him to contribute. He'd been a heck of a lot chattier on the dance floor, she thought. Why the change? Was it because now it was just the two of them? Well, whatever the reason, Elizabeth wasn't going to sit in stony silence the whole way home.

"You live in Huntington Beach, California and don't own a car?" she asked.

He shot her a sidelong glance. "Too much trouble to own one when you're never in one place more than a few years. All that hassle with changing license plates and registration..."

A veritable *flood* of information. And with it, memories. Her father, too, had never owned a car until he and Elizabeth's mother had retired to Florida several years before.

Harding lapsed into silence again, and she bit her tongue to keep from being the one to speak first this time. But maybe she shouldn't be so hard on him, she thought. She had seen the look on his face while they danced. She knew that he had been feeling the same overpowering attraction that she had experienced. All things considered, she thought, they were doing well indeed, having *any* sort of conversation.

Although, she told herself as miles of beach road disappeared behind them, perhaps it would be better all the way around if they each simply owned up to the truth of what was happening between them. She looked at his stoic profile and knew that if they were going to get this out into the open, it would be up to her to start the ball rolling.

Before she could change her mind, she said, "This won't work, you know."

His breath left him in a rush. He gave her a brief, half smile before turning his gaze back to the road. "I'm glad you see that, too."

"Of course I do," Elizabeth told him.

Shaking his head, he went on as if she hadn't spoken. "The last thing I need in my life is a woman."

"I feel the same way," she tossed in and was rewarded with a quizzical look. Correcting herself, she said quickly, "About a man, I mean. Particularly, a Marine."

He frowned at the distinction, then nodded and started talking again, as if her words had broken a dam that had stood as long as it was able. "I tried marriage once, you know."

"No, I didn't." Strange, that with all the infor mation Terry had given her about Harding Casey, the woman had never added the fairly pertinent point concerning a wife.

"Yeah," he said, almost to himself. "Only lasted a few months."

"What happened?"

He shrugged those massive shoulders. "She left me. Better in the end, I suppose. She couldn't handle being a Marine wife."

Unwillingly, she felt a stab of empathy for the woman. She remembered all too clearly how hard her mother had worked, trying to give her children a sense of permanence even while traipsing around the world. "It's not an easy job," she said.

He grinned, and her stomach flipped. She sincerely hoped he wouldn't do that often, during the next week they were to spend together.

"That's right. You *would* know. Your father is career Marine."

"Yeah, and you could say my mother was, too. Lord knows she should have gotten a medal or two."

He bowed his head slightly in acknowledgment. "It takes a special woman to handle it. My ex didn't like the idea of long absences, for one thing."

"Ah, deployment," she said softly, remembering all of the times her father had been gone in her life.

"Six months every eighteen months," he said.

Christmases, she thought. Summers, school plays...

"And," he went on, oblivious to her silence, "she wasn't real keen on the notion of packing up and moving every three years or so, never quite sure which base she'd end up on."

It was a hassle, she remembered, though her mother had always looked on it as another adventure. Terry, too, for that matter. Just because she herself didn't care for the life didn't mean that there weren't plenty of women who did. To be completely honest, her own mother had thrived on it.

Finally she said slowly, "You know, Harding, any woman who really loves a man can put up with just about anything. I think you just picked a lemon in the garden of love."

He came to a stop at a traffic signal and swiveled his head to look at her in the reflected yellow glow of a fog lamp streetlight.

"You're probably right," he conceded. "But either way, once was enough for me. I won't try it again. A mistake like that is hard to correct and almost impossible to forget."

The light turned green, and he stepped on the gas.

"I agree completely." Elizabeth settled back into her seat, more comfortable than she had been all night. What a relief it was to get this all into the open. "That's why I have no intention of marrying.

Especially a military man. Growing up with one was enough. Besides, I've yet to meet any man I would be interested in enough to even *think* about marriage." She turned her head to watch the black waves roll in toward shore. "And I like having my time to myself. I need it. To think. To work."

"I know just what you mean," he said. As they neared the Huntington Beach pier, he pulled the car close to the curb, threw it into Park and shut off the engine.

She looked at him. "What are you up to?"

"Not a thing, ma'am. Just thought you might like to take a little stroll on the beach before heading back to your place."

Odd, that once they had started talking openly about how neither of them was interested in the other, they were getting along great.

"You know something?" she said. "That sounds like a wonderful idea."

He got out, came around to her side and opened the door for her. Once he'd helped her out of the low-slung car, he released her hand and walked beside her as they crossed the street to the steps leading down to the sand.

"I'm really glad we had that little talk, Harding."

"I am, too, Elizabeth," he said. "We'll be spending a lot of time together this coming week, and there's no reason why we can't relax and enjoy each other's company. As friends."

Friends. Sure. Why not? They could do it. They were both grown-ups. Uncontrollable lust was for teenagers or for those who had no self-control.

"Friends," she agreed firmly. At the bottom of the steps, she paused to step out of her high heels.

"You should maybe keep those on at least until we're clear of the pier. There's probably broken glass all over the place."

She looked up at him briefly. "High heels and sand do not mix, Harding."

He nodded slowly, then before she could say another word, he bent down, scooped her up in his arms and cradled her against his chest.

Her heartbeat thundered in her ears. Her breathing shortened, became more difficult.

"What are you doing?" she managed to ask.

Grinning at her, he said, "Helping a *friend*."

"Oh." She swallowed with difficulty and ordered her pulse rate to slow down. "Okay."

Friend, she thought silently. Repeatedly. Maybe if she said it often enough, her body would start to believe it.

Three

Harding set his new "friend" down gently and took a step back from her. His body was on full alert. Hard. Ready. Eager. Too much more of this "friendship" and he would be a dead man.

Or maybe a live-and-in-pain one who wished he were dead.

But what was he thinking? He was a Marine. He had been in battle. Survived whizzing bullets and stupid recruits. Surely he could last out a week in the company of Elizabeth Stone.

He shot her a look from the corner of his eye and had to admit that a week with Elizabeth Stone was going to be much tougher on him than any enemy soldier with a puny little machine gun could be.

In silence they started walking along the shoreline. The tide was out, and the slow ripples of water surged sluggishly toward the beach, occasionally sneaking up close enough to them that the two people did a quick step to one side to stay dry.

Sea-air-scented wind ruffled across the surface of the ocean, and a full moon lent a silvery, almost bright, light to the darkness.

"What was Mike saying to you at the restaurant earlier?"

"Hmm?" He looked at her, thought for a minute, then said, "Oh."

"You don't have to say," she said with a gentle laugh. "I'll bet I could guess."

"Yes, you probably could." Chances were very good that Terry had been saying approximately the same things to her.

"Why do you suppose they're trying so hard to bring us together?"

He shrugged again. "They mean well."

"So did the Crusaders."

Harding laughed aloud at her gloomy tone as much as at her words.

She looked up at him and grinned. "I guess there really isn't anything we can do to stop them, is there?"

"Short of getting married?" he asked. "No."

"Well, as much as I love Terry," Elizabeth said,

and bent down to pick up a piece of driftwood, "I'm not willing to marry somebody just to make her happy."

"Amen."

She tossed the stick into the receding tide and stared at it for several long moments as it rocked on the rippling surface before being pulled back out to sea. "I haven't been down here in far too long," she said wistfully.

Smiling, he echoed her earlier astonishment that he hadn't owned a car. "What? You live in California and don't go to the beach?"

She caught on to what he was doing and said, "Touché."

They started strolling again in a companionable silence. An older couple, walking a tiny dog on a long leash, passed them with a muttered greeting. From far off down the beach they saw the wavering, indistinct glow of small fires burning in the cement fire rings. On the clear, still air, laughter and snatches of campfire songs drifted to them.

But Harding paid no attention to any of it. Instead, his concentration was focused on the woman walking alongside him, carrying her high heels in one hand. He watched the soft breeze lift her dark brown curls off her neck and thought he caught the scent of her perfume. Something light and feminine and alluring, it sent daggers of need digging into his guts.

Damn, what if he had listened to Mike a year ago when his friend had first suggested he meet Elizabeth Stone? What might his life have been like these past twelve months? Torture? Or bliss?

Torture, most definitely.

Because no matter how much he wanted her… no matter how powerful the attraction was between them…he wouldn't allow anything to come of it.

In fact, he couldn't imagine why Mike and Terry had thought to pair the two of them up, anyway. They couldn't be more different. He snorted a choked laugh and shook his head.

"What's so funny?" she asked. Reaching up, she plucked at a long strand of windblown hair that had attached itself to her eyelashes.

"Just thinking," he answered. "Mike and Terry must have been nuts to believe you and I—"

"Nuts," she agreed.

"Me, a career Marine, and—" he stopped, cocked his head at her and wondered aloud "—what is it you're called? The Princess of Party Cooking?"

Now Elizabeth laughed. "Some reviewer gave me that tag a couple of years ago." She shrugged. "My publisher loved it and ran with it. The name stuck. But all I really am is a pastry chef."

"Who writes bestselling cookbooks."

"*Co*writes," she countered, holding up one finger to admonish him. "Which means, I supply the recipes and a few humorous stories about some of my more memorable disasters and Vicki, the writer I work with, puts it all together and makes me sound brilliant."

Harding looked at her, surprise gleaming in his eyes. "Not many people would admit that they don't actually write their own books."

She smiled at him. "No point in denying it. Vicki's name is right there on the cover."

"And whose idea was that?"

Elizabeth's gaze shifted to the darkness of the sea. "Mine," she admitted. "I can cook, but I can't write, and I don't want to take bows for something I didn't do."

He knew lots of people who wouldn't have been bothered by that in the least. There was more to Elizabeth Stone than just the way she kicked his hormones into high gear.

Moving away from those ideas, he instead focused on what he had been thinking before. "Still, what could a Marine and a 'princess' possibly have in common?"

"Not much, besides knowing two people with way too much time on their hands."

"True."

She swiveled her head to look at him, and one glance from those dark, fathomless eyes of hers and he felt as keyed up and tightly strung as he did the night before a battle.

He sucked in a quick, deep breath and saw her do the same before she turned away abruptly.

Elizabeth bent down, picked up another, longer stick and turned her back on the ocean.

"What are you doing?" he asked, silently grateful that she had broken eye contact.

"Something I haven't done in years," she said, and started writing her name in the water-soaked sand at the edge of the tide.

He stood to one side and watched her.

When she had finished with her own name, she went on, inscribing his name, using the last *H* in Elizabeth as the first *H* in Harding. Her task complete, she tossed the stick aside and stood back, admiring her handiwork. Then she looked up at him expectantly.

"Very nice," he said. "Until the tide shifts." Then the ocean would run in, obliterating their names like an eraser moving over a chalkboard.

"Nothing is forever," she told him, and as she spoke a rogue surge of water rushed across her ankles and sluiced past her feet. The seawater rippled across their names in a haphazard pattern, and in a moment most of the script was gone.

"See?" she said with a lightness that didn't quite cover the note of disappointment in her voice. Then, glancing down at her soaking wet nylons, she grimaced and walked away from the ocean's edge, closer to him. "Hold these for a minute, will you?" she asked, and handed him her heels.

As she lifted the hem of her already short skirt, he tensed and asked, "What are you doing?"

Bent at the waist, she looked up at him briefly. "I'm just going to take off these nylons."

"Out here?" Did his voice sound as strained to her as it did to him?

"There's nobody around but you and me."

That only made things worse.

Harding took in another deep gulp of cold air and hoped it would do something to stop the flames erupting inside him. As a gentleman should, he half turned, to give her some privacy. Besides, there was no point in torturing himself.

She saw the movement and chuckled. "Don't worry about it, Harding. They're not panty hose."

Oh, God, he thought, closing his eyes on a quiet groan. *Garters?*

"They're just thigh-highs," she went on, when he still didn't turn back toward her.

Thigh-highs. *Black* thigh-highs. His body tightened at the mental image of lace and sheer black fabric hugging and caressing those long legs of hers.

"For heaven's sake, Harding," she said. "Look at me. You would see more flesh if I was wearing shorts!"

He turned around, then, and bit back another,

deeper groan. It was worse than he had thought. Thigh-highs indeed. Apparently Elizabeth Stone was completely unaware of just how seductive she looked.

The wide, black lace elastic band hugged the creamy white flesh of her upper thigh and gave way to sheer, black silk covering the rest of her leg. Slowly she smoothed her palms along the stocking, rolling the fragile material beneath her fingertips, exposing her pale white skin, inch by tantalizing inch.

Mouth dry, throat tight, he watched her, unable and unwilling to look away. Her hands moved down her leg, and his palms itched to help her.

By the time she had removed the first stocking, his breathing was strangled. When she started in on the second, bending over slowly to complete the task, his gaze shifted to the curve of her behind beneath the short, tight black skirt.

His fingers tightened around the shoes he held in one hand until he felt the tips of the high heels dig into his palm. He deliberately concentrated on that small discomfort in order to take his mind off the nearly overwhelming pain of his aching groin.

Finally she straightened up and tossed her hair back out of her eyes. "That feels better," she said, balling her wet nylons up in her hands. "Nothing worse than soggy stockings."

"Uh-huh." He could think of a few things worse.

"Harding?"

He swallowed heavily. "Yes, ma'am?"

"You okay?"

"Yeah," he ground out. "I'm fine." Or he would be as soon as he could get back to the base and stand under a cold shower for two or three hours. Or days.

"You don't *look* fine."

"Forget it."

She blinked, surprised at his gruff tone. "Okay."

"Look," he said, more hotly than he had planned, "we talked about this. How whatever it was we're feeling for each other won't work."

"So?"

"So, I'd appreciate you not making this any harder than it already is."

"I made it harder by taking off my stockings?"

Rock hard, he thought.

"Jeez, Harding, relax." She shook her head and turned her face into the wind. "We're both adults. We can handle this...attraction without acting on it."

"I didn't say I was going to act on it. I *said* you were making things more difficult than they had to be."

"Aren't you overreacting just a little?"

"I don't think so."

"Maybe," she said with a long look at his obviously uncomfortable expression, "you'd better take me back home, then."

Now *that* sounded like a plan. Get out from under the damn full moon, away from the soft, sea-scented breezes and the lulling, hypnotic rush of the ocean. Once distanced from this romantic setting, it would be easier to stick to the friendship they had so recently agreed upon.

"That's probably a good idea," he said abruptly.

"I'll take those," she muttered, and reached for her shoes.

She moved in close, destroying his good intentions. Her scent surrounded him. Her warmth called to him, and he couldn't withstand it. His resolve disappeared. Instead of giving her the shoes, he dropped them to the sand and grabbed her hand. Harding felt it again immediately. That sudden jolt of awareness. Of heat. Electricity. And she felt it, too. He could see it in her eyes.

Instinctively he pulled her closer. Without a word she moved into the circle of his arms and tilted her head back for his kiss. Moonlight dusted her features, and even as he bent to claim her mouth, he knew he shouldn't. Knew that once the line was crossed it would be impossible to go back.

The wind picked up, and the roar of the ocean sounded all around them.

He brushed his lips across hers gently, once. Twice. Then his mouth came down on hers with a hard, steady pressure, and a crashing wave of sensation fell on him. As if the night sky were lit up with fireworks, he felt himself come to life. He felt an intense connection with this woman, and when she suddenly broke away and took a staggering step back from him, it was as if he'd been dunked in a pool of ice water.

Breathless and stunned at her reaction to a simple kiss, Elizabeth took a step away from the man who had just touched her so deeply. It was small consolation to see her own shocked feelings etched into the Marine's stoic features.

"All right," she whispered, and started walking backward, keeping a wary eye on him. "Maybe you weren't overreacting." She shook her head and added, "We can't do this, Harding. *I* can't do this." Then she turned and ran across the sand. She raced toward the pier and the street beyond where there were lights, people and a car that could carry her back to her house.

To safety.

She heard him running after her and knew that she would never be able to beat him. He had years of training behind him while all she had to show for exercise was a folded-up treadmill that made an excellent silent butler.

Before she got close to the steps leading back to the street, Harding caught up with her. Grabbing her upper arm, he turned her around to face him.

"Why did you run?"

Why was he pretending he didn't know the answer to that?

"You know why."

He reached up and ran one hand across his severe military haircut. "You don't have to run from me," he growled. "I wouldn't hurt you."

"I know that," she snapped, irritated with herself more than him. Good Lord, she was thirty-two years old. She had been kissed before. Often. Why was she reacting like a giddy teenager on her first date?

Because, a voice in the back of her mind answered, she had never been kissed like *that* before.

"Look, Harding," she said, trying to explain something that just might prove to be unexplainable. "I wasn't scared. Exactly. Just...surprised." Stunned would have been a better word. "I guess I wasn't really running away from you—it was more like running from whatever it is that happens between us whenever we get too close."

He nodded abruptly, his mouth thinning into a grim line. "I know the feeling."

"You were right when you said we shouldn't make this more difficult than it already is." Elizabeth forced a deep breath of cold air into her lungs. "Why start something that neither one of us has any intention of finishing?"

He looked at her for a long, slow minute. "The only reason I can think of, is that Marines don't run."

She choked out a laugh. "I'm not a Marine."

"No," he said and pulled her close to him. "But I am."

This time, when their lips met, Elizabeth was prepared for the incredible sensations skittering inside her. At least she thought she was. She gasped as the opening ripples of excitement coursed through her, then she gave herself up to the inevitable. She had known from the moment she had first looked into his blue eyes that this kiss was coming, and instead of worrying about the repercussions, gave herself up to the wonder of it.

He parted her lips with the tip of his tongue, and when she opened for him, he plundered her mouth like an invading army. Daggers of desire pricked at her insides, and when he held her tighter, closer, she pressed herself into him, flattening her breasts against his chest.

He cupped the back of her head, his fingers combing through her hair and she reached up, wrapped her arms around his neck and held on as if afraid she was about to slip off the edge of the world. His right hand moved across her back, down her spine to the curve of her bottom. He followed that curve and held her against his hardness. An answering need blossomed inside her, and she moaned gently.

Tearing his mouth from hers, Harding dipped his head to lavish damp kisses along the length of her neck. His arms tightened around her like twin bands of twisted steel. Desire screamed inside her. The feeling was more, so much more than she had expected. Elizabeth had the wild, insane desire to rip off her clothes and offer herself to him there. In the sand.

She craved his touch more than her next breath.

"Harding," she whispered, "I want—"

"Way to go, soldier boy!" A loud voice, filled with laughter, splintered the moment.

Harding straightened abruptly, pulled her close to him protectively and shielded her while she pulled herself together.

Laughter floated down to them from the pier above, and after a moment or two, shuffling footsteps told them that their audience had moved on.

She buried her face against Harding's chest.

"Damn teenagers," he muttered. "They're everywhere. What I wouldn't give to get that kid in boot camp."

"Good God," Elizabeth groaned, her voice muffled. "What were we doing...thinking?"

"Thinking didn't have much to do with what we were doing," he told her and stood stock-still for a long moment, keeping his arms firmly around her. Finally though, he said, "C'mon. I'll take you back to your place."

Elizabeth drew in a long, shuddering breath as he lifted her into his arms again to carry her across the glass-littered sand. Ridiculous, but she almost enjoyed being carried around like some modern-day Jane to his Tarzan. She had never known a man strong enough to lift her not-so-small form as easily as he would have a child.

Her arm around his shoulders, she tried not to think about the hard, corded muscles lying just beneath his uniform. Or about how much she would love to feel his naked strength beneath her fingertips.

When she thought she could speak without her voice shaking, she tried to lighten the incredibly tension-filled moment. "I thought you said Marines don't run?"

He glanced at her, then shifted his gaze to a point above her head. "They don't. But they have been known to make a strategic retreat now and again... when absolutely necessary."

"Like now?"

"Princess, *exactly* like now."

Four

"Look, Harding," she said and stared up into those lake blue eyes of his. "I don't think this friendship thing is going to work."

"Probably not," he conceded as he set her down on the sidewalk.

Surprised, she nodded at him thoughtfully and pushed the button for the Walk signal. "Somehow, I had the feeling you were going to prove to be one of those die-hard Marines."

"Meaning what, exactly?" The light changed. He took her elbow and guided her across Pacific Coast Highway.

"Meaning," she said, forcing herself to keep up

with his much-longer stride, "not knowing when to give up. Surrender."

He stopped alongside the car and looked down at her. One corner of his mouth quirked, and her insides jumped. Ignoring the sudden rush of adrenaline to the pit of her stomach, Elizabeth went on. "I mean, since we both know that friendship has already been blown out of the water, we can simply call Mike and Terry and tell them that the deal's off. We can each help out…we're just not going to be doing it together."

"Nope."

It took a moment for that one word to sink in.

"What do you mean, 'nope'?"

"I mean," he said, opening the car door for her, "I have no intention of telling Mike that I can't handle being around you for a week."

"But—"

"Princess," he said, "I've been in battle. I've been stranded in jungles with nothing to eat but my own shoes." His voice deepened as he loomed over her, and Elizabeth's head fell back on her neck as she struggled to maintain eye contact. "I've taken lazy, unmotivated teenagers and made them into first-class Marines. I've been in charge of *hundreds* of men and tons of equipment."

"So?" She managed to ask.

"So, I'm damn sure *not* running up the white flag because of a couple of kisses." That said, he jerked his head toward the car. "Now, get in and I'll take you home."

Bristling at the command, Elizabeth pitched her wet shoes and stockings into the car, planted her fists on her hips and gave him a glare guaranteed to melt stone. "We're not leaving yet, Marine."

His black eyebrows lifted.

Who the hell did he think he was? Did he really think that *he* could ignore her better than *she* could ignore him? This was precisely why she had always steered clear of the military type. Giving orders was second nature to them. Well, if he thought he could tell *her* to do *anything,* he had a big surprise coming.

Poking him in the chest with the tip of her index finger, she went on. "I've never been in battle or a jungle. But I have faced down a hungry crowd with nothing to feed them but a ruined soufflé and overdone bread. I've met deadlines, done book tours that left me so tired, death looked like a vacation, and, mister, there isn't a Marine *alive* who can outlast *me*."

He opened his mouth to speak, but she cut him off.

"And as for those kisses, don't flatter yourself. I've been kissed before, buster—and if that's the best you've got, believe me, I'll be able to keep from hurling myself at your manly chest."

A glimmer of a smile raced across his features, then disappeared.

"Manly chest, eh?"

"A figure of speech," she said. A *true* figure of speech, but that was beside the point. Also beside the point was the fact that she had lied about the potency of his kisses. Sure she had been kissed before. But never like that.

"You finished?" he asked.

"For now."

He nodded slowly. "Fine, I just want to say one thing."

"What?"

"You may be tougher than you look, princess. But *this* Marine can outlast *you* anytime."

"Humph!" She'd lost track of exactly what they were talking about here, so she figured that answer was her only safe one.

"Then we're agreed?" he asked.

"Agreed," she snapped, then added, "Agreed on what?"

"That a couple of kisses are no reason to admit defeat."

"Oh. Sure."

"Fine, then, it's settled." He set one hand on the top of the car door and ushered her inside with the other. "We can't be friends, but we can last out the week in each other's company."

"No problem," she said firmly, and settled back

in the seat as he closed the car door and walked around to the other side. He slid into the driver's seat, jammed the key into the ignition, then looked at her before firing up the engine.

Blue eyes locked with brown. Elizabeth's heartbeat jumped into high gear. The palms of her hands were sweaty, and deep within her a core of heat burst into flame.

"No problem," she whispered.

"Right," he said, with as little conviction as she felt.

The South Coast Plaza mall was packed. Saturday-morning crowds teemed through the cavernous place. Moms pushing strollers, crying babies, lounging teenagers, professional types with cell phones glued to their ears all competed for walking room.

Elizabeth came to an abrupt stop beside the escalator. A stroller clipped her heel and rolled on past without even slowing down. She winced, shot the oblivious mother a glare, then turned back to the man on her right.

Harding looked hopelessly out of place. That spit-and-polish Marine exterior stood out like several sore thumbs, in the midst of suburbia. She shook her head as she looked up—*way* up at him. Without the benefit of her three-inch heels, Elizabeth felt short for the first time in her life.

Mercy, he was gorgeous. Just for a moment she allowed herself to remember how it had felt to be cradled against that massive chest of his. Memories rushed into her brain. The strength of his arms. The warmth of his kiss.

The abrupt way he'd left her at her front door the night before.

She drew one deep, shaky breath. This was going to be a long week.

"So what's first?" Harding asked, startling Elizabeth out of her reverie.

"Oh!" She glanced down at the list in her hand. Her sister, Terry, was nothing if not efficient. On the small memo pad, there was a different list for every day during this last hectic week before the wedding. Looking under Saturday, Elizabeth read out loud, "Pick up going-away dress at the Flim Flam."

"Flim Flam?" Harding echoed.

"A new dress shop here in the mall."

He nodded. "Anything else?"

"Yeah, she wants us to pick up Mike's wedding present at Macy's."

"Where's that?" Harding asked, staring into the distance.

"At the other end of the mall." Elizabeth checked her watch. They had plenty of time, actually, but it gave her something to do. "Why don't you go to Macy's, I'll pick up her dress then meet you at the coffee bar."

"All right," he said. "What am I picking up?"

She laughed shortly. "Sorry. Go to the jewelry counter. Terry bought him a watch last week, and the engraving is finally done. They'll be holding it for her there." She dug into her shoulder bag and came up with a receipt. Handing it to him, she said, "Show them this. You shouldn't have a problem. It's already paid for."

He glanced at the paper, folded it neatly into fours, then tucked it into his pants pocket.

"Macy's is right at the end of that concourse," she told him, pointing off to the left.

He smirked at her. "I think I'll be able to find it."

She shrugged. "Okay then, see you at the coffee bar in one hour."

Elizabeth turned to go, but he grabbed her hand, pulling her back to his side. Carefully he checked the time on her wristwatch, then adjusted hers to match his exactly.

"Synchronizing our watches?" she said on a muffled laugh.

"Yep." He gave her a brief nod, then said, "Coffee bar, eleven hundred thirty hours."

She stifled the groan building in her chest. Memories of all the years she had spent living according to military time flashed through her brain and left again just as quickly. It didn't matter. She was through with all of that. She and Harding were

only going to be around each other for a week—
there was no point in arguing with him all the
time.

"Fine. Eleven-thirty. The coffee bar's on the
second level," she said, "right next to—"

"I'll find it."

"But this mall is really big, Harding. It can be
very confusing." Elizabeth shopped there all the
time, and even she had been known to lose her
bearings a time or two.

He gave her a slow, patronizing, infuriating smile
as he shook his head. "Elizabeth, in the Corps, I am
what is known as a pathfinder."

That was a new one to her. One eyebrow rose as
she asked, "As in *Last of the Mohicans?*"

He frowned briefly. "As in I am trained to be
able to survive in a jungle with nothing but a piece
of string and a knife. I *think* I'll be able to find my
way around a shopping center."

She felt she should point out that very few jungles
are equipped with banks of elevators, hundreds
of people, strolling musicians, a double-decker
carousel and dozens of corridors, each of them just
like the last. But...who was she to argue with a
pathfinder?

"Okay, Hawkeye," Elizabeth said with a half
smile. "Go to it! On my mark, I'll meet you in one
hour." She looked down at her watch, snapped out

"Mark!" then turned on her heel and disappeared into the crowds.

Amazing. One minute she was there and the next she wasn't. In the constantly shifting crowd of people, he couldn't even catch a glimpse of her. He didn't even want to *think* about what this place must be like during the Christmas shopping rush.

Minutes ticked by before he told himself to get moving. He wanted to be sitting at that blasted coffee bar having a nice, leisurely snack by the time she arrived. Mumbling "Excuse me" to the elderly woman who crashed right into him, Harding stepped onto the escalator and descended into Suburban Hell.

Fifty-five minutes later, Harding tightened his grip on the small Macy's package in his hand and started down yet another corridor. He glanced from storefront to storefront, sure he'd been that way before. Frowning, he came to a dead stop in front of a kitchenware shop. Dammit, he recognized that three-foot-tall chicken in the display window. Either he was walking in circles or there was more than *one* chicken wearing a chef's hat decorated with big red hearts somewhere in this blasted mall.

Scowling furiously, he glanced at his wristwatch. Nearly time. So much for having a leisurely snack while waiting for Elizabeth. At this rate he'd be lucky to find the damned coffee bar before the wedding.

A logical voice in his head told him he should just find a directory kiosk. He seemed to recall seeing one…somewhere. But that went sorely against the grain. Of course, he could simply ask someone for directions. He shook his head at the thought. No. He'd made his brag. He'd told Elizabeth that he could find his way through this overpriced maze, and blast it, that's just what he was going to do.

He still had five full minutes. Plenty of time. He would not be beaten by a shopping mall!

"Excuse me, private," a soft voice said from behind him.

Private? He stiffened at the insult, turned around and looked down into the sharp green eyes of a woman at least seventy years old. Her silvery hair was permed and sprayed into submission, and her bright pink sweatshirt had the words Mall Walker emblazoned across the front. He assumed the term had nothing in common with another well-known phrase… *street walker.*

"Yes, ma'am?" he asked.

"Don't you look handsome?" she said softly, with a slow shake of her head. "My, I always *did* love a Marine uniform better than just about anything…."

"Thank you, ma'am," he started, already looking for a chance to get away. He had only five minutes to find that coffee shop. Harding glanced at the short woman planted firmly in front of him. What was it about a uniform that got people talking?

"You know, my dear late husband, Edgar, was a Marine."

"Yes, ma'am?" He gave a mental sigh and wondered how he would be able to escape without hurting the woman's feelings. He didn't want to be rude, but he simply didn't have the time to listen to a stream of memories from a military admirer.

"Oh my, yes. He was a private, too."

He winced inwardly at the slap at his rank. It couldn't hurt to straighten her out a little. "Actually ma'am, I'm a Sergeant Major."

"No matter." She waved one hand at him and gave him a small smile. "My Edgar was a part of D Day, you know."

"Really?" People streamed past him like a swiftly moving river rushing past a rock. A rock buried deep in the mud and moving nowhere. Fast. He resisted looking at his watch again.

"Oh, yes. Why, if it hadn't been for my Edgar, who knows what might have happened on that horrible day." She paused, and when he didn't prompt her, she added, "World War II? D Day? The Normandy Invasion? Surely they teach privates about World War II these days."

"Yes, ma'am," he said, and bit down on the inside of his cheek to keep from smiling wryly. "I believe it's been mentioned a time or two."

"Well, thank heavens. I'd hate to think Edgar's sacrifice was in vain, you know."

Sacrifice? Immediately contrite that he hadn't given her his complete attention, he told himself that the widow of a fellow Marine deserved better. Quietly Harding said, "I'm sorry ma'am. He died at Normandy, then?"

She jerked her head back and stared at him, horrified. "I should say not! Why he's at the Golf Pro shop this very minute."

Now he really *was* lost. "But you said 'his sacrifice'?"

She frowned at him. "My Edgar was deathly ill at the time…his sinuses have always been a source of travail for the dear man…yet he put his own misery aside in order to drive the men to the harbor where they boarded the ships to mount the invasion. If not for my Edgar—" she shook her head slowly "—why, everything might have turned out differently."

Oh, for— Giving her a polite nod, he sent his best to Edgar and made his escape as quickly as possible. Pick a direction. Any direction. Some pathfinder, he told himself. Yet in his own defense, he had to admit that the people now rushing through familiar territory would be completely lost in a jungle. He, on the other hand, would shine in such a situation.

He glanced at his watch and grumbled in irritation. Eleven thirty-five. Shifting his gaze to sweep across the crowded mall, he was almost ready to cry defeat and look for a directory when he had a better idea.

Casually he strolled toward a group of four teenage girls and stopped just a foot or two short of them. Then he wondered aloud, "Now where was that coffee bar?"

One of the girls giggled and elbowed her friend who was staring at Harding in wide-eyed appreciation. "Are you looking for Lola's Latte?" the giggler asked.

Lola? Latte? "Would that be the coffee bar on the second level?" he asked, just to make sure.

"That's the one," another girl piped up.

"Then, yes," Harding told them. "I am looking for Lola's." He swallowed what was left of his pride and asked, "Do you know where it is?"

"Sure," the giggler spoke up again, pushed past her friends and sidled up close to Harding.

She couldn't have been more than seventeen, so he took a hasty step back. Quite a day. First Grandma, then a kid.

"Go right along here," the girl said, "turn right at the Pokey Puppy, go past the Discovery store and Lola's is right next to Potato Pete's."

Potato, Pokey, Discovery, he had to get out of this place. "Thanks, ladies," he said, and started moving, ignoring the giggler's heavy sigh as he brushed past her. He was already late, but if he hurried, maybe he'd get lucky. Maybe Elizabeth had gotten held up at the dress shop. Maybe he would still beat her to their appointment.

Then again, maybe not.

He slowed down purposely when he saw her sitting at a small round table outside Lola's, leisurely sipping from an oversize yellow coffee cup. Bad enough that he was late. No sense in looking like he was running.

In the instant before she saw him, Harding took a long minute to appreciate the picture she made.

No one should be able to look as good in jeans as she did in black silk. But somehow, Elizabeth managed it. Those worn, faded Levi's of hers hugged her long, slender legs like the hands of a familiar lover. Her tight blue T-shirt clung to her full breasts, defining a figure made to drive a man crazy. She shook her soft brown hair back from her face, and her gold hoop earrings glinted in the sunshine spilling in from the overhead skylight.

Harding gritted his teeth. He'd already had one long, sleepless night, thanks to memories of her and the kisses they'd shared on a moonlit beach. Studying her in such close detail wasn't helping any.

She spotted him and raised a hand to wave at him. He swallowed the groan rising in his chest as his gaze locked on the smooth expanse of lightly tanned skin exposed between the hem of her shirt and the waistband of her jeans.

He walked to the coffee bar as quickly as he could, ignoring the ache in his groin caused by just the sight of her. He had the distinct feeling that as long as he was around Elizabeth Stone, he wouldn't be walking in comfort.

A smile curved one corner of her mouth as he dropped into the chair opposite her. Glancing first at her watch, she looked at him through amused brown eyes. "Eleven forty-five, Sergeant Major."

"I know." He shifted in the chair, set the Macy's bag on the table and tried to ignore the tantalizing temptation of her luscious mouth.

She grinned, and something inside him tightened.

"Lost?" she asked.

"No," he corrected. "Just...delayed."

"Uh-huh," Elizabeth nodded, set her cup down and signaled for the waiter. Looking back at Harding, she asked, "Would you like a cup of coffee? A compass? Or perhaps just a knife and a piece of string?"

The glimmer of amusement in her eyes couldn't be ignored. Neither could the knot of need centering low in his belly. Humiliating as it was to admit, he wanted her more than anything. Even her laughter at his ineptness wasn't enough to quash the desire building within him.

Determined to ignore the direction his thoughts were taking, he forced a smile and admitted,

"Coffee would be great. And if you're going to leave me alone in this place again…a compass wouldn't be out of line."

Elizabeth looked surprised, then a short chuckle rippled past her throat and settled over him. Reaching across the table, she lightly laid her hand atop his.

"Congratulations, Harding. You're the first man I've ever known to admit to being lost."

He looked down at their joined hands. Jagged streaks of heat stabbed at him. Lifting his gaze, he met hers and saw the same staggering sense of awareness reflected in her eyes.

Immediately she pulled her hand back and buried it in her lap.

A waiter silently came up to the table.

And the moment was lost.

But Harding had a feeling that during the next week with Elizabeth, there would be plenty of such moments.

Five

That was a mistake.

Under cover of the tabletop, Elizabeth rubbed the fingers of her right hand together. It did no good, though. Her flesh still tingled as if she'd received a small electrical shock.

She should have known better than to touch him. Hadn't the memory of his kisses kept her up half the night? Yes, but by the time dawn had streaked across the sky, she had managed to convince herself that she had imagined her strange, overpowering reaction to Harding Casey. So much for that theory.

"Elizabeth?" he asked. "Are you all right?"

No. Definitely not. "Sure," she said, forcing a lightness she didn't feel into her tone. "I'm fine."

"Then, you don't want another cup of coffee?" he asked, nodding his head toward the impatient-looking waiter standing alongside their table.

Lord. Apparently a simple touch of Harding's hand could send her into a zombielike state where she didn't even hear conversations going on around her. How long had the two of them been waiting for her attention?

"Actually," she said, pushing her nearly empty cup to one side. "I'd love another, thanks."

Harding nodded at the young man, who shook his head in exasperation before picking up her cup and moving off.

"So where were you?" he asked when they were alone again.

"What do you mean?" Dumb. She knew exactly what he meant.

He smiled knowingly. "Your body was here, but your mind was someplace else entirely. Thinking up new recipes?"

"All right. I mean, yes." It was better than anything she could come up with at the moment.

He nodded slowly. "I guess your ideas must come to you all the time."

"Oh, yes," she answered honestly. "My imagination is always active." Way *too* active at times, but she didn't need to tell him that.

"Mike tells me that you're making the wedding cake."

With the conversation moving to safe ground, Elizabeth smiled and breathed a sigh of relief. "I couldn't let my own sister get married with just any old cake, could I?"

"No, I suppose not." He folded his large, callused hands together on the bright yellow tabletop. "Still, it's a lot of work, isn't it?"

Elizabeth, despite her best intentions, was staring at those hands of his, imagining what it would be like to feel them moving over her flesh. Stroking. Caressing. Exploring.

"Elizabeth?"

"Hmm?" She snapped out of her dangerous daydream and caught his wary stare.

"Are you *sure* everything's all right?"

"I'm fine, Sergeant Major," she said firmly, determined to get past this ridiculous fascination she had for him. "As to the cake—" she sincerely *hoped* they had still been talking about the cake when she zoned out "—it will take some time, but it will be worth it."

"I can hardly wait to taste it," he said softly.

Unwillingly her gaze shifted to his mouth. A slow chill slithered up her spine, and she shivered. Thankfully, the waiter chose just that moment to appear, drinks in hand.

Setting them down in front of her and Harding,

the young man gave her another glance, then moved away quickly.

Terrific. Even strangers were noticing her odd behavior. What had happened to all of the strong words she'd thrown at him the night before? Wasn't she the one who had said that she could outlast any Marine? Wasn't she the one who had said that spending a week with him wouldn't bother her in the slightest?

Well, it had only been two days, and not only was she bothered, she was *hot* and bothered.

"So," Harding asked, picking up the fire-engine red cup, "what am I having?"

"I beg your pardon?"

"I told him to bring me one of whatever you were drinking. It seemed easier than trying to decipher that menu."

She smiled. True, there were far too many different types of drinks listed on the chalkboard over the counter. Being a creature of habit, Elizabeth always ordered the tried and true. "It's café mocha."

He raised his cup to his lips, sniffed, smiled and tasted. "It's good."

"Darn right," she said, taking a sip herself. "It's chocolate. Hard not to be good."

"Mike told me you were a fanatic about chocolate."

"*Fanatic* is a hard word."

"But appropriate?"

She smiled. "Definitely."

"And is the wedding cake chocolate?"

"On the inside, you bet. The outside will be traditional white...with a few surprising elements."

"A lot like the chef, then. Traditional, but with surprises."

"What do you mean?"

He reached across the table and captured one of her hands. Instantly a jolt of electricity skittered up the length of her arm. Judging by the flash of awareness in his eyes, Harding had felt it, too.

"That's what I'm talking about," he said softly. "Every time I touch you, I feel it. Something out of the ordinary. Something surprising. Startling."

She pulled her hand free, not because she wanted to, but because it was the only prudent move. "I thought we decided last night, that this...*thing* between us wasn't going to go anywhere."

"I know what we said." He spoke softly, keeping his already-deep voice pitched to a level that made her think of moonlight. Firelight. Naked passion. "But this is damned hard to ignore."

"We have to try." She held her coffee cup in both hands and took a long sip before continuing. "Look, Harding," she said, "we're not kids. We don't have to give in to what is basically just a hormonal urge."

Just the thought of surrender, though, brought another chill to her spine.

"Is that all it is?" he whispered.

"It's all it can be." She pulled a deep breath into her lungs and prayed that her voice would be steady when she spoke again. "Neither one of us is interested in a relationship. You're a career Marine—and though there's nothing *wrong* with that—"

"Gee, thanks."

"I grew up in the military. I've had enough."

"I didn't ask you to marry me."

She blushed. Dammit, she could feel heat and color race up her neck and blossom in her cheeks. Served her right. He *hadn't* suggested any long-term relationship. All he had talked about was their obvious attraction for each other. Hardly a declaration of undying love, for goodness' sake.

What was wrong with her, anyway? She hadn't felt so clumsy and nervous around a man since she was seventeen. And this was no time to lose her sense of balance.

"You're right." Elizabeth forced a choked laugh past the knot in her throat. "You didn't. And if you had, I would have said no."

Something flickered in his eyes, but was gone before she could identify it. He nodded slowly, his mouth grim. "So, what's the problem with talking about whatever this is that's going on between us?"

"It's pointless, Harding," she said. "And dangerous."

"How do you figure?" His index finger curled through the handle of the coffee cup. He lifted it, took a drink and waited for her answer.

"Neither one of us wants this relationship to last beyond Mike and Terry's wedding, right?"

"Yeah, but—" he shrugged again and set the cup down "—we'll probably be seeing each other off and on for years as we visit them."

Years. Years of torture. Years of watching him. Wanting him. Swell.

"All the more reason to stop this before it starts," she told him briskly. "If we were to give in to this... *thing,* imagine how awkward the situation would be every time we met."

One corner of his mouth turned up in a half smile. Damn. Why did he have to be so good-looking? Why couldn't Mike's best friend have been a one-eyed troll with a bad leg?

"You don't think this is awkward already?"

"Difficult, not awkward. Awkward is making polite conversation with someone you've seen naked."

Now she couldn't mistake the emotion flaring up in his eyes. Desire. Instantaneous, combustible desire. She recognized it immediately, because she was feeling the same thing. Just the thought of Harding Casey, naked, invading her body with his own, was enough to start small tingles of expectation thrumming in her center. She shifted uncomfortably in the seat.

A long, tension-filled minute passed before Harding tore his gaze from hers. "You're right," he said.

"I am?" She cleared her throat. "About what in particular?"

"About this. Talking about it. Thinking about it. It's pointless. Not to mention frustrating as hell." He stood up abruptly. Checking the total on their check, he pulled a bill from his pants pocket, tossed it onto the table and said, "We'd better get going, Elizabeth." Picking up their packages, he held his free hand out to her, to help her up.

She stared at it for a long moment, then lifted her gaze to his. If she put her hand in his, the flames would ignite, and they would be right back where they started.

"Oh," he said, finally understanding her hesitation. "Yeah. Okay." His hand fell to his side, and he stepped back, giving her plenty of room to walk past him into the milling crowds.

Safety in numbers, Elizabeth told herself. As long as they surrounded themselves with people, neither of them would be tempted to give in to what they both really wanted.

A long, hot, incredibly satisfying night of love-making.

Mentally grasping for a change in subject, she blurted, "What else has Mike told you about me?"

Anaheim Stadium was crowded. Too early in the season for the Angels' die-hard fans to be disgusted at yet another lost chance at the Pennant, the stands were filled with people telling each other that this year would be *the* year.

Harding looked to his right briefly. Mike and Terry were so wrapped up in each other, they probably hadn't noticed that the game was half-over. Shifting his gaze, he looked at the woman sitting on his left. Three days. He'd only known her for three days…and yet, it felt like forever. He hardly remembered a time when he hadn't had the image of her soft brown eyes in his mind. Her scent haunted him and every moment spent with her was a strange combination of pleasure and torture.

No woman had ever affected him like this.

Elizabeth made a notation on the score book page of the program laying across her lap, then shouted at the home plate umpire.

"If you can't see any better than that, I'll give you a ride home. You shouldn't be driving!"

Harding suppressed a chuckle and only half heard the man sitting behind them mutter, "You tell 'im, lady!"

Who would have guessed that Elizabeth Stone, the Princess of Party Cooking, was such a rabid baseball fan? Sure, Mike had told him that she enjoyed the game...but she actually kept score. Not just listing home runs, but pitcher substitutions, pinch runners...everything.

He smiled to himself as she reached up to push her hair behind her ears. Her gold hoop earrings winked in the glare of the overhead stadium lights. Harding curled his fingers into his palms to keep himself from touching her. All day, every day, he had been quelling that impulse. And it wasn't getting any easier.

His body tightened. He clenched his jaw at the discomfort. A discomfort he was becoming all too accustomed to.

He stood up abruptly, and Elizabeth looked at him.

"I'm going for something to eat," he said, more gruffly than he had intended. "You want anything?"

She glanced at Mike and Terry. Her sister was leaning in to accept her fiancé's kiss. Muttering under her breath, Elizabeth stood, laid her program on her seat and said, "I'll come with you."

So much for getting a little distance, he told himself. Glancing over his shoulder, he asked, "Mike. You two want anything?"

Mike didn't even look up. He just shook his head and kissed Terry again. Grumbling softly, Harding stepped out onto the stepped aisle and followed

Elizabeth to the upper level. He tried to keep his gaze from locking on to the seductive sway of her bottom in those worn jeans. But he failed.

The line at the snack bar was ten people deep. They joined the crowd silently, Harding standing directly in back of her. An inch or so of space separated them, and still he could feel the heat emanating from her and taunting him with her nearness.

Where had all of his resistance gone? What had happened to the man who had insisted that he could spend a week in this woman's company without giving in to desire? Humph. The answer was easy. Three days into the week, that fool of a man was discovering that he was feeling something *more* than desire. Something that wouldn't be ignored and apparently had no intention of going away.

"Enjoying the game?" she asked over the noisy hum of the crowd.

"Not as much as you are," he said. Conversation was good. Maybe talking would help keep his mind too occupied for dangerous daydreams.

She glanced at him over her shoulder and smiled. "Baseball was the one thing my father and I shared. We never stayed in one place long enough to call any team 'ours,' so we always cheered for the Yankees. Since I moved to California, I've finally got a home team to root for. The Angels beak my heart annually, but I won't give up on them."

"Never surrender?"

"Exactly."

The crowd moved as one, inching closer to the snack counter. Mingled scents of popcorn, roasting hot dogs and beer floated in the air.

Someone jostled Elizabeth, pushing her backward, into Harding. Her bottom brushed against his already aching groin, and he sucked in a gulp of air in response. He grabbed her upper arms and held her still. If she moved again, he was a dead man.

"Harding," she muttered, pressing herself closer against him. "This isn't working."

"Tell me about it." His teeth ground together when she leaned into him.

"I'll never last out the week."

He dipped his head to whisper in her ear. "Me, either."

She shivered slightly as his breath brushed across her skin. He dropped one hand to her waist. Sliding his arm around her front, he held her tightly to him.

Elizabeth let her head fall back onto his chest. Her eyes closed as she concentrated on the feel of his hard readiness pressed against her bottom. She shifted her hips slightly and felt his quick intake of breath.

"How hungry are you?" he whispered, once more tickling her flesh with his breath.

She licked suddenly dry lips. It didn't matter that

they were standing in the middle of a rowdy crowd. If anything, that fact only made their private dance more exciting. Dangerous.

During the last few moments, she had forgotten all about the baseball game, the snack bar, even her sister and Mike, still sitting in the stands. For now, all she knew or cared about was the man holding her. The man whose touch electrified her. The man she wanted more than she wanted her next breath.

It was pointless to deny this attraction. This desire. Even now the flames of passion were licking at her center, stirring her senses into a whirlwind of need that threatened to choke off her air.

"I'm not hungry, Harding," she answered softly. "Not for a hot dog, anyway."

"Then let's get out of here," he muttered thickly. Keeping one arm around her waist, he guided her through the crowd until they were clear. He kept walking until they were half-hidden behind a concrete pillar.

Every breath strained her lungs to the bursting point. Elizabeth looked up into his eyes, then lifted one hand to cup his cheek. "This is crazy, Harding. We've only known each other three days."

He turned his face into her hand, kissing the palm. Lifting one hand, he captured hers and squeezed it before saying, "We *met* three days ago. But we've heard about each other for a year now."

"Still..." She shook her head, some rational

corner of her mind trying to deny what was happening.

"I know your favorite color is blue," he whispered. "You hate cats, love dogs and always wanted three children—two boys and a girl."

She swallowed heavily before speaking. "I know you have no family beyond the Corps. You kill plants by overwatering them, and you like your coffee black with two sugars."

He gave her a slow, lopsided smile. "We're not strangers, Elizabeth. From the moment we met, I knew this was where we were headed."

Her heartbeat skittered, then accelerated, slamming against her rib cage. Every inch of her body felt as though it was on fire. She ran the pad of her thumb across his lips, and when his tongue darted out to taste her flesh, she gasped, feeling the intimate caress down to the soles of her feet.

"I knew it, too, Harding," she managed to say. "And I don't want to fight it anymore."

He groaned slightly and moved in even closer to her, until they were both hidden in the shadows. "Fighting's not what I have in mind," he whispered. Then he dipped his head and claimed her mouth for the kiss they'd both been waiting for.

She sagged against him, offering herself up to the flames of desire raging through her. His tongue parted her lips and swept inside her mouth, stealing what was left of her breath and charging her with a hum of energy that lit up her insides like a fireworks display.

Time stopped. His fingers speared through her hair at the sides of her head and held her still for his gentle assault on her senses. Every stroke of his tongue brought new sensations, sharper pangs of need. She met him, touch for touch, caress for caress, their tongues twining together in an ancient dance of desire.

A distant roar of applause and cheers from the stadium crowd finally broke them apart, reminding them both where they were. Harding took a half step backward, clearly reluctant to leave her.

"I'll go back to our seats," he said softly. "Tell Mike and Terry that you're not feeling well. I'm going to take you home."

She nodded, her throat too full to speak, her emotions too near the surface. She could still taste him. Running her tongue lightly over her lips, Elizabeth shivered as his gaze followed the sultry motion. There was no way she would be able to simply sit and watch a baseball game. Not now. Not when her body was alive with expectation.

"Wait here," he told her. "I'll be back in a minute."

He turned, took a step, then stopped. Looking back at her, Harding stared directly into her eyes for a long, slow minute. Finally he asked, "Are you sure this is what you want, Elizabeth?"

There it was. Her chance to call a halt to this insanity that had overtaken them. With the word *No* she knew Harding would escort her back to her seat, and they could go on as they had been...each pretending that this magic between them didn't exist. Each trying to forget what had happened in the past few stolen moments.

"Hurry back, Harding," she whispered brokenly, making the only decision she could.

Six

The twenty-five-minute drive from the stadium to her condo had never seemed so long before. Freeway miles flew past, but once on the side streets, they were caught by every red light.

Elizabeth shifted in the Mustang's bucket seat and shot a glance at the man beside her. Immediately, her stomach began to pitch and turn. She wasn't regretting her decision——but the strained silence arching between them made the whole situation a bit...strange. She'd never known such passionate urgings before she'd met Harding Casey. But then, she'd never known a man like him before, either.

Spirals of need curled within her, prompting another uncomfortable shift in her seat. Her favorite jeans felt too tight. Too constraining. The seat belt slashing across her front pressed against her breasts, increasing the ache already planted by want. She bit her lip and groaned her frustration when yet another red light stopped them only a few blocks from her condo.

"Think somebody's trying to tell us something?" Harding asked tightly.

She looked at him sharply. Was *he* regretting their hasty decision to leave the ballpark for her house?

"Changing your mind, Harding?" Somehow, she squeezed those words past the knot in her throat, then held her breath as she waited for his answer.

He turned his head to look at her, and she knew immediately that nothing had changed. Even in the darkness his eyes seemed to burn with the same fires streaking through her. His right hand dropped from the steering wheel. He reached across the automatic gearshift, laying his palm on her left leg. Slowly, firmly, he stroked her thigh. She felt the heat of his touch slip through the worn denim fabric and sink down into her bones. She held her breath as his hand moved to her inner thigh.

"What do you think, Elizabeth?" he asked quietly, shifting his hand until his fingers cupped her aching center.

Breath rushed from her lungs. She stared into his eyes and saw her own need and hunger reflected back at her. His fingers smoothed up and down over the denim stretched across the joining of her thighs. His gaze held hers, refusing to let her look away. The lake blue of his eyes darkened with every ragged breath she drew, and when she parted her legs farther, she watched his features tighten.

The driver behind them honked his horn, demanding they notice that the light had turned green. Elizabeth squelched a groan threatening to erupt from her chest. She didn't want him to stop touching her. She suddenly couldn't bear the thought of not having his hands on her.

Harding scowled into his rearview mirror and stepped on the gas. He guided the responsive car with one hand on the wheel. Though he kept his eyes on the road, his right hand continued to torture Elizabeth. As if responding to a need as deep as her own, he didn't break the contact between them.

She let her head loll against the seat back, and she closed her eyes to the streetlights whizzing past. In the enclosed shelter of his car, it was as though the entire world had disappeared, leaving only the two of them.

As the Mustang slowed down again, she thought she heard him mutter a curse, but she wasn't sure. She wasn't sure of anything beyond the incredible sensation of his fingers moving on her body.

The Mustang's engine hummed as they waited out another red light. Elizabeth turned her head and opened her eyes to look at him. Their gazes locked and held as she felt his nimble fingers undoing the button fly of her jeans.

"Harding," she whispered, suddenly all too aware of the cars behind and alongside them. True, it was dark, but what if someone saw them anyway? "You can't—"

"I already have," he countered, and slid his fingertips down over her abdomen and beneath the band of her panties.

"Oh, my," she gasped and lifted her hips, unconsciously helping him toward his goal.

"Oh, Elizabeth," he said softly. His fingertips slowly caressed her damp heat—without the barrier of her jeans.

Embarrassed, excited and tortured almost to the breaking point, she looked away from him, directing a blank stare toward the traffic streaming across the intersection in front of them. Dangerous, her mind screamed. Scandalous.

She was allowing a man to make love to her while they sat at a red light on Beach Boulevard. What was worse, she had no intention of stopping him.

What was happening to her? Where was the safe, sane woman she had always been? She grabbed the armrest, curling her fingers into the padded black vinyl. The stream of traffic in front of her blurred. Half closing her eyes, she bit down hard on her bottom lip to keep from crying out at his tender, intimate touch.

"Not much farther," he said as the light turned green and they were able to go again.

She nodded, swallowed, then heard herself say, "Hurry, Harding. Hurry."

His fingertips found her most sensitive spot. Unable to help herself, she moaned softly and spread her legs wider in response. She lifted her hips off the seat slightly, instinctively trying to draw him in farther. But the strong denim fabric would only give so far.

Frustration and expectation warred within her. She glanced at him again and noted the taut lines of strain etched into his face. Shifting for a quick look at her surroundings, Elizabeth saw that they were only a block or two from her house now.

So close.

And still so far.

She leaned toward him as far as her seat belt would allow. Harding shot her a look from the corner of his eye as she came nearer.

"Elizabeth?"

The deep rumble of his voice filled the car, but she didn't answer him. Instead, she laid one hand on his powerfully muscled thigh and felt it tighten reflexively. His fingers clenched around the steering wheel. Running her palm lightly up and down the inside of his thigh, she tried to share the incredible sensations he was showering on her. Her fingers brushed across his groin as he made the left turn into her condominium complex.

He muttered something unintelligible as he reluctantly pulled his hand free of her jeans and maneuvered the car into a parking slot in front of her condo. Yanking on the emergency brake, he turned off the engine, snatched the keys out of the ignition, then got out of the car. She fumbled with the buttons on her jeans and still had her own door open before he arrived.

Reaching into the car, he helped her out, kept a tight hold on her hand and marched up the flower-lined walkway to her front door, Elizabeth stepping quickly to keep up with him.

She tried to get the key into the dead-bolt lock three times before Harding took it from her, slid it home and turned it, opening the door in a rush. They stepped inside, he slammed the door, set the lock again and grabbed for her.

Elizabeth clutched at his shoulders in the dimly lit foyer. His hands were everywhere. Touching, caressing. He lifted the hem of her shirt and dragged it up and over her head. She shook her hair back from her face and reached for the buttons on his uniform.

"This is crazy," she whispered as the last button was freed.

"Completely nuts," he agreed, shrugging out of

his shirt, then pulling his white undershirt off as well.

"We're not thinking," she muttered, and gasped as his knuckles brushed her skin. He undid the front clasp of her bra, then pushed it off her shoulders so he could admire her breasts unhampered. "We should be thinking."

"Probably," he said, lifting one of her breasts and rubbing his thumb across the distended nipple.

"Ohh...." She moaned helplessly, took his free hand and placed it on her other breast. Shudders wracked her body as ribbons of pleasure swirled through her. "What if we regret this tomorrow, Harding?"

He bent his head, drew one nipple into his mouth and slowly, lovingly, circled it with his tongue. After too brief a time, he straightened again. "It'd still be worth it," he whispered.

Lifting her hands to his broad, naked chest, her fingers entwined themselves in the dark hair sprinkled across his flesh. His shining, silver dog tags tinkled musically as she stroked his skin. Her thumbs dusted over his flat nipples, and he groaned, grabbing her to him tightly.

Sliding his fingers into her hair, he tipped her head back and held her for his kiss. His mouth came down on hers like a dying man who'd been offered a last drink of water. His tongue plundered her mouth, taking all she had to offer and silently demanding more.

Everything in her was on fire. She felt the rush of passion building into an inferno and gave herself over to the flames. Clutching at him, she dug her fingernails into his shoulders and hung on as if he was the only steady point in her universe. Whatever it was that lay between them, it was more powerful than anything she had ever known. Though her mind still worried about what she was doing, her body knew it was right.

She twisted slightly in his arms, rubbing her breasts against his chest, loving the feel of her own soft flesh brushing over his hard muscles. She luxuriated in the feel of his strong arms wrapped around her bare back. Then one of his hands dropped to her behind, pulling her tightly to his hard readiness, and she groaned again, louder this time.

She needed him now.

She had to feel him entering her body, becoming one with her.

"Harding," she gasped as she broke their kiss.

"Now," he muttered, and buried his face in the curve of her neck and shoulder.

"Yes," she whispered. "Upstairs. First door."

He lifted her easily, and she didn't even have time to enjoy the sensation of being carried before he set her on her feet beside the queen-size bed. He took a step back and tore at his belt buckle.

Frantic now, Elizabeth unbuttoned her jeans and pushed them and her panties down her legs, only to be stopped by her running shoes. Hurriedly she toed her shoes off, then kicked off her pants. She turned to face him and stared silently. He was more amazing than she had expected. Tall and muscular, his body was a testament to the rigorous training of the Marine Corps.

Her gaze dropped to his groin, and she felt a momentary pang of worry when she realized how large and ready he was.

But then he came to her, sweeping her into the circle of his arms and laying her down onto the mattress. And at once, the inferno between them leaped into life again. She parted her legs as he moved over her and positioned himself between her thighs. She felt the featherlight touch of his hands smoothing up and down the insides of her legs. The tips of his fingers explored her most tender flesh, dipping in and out of the moist heat of her body until Elizabeth was ready to shatter into a million tiny pieces.

"Harding," she gasped, looking up into his darkened blue eyes. "Harding, I need…"

"Just what I need, Elizabeth," he finished for her, and came up on his knees. Slipping his hands beneath her, he lifted her hips slightly and drove himself home.

She arched into him, her head digging into the mattress, her arms up, blindly reaching for him. He shifted, moving his hands to the mattress on either side of her head. Bracing himself, he leaned over her, stared down into her wide eyes and moved within her.

Over and over, he retreated and advanced, hurtling them both ever closer to the mindless explosion of sensation awaiting them. She felt it building, humming along her nerve endings, toying with her. Teasing her with its nearness. Her fingers clenched tightly behind his neck, she rocked her hips in time with his, their dance racing to its conclusion.

When the first tremor shook her, she held him tighter, closer. Taking a deep breath, she threw herself over the edge of caution and into the whirlpool of release. Each rippling explosion of satisfaction rocked her harder than the one before. She cried out as her pleasure crested, and held him tighter still when he stiffened, moaned her name and emptied himself inside her.

Harding had never known anything like it. His groin ached with satisfaction, and already, a new, stronger need was rising up within him. The blood rushed through his veins and his own heartbeat thundered in his ears.

She moved beneath him, and he immediately levered himself up onto his elbows.

"Don't," she said quickly.

"Don't what?"

"Don't pull away yet."

His body hardened and thickened inside her. Her damp, tight warmth surrounded him, and he felt as though he would never leave the sanctuary he had found. Instinctively he rocked his hips against her, showing her without words that he had no intention of pulling away from her.

Her hands slid up and down his back, and everywhere she touched came alive. Her palms dusted his flesh and he groaned quietly. "I want you again," he whispered, and bent to take one of her nipples into his mouth.

She arched against him, and he grazed the distended bud with the edges of his teeth. His tongue worked her nipple, circling, flicking at the tender flesh with short strokes.

"This can't be happening again," she said on a half sigh. "So soon…"

"Again," he whispered as he lifted his head and looked down into her eyes. "And again and again. I can't get enough of you, Elizabeth. The taste of you, the feel of you." He pushed his body deeper inside her, enjoying the sparkle of pleasure he saw flickering in her eyes. She wanted him as badly as he did her. That knowledge fed the flames of his own passion.

Harding wrapped his arms around her, and when he eased himself up onto his haunches, he kept her with him, his body buried within her. She straddled him, her legs on either side of his thighs. Wiggling her hips slightly, she took him even deeper inside as his hands dropped to her hips.

Her head fell back, and Harding looked his fill of her. In the moonlight streaming through the second-story window, her brown hair glimmered and shone. Curls fell in a tangled mass around her head, and her gold hoops swung in abandon, making her look like some ancient, pagan goddess—naked but for the gold at her ears.

His hands encompassed her narrow waist briefly before he allowed one of his hands to slide down her abdomen to the nest of pale brown curls at the juncture of her thighs. She tensed, waiting. He smiled to himself and stroked her most sensitive spot.

She straightened up on his lap, shifting her hips from side to side, cradling his body with hers. Her hands at his shoulders, she bent to claim his mouth, and this time he let her be the aggressor. She branded him with strokes of her tongue, stealing his breath and giving him hers.

Unable to wait another moment, Harding placed both hands on her hips. Then, guiding her, he helped her move on him. Each time she took him inside her, he felt his world shift. When completion roared toward them, he clamped his mouth to hers, devouring her sighs and muffling his own shout of satisfaction.

She didn't remember moving, but when she opened her eyes again, she was lying on fresh, cool sheets, the quilt pulled neatly over her.

And Harding.

She glanced down at her waist and laid one hand on the arm he had wrapped around her. Her body still humming with the lingering effects of their lovemaking, she was embarrassed to admit—even to herself—that she wanted more. Needed more.

"Awake?" he asked quietly.

"Uh-huh," she said on a sigh. "What time is it?"

"Around midnight."

Nodding, she turned in his arms until she could see him.

Bracing himself on one elbow, Harding looked down at her steadily. Somberly.

A warning sounded somewhere deep inside her. Whatever afterglow she was experiencing, Harding apparently wasn't.

"What is it?" she managed to ask.

He frowned slightly, released her long enough to

rub one hand across his face, then said, "We have to talk."

Something cold slithered along her spine. She pulled the sheet up higher over her breasts, scooted a couple of inches away from him. "If you're thinking about apologizing to me, don't."

"Elizabeth…"

"I mean it, Harding." Strange how quickly a glow could disappear. Stranger still how much colder she felt now that it was gone. "We're both grown-ups. We knew what we were doing."

"Not entirely."

She pulled a bit farther away from him, pushed her hair out of her eyes and asked, "What's that supposed to mean?"

"We didn't take any precautions," he said flatly.

"Precau—" Good heavens. Her stomach dropped, and she thought she even felt her heartbeat skitter a bit as the implications of what he was saying sunk in.

Sitting up, she crossed her legs Indian style and clutched the quilt to her like a frightened virgin. Despite the situation, she almost laughed. A bit late for trying to protect her virtue.

"I don't see a damn thing funny in this," he pointed out.

"Not funny," she corrected. "Ridiculous. Embarrassing."

"Embarrassing?"

"Of course. These days, any teenager knows better than to do what we just did!"

He pushed himself off the mattress and began to pace. "I don't suppose you take the Pill?" he asked on one of his trips around the room.

"No," she said, shaking her head. "There didn't seem to be any point." Flopping back against the headboard, she frowned and admitted wryly, "I don't exactly have what you would call a busy love life."

He stopped dead and looked at her, one eyebrow lifted into a high arch.

"Sure, tonight," she shot at him. "But before you there was only——" She broke off and stared at him.

"What?"

"Is that what your concern is for? Trying to find out if I've got anything *contagious?*"

"Dammit, Elizabeth."

"Rest easy, Harding." She clumsily got out of bed, still dragging that quilt with her. Wrapping it around her, she tossed the tail end of the blanket over one shoulder, lifted her chin and said, "I'm completely safe. I've only been with one other man and——"

"One?"

A flush of heat stormed up her neck and stained her cheeks. "Apparently I've given you the wrong impression, here. Believe me, the way I acted with you tonight is not my normal behavior. I don't ordinarily hop into the sack with someone I've known for three days."

"That's not what I meant—"

"I can understand why you might not want to believe me, what with the evidence all to the contrary..."

"Elizabeth," he said, and took a step toward her.

She jumped backward. As insulting as his comment had been, she didn't trust herself if he was to touch her. Damn his eyes, anyway, she would probably melt into him and find herself flat on her back again.

He took a deep breath before speaking in a slow, too calm voice, "I didn't mean that. I was only surprised that a woman like you—"

"Fast and loose?"

"Dammit, stop putting words in my mouth!"

Her bottom lip trembled, and she bit down on it, hard. She wasn't going to cry, blast it. Not now. Not in front of him.

Harding saw the sheen of unshed tears swimming in her eyes and cringed inwardly. Damn, he'd made a mess of this. When he'd awakened with her in his arms, he had experienced an inner peace that he had never known before. Staring down at her features while she slept, his mind had taken an incredibly wild turn.

His imagination had leaped from this one night of passion to a lifetime of promises and children. Just the thought of it had terrified him—and yet, somehow intrigued him almost as much. *That* was the moment he had realized that he'd been a careless idiot.

Children? A baby?

Hell, how could he *not* have used a damn condom? Fine, he had the excuse of being somewhat out of practice. He'd been living a practically celibate life since his divorce. One-night stands didn't interest him—and anything more might have led to a relationship. Definitely something he didn't want.

Even the threat of which he'd managed to avoid neatly.

Until Elizabeth Stone.

Gritting his teeth, he started toward her again, determined to say his piece. She backed up, her feet tangling in the quilt she clutched to her chest as if it was Superman's cape. Her balance dissolved, and she swung one arm wide, searching for a handhold. Before she could fall, Harding caught her, dragging her up tight against him.

"Let me go."

"Not yet," he said, and lifted her chin with his thumb and forefinger until she was looking at him.

Those eyes of hers mesmerized him. The deep brown color shimmered beneath a teary film. He wanted to hold her, kiss her, make love to her again until they rekindled the fire between them. Instead, though, he said, "All I meant was that I couldn't believe there were so many stupid men in the world." Not that he was complaining. He much preferred the fact that there hadn't been many men in her life.

She stopped twisting and wriggling to get free.

"A woman as beautiful and warm as you should be fighting them off with a stick."

"I have," she said pointedly.

"Until me." He smiled sadly. It wasn't an easy thing, knowing that he had allowed his hormones to rage so out of control that he'd put her at risk.

She stiffened in his arms. "Harding, let me go."

"Not until I say what I started to say before."

"Which is *what* exactly?"

The watery film in her eyes had dissipated some, to be replaced by a flash of anger. Anger, he knew, was much easier to deal with.

"Elizabeth, I wasn't worrying about diseases." Hadn't it occurred to her yet? Apparently not. He paused, still holding her gaze with his own. "I was thinking more along the lines of a *baby*."

Her jaw dropped.

"Oh, my God," she whispered.

"Is there a chance?" he asked.

"Of course there's a *chance,*" she muttered, moving away from him as his hold eased up. Sitting down on the edge of the bed, she continued to talk. "Not much of one, probably. It was only the one time."

"Two times."

She flushed again. "Two."

He hadn't known that there were still women who blushed. "I'm sorry, Elizabeth, this is all my fault."

"Stop saying you're sorry," she snapped.

"What?"

"I mean it, Harding." Glaring up at him, she went on. "Tonight happened because we *both* wanted it. You're in the clear, Sergeant Major."

The clear? Did she expect him to disappear? Leave her to pay whatever consequences might arise because of tonight? A strong surge of anger shot through him. "What the hell does that mean?"

"That means that if I hear another apology from you, I'll scream." She scooted back onto the bed, wrapped in the cocoon of her quilt. "Will you please leave, now?"

He inhaled sharply and blew the air out of his lungs in an exasperated rush. Staring at her, he saw that she had closed herself off from him as effectively as if she had slammed a door in his face. There wouldn't be any talking to her tonight. Not if he expected her to listen. *Really* listen.

Fine then. They could talk tomorrow. When she would hopefully be reasonable. Bending down, he snatched at his clothes and hurriedly pulled them on. Glancing at her, he noted that she kept her gaze averted.

In a matter of minutes he was standing beside the bed, waiting for her to acknowledge him. Finally she shot him a look from the corner of her eye.

"We'll talk about this tomorrow. I'll call you in the morning."

"I'll call you," she countered firmly, "when I'm ready to talk about it."

Harding bent down, picked her up by the shoulders and planted a hard, quick kiss on her lips. Briefly he thought he felt her kiss him back, but then her defenses went up and she turned into a block of wood. Disappointed, he dropped her back onto the bed, turned and marched to the door. There he stopped, pointed at her and ordered, "Zero nine thirty hours, Elizabeth. You pick up the damned phone."

Seven

She pulled up to the main gate at Camp Pendleton just as dawn was streaking the sky. Sparing a quick glance for the deep rose-colored clouds, she turned her complete attention on the young Marine guard standing beside her car. She must be getting old, she thought. The kid didn't look more than nineteen. She rolled down the window.

"Can I help you, ma'am?" he asked.

Boy, she hated being called ma'am. Dismissing the distraction, she got straight to the business that had brought her to the Marine base.

"I'd like to see Sergeant Major Harding Casey, please."

"Yes, ma'am," the Marine said, his gaze drifting

over a paper attached to the clipboard he carried. "Is he expecting you?"

"No," she confessed. "He's not."

"Which battalion is he with, ma'am? I'll have to call the Sergeant Major before letting you in."

Battalion. Dammit. Of course they would have to know which battalion. And which regiment. Why hadn't she thought of that? She'd been raised on Marine bases. She knew firsthand the thoroughness of the gate guards.

And she didn't have the slightest idea which battalion Harding was assigned to.

Lifting one hand, she rubbed her forehead right between her eyes. Her head was pounding, and her eyes felt gritty from lack of sleep. All night, she'd lain awake, remembering everything that had passed between Harding Casey and her. Everything from the incredible passion and closeness they'd shared, to the moment when he'd destroyed the magic by apologizing and then capping that off with an order to answer her telephone.

Just who the hell did Hard Case Casey think he was, anyway? One night of lovemaking…no matter how mind-shattering…did *not* give him authority over her.

But it *might* have given her a baby.

No, no, no. Don't even think it. The chances had to be astronomically slim. Surely the odds were with her. And yet, something inside her turned over.

She had always wanted a child. Three, actually. And lately she had begun to think it would never happen. What if it *had,* now? What if she was pregnant this very moment? She glanced down at her flat belly, covered by the jeans Harding had manipulated so nicely the night before, and cautiously laid her palm protectively over it.

"Ma'am?" The young Marine cleared his throat meaningfully. "His battalion and regiment?"

"I don't know," she admitted, not sure what to do now.

He must have seen the indecision in her face because he almost smiled. "If you'll pull your car off to the side there, ma'am, I'll see what I can find out."

She did as she was told, turned the engine off and waited. Watching the Marine, she saw him step into the small cubicle inside the gate and reach for a phone. Before he could use it, though, another guard appeared from behind the building. The two men spoke in tones she couldn't quite hear, until the second Marine said loudly, with a glance in her direction, "A *woman* to see Hard Case?"

She didn't know whether to be relieved or insulted. But there was definitely a part of her delighted to hear that women weren't streaming in and out of this gate visiting Harding. Elizabeth watched the second guard grab the phone, speak to someone for a moment, then hang up. He walked to her car, briefly gave her directions to Harding's quarters, then smiled and stepped back out of her way.

As she steered her Toyota along the streets of the base, an eerie feeling began to creep over her. Though her father had never been stationed at Pendleton, the base was so much like all of the others she'd lived on, she felt almost as if she were coming home.

Memories rushed into her brain, and even the air seemed almost too thick to breathe. The drive to Harding's quarters became a short, personal tour of her past. She noticed tricycles and skateboards that had been left out on front lawns, and immediately remembered bravely pedaling her first two-wheeler down a sidewalk while her father ran along behind, tightly gripping the back of the bike to keep her safe.

She saw basketball hoops and chalk-marked sidewalks, which released the memory of her, Terry and her mother playing hopscotch on hot summer afternoons. Shadow pictures raced through her brain as she passed a tidy church, the PX, restaurants and the parade grounds. All of it so familiar.

Strange, but for years, whenever she thought about her childhood, all she remembered was the pain of always moving around—never belonging anywhere—constant uncertainty. Now, though, other images reared up and demanded to be noticed.

The good times. And there had been many of them. Life on a military base wasn't always easy. But almost in compensation for the trials, came the joy of feeling as though you were part of a huge family. A family where each member looked out for the other. A family where arguments and old injuries were put aside in times of need.

An unexpected sheen of tears filled her eyes, and she was nearly blinded by the past. But she blinked them back as she pulled up in front of the senior staff NCO billeting barracks. Determinedly, she put her past where it belonged. She would need all of her wits about her during this little confrontation with Harding.

Especially since she wasn't at all sure what it was she'd come to say.

As if the thought of his name had conjured him up, a door in the barracks building opened and there he was. Standing on the threshold of his quarters with a frown on his face and his silver dog tags gleaming against his tanned flesh, he had one bare shoulder propped against the doorjamb, his arms folded across his chest. He had pulled on a pair of uniform trousers, but otherwise he was naked.

Instantly memories of the night before flitted through her already-tired brain. Elizabeth's mouth went dry, and she had to force herself to move suddenly shaky legs. Once out of the car, though, she walked directly to him without stumbling once.

She stepped past him, entering the apartment. He followed her in and silently closed the door. Taking a deep breath, she turned around slowly and her gaze collided with his.

"Good morning," he said. "Zero nine thirty already?"

"No," she snapped, refusing to rise to the sarcasm. "I had to talk to you and couldn't wait for my 'assigned time.'"

He looked mildly surprised, but he nodded and started for the kitchen. "Come on. I think we're both going to need coffee." Over his shoulder, he added, "Sorry, but I'm fresh out of café mocha."

"I'll suffer," she countered and wanted to bite her tongue. If she expected to have a civilized conversation with the man, she shouldn't start by firing a warning shot.

The kitchen was small, barely big enough for two people. Faded green curtains graced the only window and on the tiny, two-seater table, was a plastic basket filled with apples and bananas.

While he started the coffee, she walked a slow circle around that table. "Look, Harding, I think there are a few things we have to get straight."

"I agree."

"Good." That was a start, wasn't it?

Finished, he turned, propped himself against the countertop and crossed his arms over his chest again. Above the gurgle and hiss of the coffeemaker, he asked, "So who goes first? You or me?"

"Me," she said quickly. "I've been thinking about this all night."

He gave her a slow nod, but his expression was unreadable.

She stopped behind one of two ladder-back wooden chairs. Curling her fingers over the top slat, she said firmly, "What you did last night was way out of line."

He smiled wryly. "I think we established *that* much before I left."

"I'm not talking about the sex," she snapped. "I'm talking about the way you apologized, took all responsibility, then walked out."

"You asked me to leave."

She waved that comment aside for the moment. "I'm a big girl, Harding. I make my own choices, and I take responsibility for those choices myself."

"Fine."

"And," she added, "nobody *orders* me to be waiting at a telephone at a certain time and place."

"All right." He half straightened and reached up to rub one hand across his hair. "We're both to blame. Happy?"

"Yes, thanks." She sat down on the chair and waited while he poured them each a cup of coffee.

When he was seated in the chair opposite her, he started talking before she could say another word.

"Look, Elizabeth," he said, and she knew she wasn't going to like whatever was coming next. "I did some thinking last night, too. And whoever is to blame, what happened last night was a mistake. A big one."

Even though she'd thought the same thing herself earlier, hearing him say it out loud sent an aching emptiness ricocheting around inside her.

"And," he went on, staring into his coffee cup as if looking for the right words, "once this wedding is over, I think it's best if we don't see each other again."

"You do?"

"Yeah." Leaving his drink untouched, he jumped up from the chair, walked the short distance to the sink, then turned around to face her. In the dish drainer behind him, there were one plate, one glass, one cup and one set of silverware left overnight to dry.

Rubbing a hand across his naked chest, he added, "There's no point. Neither one of us wants a relationship, Elizabeth. If we keep seeing each other, it'll only cause a lot of pain."

Speechless, she stared at him. Well, what had she expected? Hadn't she come to the base to tell him the same thing? Wasn't this the only reasonable solution to a situation that was already getting out of hand? Why, then, did it hurt to have him say it to her?

She took hold of her coffee cup with both hands and scrambled for something to say. "I thought Marines were supposed to be able to take pain." Did her voice really sound so soft and injured? Or was it only her imagination?

Harding crossed to her and squatted alongside her chair. Looking directly into her eyes, he said, "Yeah, we can take it. We just don't like *causing* it." Trying for a smile, he added, "Except, of course, to the enemy."

How strange this all was. A week ago she had never met this man. Now she was sitting in his kitchen, talking about dissolving a relationship that didn't really exist, not knowing if she was or wasn't carrying his child.

"It's better this way, Elizabeth," he said softly and reached for one of her hands. He paused for a long moment before saying, "I deploy in less than a month."

Her gaze shot to his. Deployment. More memories rose up to kick her in the stomach. Memories of her father, gone for six months at a time. Summers missed, lonely Christmases, cards and letters and posing for pictures that Mom could send to Dad, so far away. She remembered occasional phone calls and listening to the sound of his voice, so faint and distant.

Visions of her mother, trying to be both mom and dad to Terry and her. Echoes of her mother's lonely tears when she thought her daughters were asleep. So many absences. So many missed birthdays and kisses and hugs. So many missed chances.

She swallowed back the images and forced herself to ask, "Where?"

Grimly he said, "Okinawa."

The other side of the world. In less than a month he would be thousands of miles away from her. Elizabeth nodded and pulled her hand free of his, missing the electrifying warmth of his touch even as she told herself to get used to missing it.

Unable to sit still a moment longer, she stood up and walked back into the small, neat living room. For the first time she noticed the military beige walls and carpets. So familiar and yet…so different.

Her mother had always prided herself on making all of the different quarters they'd lived in home. Photos, framed postcards, hers and Terry's artwork splashed across the refrigerator, rag rugs and always, fresh flowers. Things to let people know that a family lived there. People. Not just Marines.

Small personal touches that were sadly lacking in Harding's place.

A handful of framed photographs lined the mantel over an empty fireplace, and one lone plant stood limply in the corner. Otherwise the place might have been vacant.

Noting her observation, Harding said softly, "I don't keep a lot of *things*." She turned to look at him. "And a man alone can't have pets." He half shrugged. "When I'm deployed, who would I get to take care of a dog?"

Loneliness tinged his voice, and the sharp edge of it slashed at her. She wondered if he even knew it was there. "At least you've got a plant. Mike told me you couldn't be trusted with one."

One corner of his mouth lifted slightly. "It's on loan from First Sergeant McCoy's wife. She said the apartment needed something alive in it. She'll nurse it back to health when I ship out."

Elizabeth nodded, but her thoughts were already spinning. How different their homes were. His was empty. Hers was crammed full of things. *Things*. Not people. For years, she'd been concentrating on building the secure home she'd always longed for. She had gathered up furnishings and knickknacks as if they would be enough to anchor her. But except for Terry and an occasional visit with her parents, her life was empty of people.

A chill raced along her spine, and she shivered. Was she any better than Harding? Had she really made herself a home? Or had she only stacked her possessions high enough to hide the emptiness surrounding her?

Harding watched the play of emotions darting across her features and would have given anything to know what she was thinking. Having her arrive at the base, so unexpectedly, had been like a gift. He'd lain awake all night, thinking about her, worrying about what they might be starting, knowing he should distance himself from her and wondering how in the hell he would be able to do that without dying a little every day for the rest of his life.

How had the world managed to change so completely in so little time? And how could he ever go back to living without her?

She took a breath and it caught in her throat. A tiny, choking sound issued from her, and it was like a bayonet in his back, urging him to her. He crossed the few feet of worn carpet separating them and pulled her into his arms. She buried her face in his chest, and for several long moments Harding simply stood there, holding her. He inhaled her soft, flowery scent, drawing it deep into his lungs, as if he could keep it with him always. He stroked her short, curly hair and listened until her breathing settled into a steady rhythm again.

Looking down, he let go of her only long enough to cup her face in his hands. Smoothing his thumbs across her cheekbones, he was relieved to see she hadn't been crying. But there was something in her eyes—some change that he couldn't quite identify.

"Harding," she said softly, hesitantly, "what are we going to do?"

His gaze drifted over her features slowly, like the most loving of caresses. He would remember this moment, this woman for the rest of his life. Again, the pads of his thumbs brushed over her cheeks. His fingers brushed her hair at her temples. Soft. So soft. "I don't know, Elizabeth. I don't have any answers."

"Then let's not ask each other any more questions," she said thickly. Her palms slid up his chest, her fingertips outlining his flat nipples.

He squeezed his eyes shut at the featherlight strokes of her flesh on his. His groin tightened and he ached to be with her. Inside her.

No questions? No answers? Was that enough?

"Elizabeth," he ground out, "I'm still leaving in a month. Six months I'll be away."

She reached up and laid one hand across his mouth. "We have now, Harding. For whatever reasons, we have now."

"This will only make the leaving harder," he said, feeling that he should remind her that pain was the only possible outcome of their being together.

"But it will make the now so much easier," she said, and went up on her toes to kiss him.

Even a saint couldn't have resisted her kiss— and Harding Casey was no saint. He groaned in the back of his throat, and his arms closed around her, tightening until he felt the buttons of her jeans pressing into his belly. Slipping one hand down lower, he cupped her behind and pulled her hard against him. Another groan escaped from his throat, and he lowered his mouth to take hers.

Her lips parted for him, and his tongue swept into her warmth, claiming her, branding her with each stroke. She wrapped her arms around him, running her palms up and down his back, creating a friction of heat that shot through him with the force of a sustained artillery attack.

In seconds he was more hungry for her than he had been the night before. Now he knew what awaited him in her warmth. He had experienced the wonder of her and couldn't wait to find it again. Gasping for air, he broke their kiss, tossed her up and over his shoulder and headed for the bedroom.

As he walked, Elizabeth lavished kisses over his broad back. Then, sliding her hands down beneath the waistband of his trousers, she smoothed her palms over his behind, dragging her nails across his skin until he thought he might explode from want before he was even deep within her.

In his bedroom, Harding dipped to one side, flipped her onto his mattress and quickly helped her out of her clothes. As he stepped out of his pants, he yanked open the drawer in the bedside table and fumbled in its depths for a long minute. When he finally found one of the condoms he'd had stashed there for two years, he straightened up and slammed the drawer shut again.

This time they would do things right. This time there would be no chances taken. This time, he would care for her the way she should be cared for. He glanced at her and saw her watching him. Raking his gaze over her body, he felt his own stir and ache in readiness. He tore the foil slightly before her hand on his stopped him.

"Let me," she said and took the packet from him.

His groin tightened even further at the mental image of her hands on him, but he gritted his teeth and stood very still, waiting. She opened the packet, removed the condom and slowly positioned it over the sensitive tip of him. Harding sucked in air through clenched teeth and kept his gaze locked on her and what she was doing to him. Inch by glorious inch, she slid the fragile material down his length, smoothing and caressing as she went. When she was finished, she cupped him tenderly, her fingers stroking, exploring him. Harding's blood pounded in his veins, and his heartbeat sounded like the bass drums in the Marine Corps band.

"Enough," he growled and eased her down onto the bed. Parting her thighs, he looked his fill of her. His fingertips explored her opening, gently readying her for his entry. But her body was as tensely strung as his. She was molten heat, calling to him, urging him closer. A moment later he leaned over her and drove himself home. Her tight warmth surrounded him, and when he was buried deep within her, he allowed himself a groan of satisfaction at having found the wonder again.

Then need hammered at him as desperately as her fingernails raked across his back. Her hips lifted and fell, and her breath came hot on his neck.

Taking a handful of her hair, he pulled her head back gently, and stared down into the eyes that had been haunting him since his first sight of them.

"Whatever happens, Elizabeth, we will always have this between us. This...*magic*."

He withdrew and plunged even deeper inside her. She gasped, shuddered, met his gaze and echoed, "*Magic*."

Desire and the flames of an all-consuming passion licked at them, driving them both to the conclusion that brought them each, however briefly, peace.

Eight

"We have *got* to stop meeting like this," Elizabeth said, her body still humming with the aftershocks of their lovemaking. She hadn't intended for this to happen again. All she had wanted to do was *talk* to him.

Harding rolled to one side, stifling a deep-throated groan as he moved. Grabbing a pillow, he jammed it beneath his head. Then, glancing at her, he agreed, "Too many more of these 'talks' and I'll be a dead man."

Pushing one hand through her hair, Elizabeth scooted backward until her back was propped against the headboard. She tugged one of the rumpled sheets up over her breasts and looked at the man lying beside her.

"This is nuts, Harding," she said with a quiet laugh.

"Don't I know it." Ruefully he shook his head, stood up and walked into the bathroom. A few seconds later he joined her on the bed again. Drawing her up close to his side, he kissed the top of her head. "So much for all of our fine notions about self-control."

"I don't know what it is about you, Marine," she said, and tucked her head underneath his chin. "But every time you touch me, I tend to burst into flames."

"I'm getting a little singed myself."

"What are we supposed to do about this, Harding?"

"Enjoy it while it lasts?"

She pushed back a bit and cocked her head to look at him. "Isn't that asking for trouble?"

"Not if we remember to be more careful than we were last night."

Elizabeth settled back against him and nodded slowly. Enjoy each other. Somehow it sounded so... empty. Ridiculous, she knew. After all, they were both adults.

"Regrets?" he asked quietly.

"Not really," she answered, and knew she sounded unconvincing.

"Elizabeth," he said, "just because we can't see a future together...that doesn't mean we can't have a present."

"I know that." She shook her head gently, then pushed her hair back behind her ears. "It's only that I've never—"

"Had a lover?" he finished for her.

She smiled wryly. "You make it sound so reasonable."

"Isn't it?"

"I suppose so," she said thoughtfully. "I guess I never considered myself the take-a-lover kind of woman."

"More of a white-picket-fence type of girl?"

"No." She laughed again at the notion. "I was always too concentrated on my career to think about husbands and cute little houses and station wagons."

"Ah..." He ran one hand up and down her arm in long, soothing strokes. "Well, all of your concentration worked. You *are* the Princess of Party Cooking."

She gave his hand a playful smack.

"Isn't it what you thought it would be?" he asked. "Your career, I mean?"

"Oh, I love it," she admitted softly. "There is nothing more fun than being in a well-stocked kitchen, dreaming up some new and tantalizing dessert."

"Nothing?" he asked, letting his fingertips trail along the edge of her breast.

She sucked in a breath. "Well, *almost* nothing."

"Thank you."

"You're welcome."

"So," he said, "if your career is all you wanted it to be, and you don't particularly *want* a husband, what's wrong with having a lover?"

There was a long pause while she thought that one over. Nothing wrong with it, she supposed. But, if that were true, why did she suddenly feel so...debauched? Her traditional upbringing must be rearing its ugly head, she decided. Well, if that was all it was, she would just have to get over it. As she had when she'd first decided to have a career instead of a husband. Either that or live the life of a well-fed nun.

Making up her mind, she nodded against his chest. "You're right. There's nothing wrong with having a man in my life occasionally."

His hand on her arm stilled, then continued its gentle stroking.

Of course, she would have to give up the one little corner of her dream that she hadn't allowed herself to think of for years. Children. Lovers do not necessarily make good fathers. And 1990s or not, she didn't know if she could be a good enough single parent to risk having a child alone.

Oh, she knew lots of women were doing it these

days. Most of them doing it quite well, too. But the staggering responsibility of being both mother and father was one she wasn't sure she was strong enough to carry.

Immediately she remembered the night before, the first time they'd made love and the fact that there had been no protection. Was it possible that one slip had already resulted in a child? Was she, even now, pregnant with Harding's baby?

She closed her eyes, telling herself firmly not to think about that yet. It was too early to worry. Especially since she wasn't sure if she had anything to worry about. Yet.

Imagine, all of this had come about because her sister had fallen in love.

Her mind racing, Elizabeth suddenly wondered what Mike and Terry would have to say if they could see her and Harding right now. She chuckled gently at the envisioned expression on her sister's face.

"What's so funny?"

"I was just thinking about Mike and Terry and how they worked at trying to get us together for a solid year with no success."

He laughed shortly, and the sound rumbled beneath her ear. "Yeah, all I heard about was how great we would be together."

"Me, too." She tipped her head back again to look up at him. "Can you imagine the 'I told you so's' we'd have to listen to if they found out about this?"

He pushed one hand through his short hair. "Mike would never let me forget it."

"Terry, either. She lives for this sort of thing."

"So, then," he said, cupping her cheek with one big palm, "we don't tell them?"

"My lips are sealed," she said.

"Not permanently, I hope." He smiled wickedly and wiggled both of his eyebrows.

Shaking her head, she grinned at him. "It's better if they don't know, anyway. After all, they were hoping for marriage, not—"

"A red-hot, fire-breathing affair?" he finished for her.

"Exactly." She ran the flat of her hand across his chest.

He caught her hand, holding it tightly. "But just because we don't want to get married, that doesn't mean we can't enjoy what we have for as long as we have it, right?"

"Right," she said, despite the pang of regret echoing deep inside her. Less than a month, he'd said. He was leaving in less than four weeks and would be gone for six long months. And when he returned, there was no guarantee that they would reconnect. Maybe he wouldn't even want to see her. Regret slithered through her again. Already she missed him.

She could admit, if only to herself, that she was dreading his leaving. How terrible could it be for her to have these moments with him to remember when he was gone?

"What's making you frown?" he asked.

"Nothing," she lied, and forced a smile she didn't quite feel.

"You're thinking about last night, aren't you?"

"No, I wasn't."

"We have to talk about that, Elizabeth."

"Yeah, I know," she said, and thought, Not now. Not this minute.

He sighed and held her closer. "Whatever happens, we'll work it out together."

"Harding, you don't have to worry about it, all right?" she said. "Like I told you, I'm a big girl. I can take care of myself."

"I know you can," he countered, staring down into her eyes. "But if you are pregnant, there would be someone else to consider besides yourself."

"Oh, my, a baby." Mixed emotions blended together in the depths of her soul. One minute she saw herself cuddling a newborn to her breast. She blocked the next image, refusing to entertain the notion at all. Banishing both mental pictures, she shook her head firmly. "No, it won't happen."

"When will we know for sure?"

"*I'll* know in about two weeks."

"Good. I don't ship out for three weeks yet, so we'll have time to decide what to do."

"Harding," she tried to ease away from him, but he held her tighter. "I won't try to keep you out of this, and of course you'll get a chance to give me your opinion on what I should do, but the final decision will be mine."

He was quiet for several long minutes, and Elizabeth held her breath, wondering what he would have to say. She hadn't known him long, of course. But through Mike and Terry she knew what kind of man he was. She couldn't imagine him *not* having an opinion.

Finally he inhaled sharply and blew it out in a rush. "We have two weeks. Two weeks before we know if a decision will be necessary. I suggest we wait to discuss it until we know if we have something to talk about."

She sighed her relief. Now that she was here, with him, she didn't want to ruin what time she had with him by fighting over what was still a *theoretical* baby.

Slipping one of his hands beneath the sheet she'd pulled up over her breasts, he found one of her nipples and gently teased it until she was curling into him, nearly purring with pleasure.

"Elizabeth," he whispered in her ear.

"Hmm?"

"Are we going to be spending the entire day in

my bed?" He dipped his head to nibble at the base of her throat.

"Have you got some official Marine business to take care of?" she asked, tilting her head back to give him easier access.

"Nope," his tongue flicked against her pulse point. "I took this whole week off as leave time. I'm officially a free man."

"Did Terry give us chores for today?" she mumbled, and bit his shoulder gently.

"Finished the last ones yesterday." He shifted, moving down the length of her body, trailing hot, damp kisses along her flesh. "All that's left is you making the cake."

"Then, Sergeant Major, I suggest we spend the day in bed, resting up for the rest of the week."

He looked up from her abdomen and gave her a quick, wicked smile. "We stay in this bed, princess, there'll be no resting."

Elizabeth shifted on the sheets, parting her legs when he moved to kneel between them. His fingers dusted along the insides of her thighs, and she felt herself jump in response. "Princess, huh?" she murmured as his hands slid beneath her bottom. "Well, Hard Case—" she broke off and looked at him quizzically. "Why do they call you Hard Case, anyway?"

"Do you really need to know that *now?*" he

asked quietly, and lifted her hips high, easing her legs into place over his shoulders.

Suddenly aware of what he was about to do, Elizabeth gasped, "Harding!"

"Just lie back, princess," he said with a knowing smile.

Then his mouth covered her, and all of her thoughts dissolved into a hazy mist of delicious sensations.

At 10:00 p.m. the night before the wedding, Elizabeth sat at her kitchen table, listening to her mother and Terry as she decorated the cake.

"I just don't understand why the bachelor party *has* to be held the night before the wedding."

"Tradition," Sally Stone told her younger daughter for the third time.

Terry stuck her index finger into the small, stainless steel bowl containing lilac-tinted frosting and winced when Elizabeth smacked her hand.

"Hey, I just wanted a taste."

Elizabeth shook her head, filled the pastry bag with the lilac confection and prepared to create rosettes. "Taste it tomorrow."

"Your sister's right," Sally said.

"Naturally." Terry gave her mother a sly grin. "Lizzie was always your favorite."

Elizabeth laughed.

"Let's not start that again," their mom said and

stood up. "Anyone like a cup of tea before I send Terry to bed to get some sleep?"

The woman in question frowned. "The men are out drinking beer, and I get hot tea and an early bedtime?"

"I think we can do better than that," Elizabeth told her sister. She nodded toward the slate blue side-by-side refrigerator in the corner. "There's wine in the fridge."

Terry smiled and jumped to her feet. "How about it, Mom? Feel like giving me a grand send-off?"

The older woman looked at first one daughter, then the other. Eyes twinkling, she said, "Sure. We'll have a toast. But then, the bride goes to bed. I don't want my beautiful daughter posing for her wedding pictures with bags under her eyes."

"Okay, okay," Terry agreed, and reached into the refrigerator. She grabbed a bottle of white Zinfandel, set it on the table and crossed the wide, well-appointed kitchen. "Glasses in the same place?"

"Of course." Elizabeth kept her eyes on her job. She still had two layers to pipe rosettes on, before she could add the final flourishes to what she hoped would be a masterpiece. Naturally the job would go a lot faster if she was working as she preferred to work. Alone, with Beethoven on the CD player. But with her parents spending the weekend at her condo and Terry opting to join them for one last night of family togetherness, that wasn't an option.

"Okay, Lizzie," Terry said as she filled the third glass, "take a break. That's an order."

"Hey, if you don't want a cake at the wedding," she teased, "just say so. It's all right with me."

"One minute, master chef. One minute to give your baby sister a toast."

Elizabeth sighed, set the pastry bag down onto the table and picked up her glass. Standing, she looked at the other women, each in turn. Terry looked wonderful, eager and happy. Their mother was still beautiful, even though there was more gray in her hair than blond these days. Those blue eyes of hers shone with pride, and Elizabeth was suddenly struck with an almost overpowering surge of love for the family she had sometimes taken for granted.

In the next instant the three of them lifted their Waterford crystal glasses and brought them together, less than an inch apart.

"Here's to—" Terry hesitated, then grinned "—Mike getting to the church on time."

"He'll be there," Elizabeth told her. "Harding will watch out for him."

Sally Stone shot a long, thoughtful look at her older daughter before saying, "Don't worry, Terry. Your father promised me that your groom would be at the church on time and clearheaded." Tapping her glass to the other two, she said, "Here's to my baby. May she always be as happy as she is tonight."

"Hear, hear," Elizabeth echoed.

"I will be," Terry whispered.

"Now go to bed," Sally said after a sip of wine.

"Mother," Terry answered with a laugh. "Ten is a little early, don't you think?"

In response, Sally took her daughter's glass and set it on the table. "I've seen the way you and Mike look at each other," she said with a knowing smile. "No doubt you'll be up all night tomorrow night. Wouldn't you like to be well rested and um... *energetic?*"

"Mother!" Terry laughed outright.

"What?" Sally looked at each of them. "We're all grown-ups, aren't we?"

"Apparently," Elizabeth said ruefully. It was the first time their mother had ever talked about sex and one of her girls in the same sentence.

Terry hugged her mother tightly, gave her a resounding kiss on the forehead, then said, "You're absolutely right, Mom. I'm going to bed." She walked to the doorway, then stopped and turned around. "'Night, Lizzie," she said. "And thanks for everything."

Elizabeth took another sip of wine, letting the chilled, fruity drink slide down her throat slowly before answering. "You're welcome. I'll see you in the morning."

Terry nodded brightly and disappeared down the hallway. They heard her run up the stairs and the soft echo of a door closing.

Taking her seat beside Elizabeth again, Sally turned her wineglass between her hands. "Is everything all right, dear?"

She glanced at her mother. "Sure. Why wouldn't it be?"

"No reason," Sally said with a shrug. "It was good of you to offer to make Terry's cake."

Elizabeth smiled to herself and moved on to the next frosted layer. "I couldn't very well let her order some ordinary-looking, dry-tasting cake from a bakery, could I?"

"No, I suppose you couldn't have."

Shooting a sidelong glance at her mother, Elizabeth wondered what the woman was working up to. Her mom had never had trouble saying what was on her mind.

"I do wonder, dear," Sally said softly.

"About what?"

"Well, how you feel about your younger sister getting married before you."

"Mom," Elizabeth paused in her decorating, smoothing the pastry bag and forcing the frosting down closer to the tip. "You can't be serious."

Sally kept her gaze fixed on the wineglass between her palms. "It might bother some women, you know. Make them feel like...old maids."

Elizabeth laughed, ignoring the tiny stab of pain deep inside her. "Come on, Mom. These are the 1990s not the 1890s."

"I know that, but still, some women might have tender feelings about such a thing."

"Some women maybe. Not me."

"I hope not."

Elizabeth laid the pastry bag down and reached over to cover her mother's hand with one of hers. "Remember me, Mom? I'm the daughter who didn't *want* to get married?"

"People change."

"Not always."

"I'm not blind, Lizzie," her mother said softly.

"What's that supposed to mean?"

"I've seen the way you look at Harding Casey."

Uncomfortable with the turn the conversation had taken, Elizabeth picked up the pastry bag and went to work. It gave her a good excuse to keep from looking into her mother's eyes. Eyes that had always been able to tell truth from lies.

"Your father and I like him very much."

"Of course Dad likes him. Harding's a career Marine. What's not to like?"

"It's not just that," Sally said quickly, "though for your father, I admit it *is* a positive sign. But I think Harding is a nice man. He's polite, charming, witty and looks at you as though you're one of those desserts you're so famous for."

Heat stained her cheeks. She felt the color race up her neck, blossoming on her face like wild roses. Dipping her head closer to her work, she said, "Don't look for things that aren't there, Mom."

"I don't think I am," Sally answered quietly. Reaching for her daughter, she tipped Elizabeth's chin up with her fingertips until their gazes met and locked. "And at the same time, sweetie, don't you try to hide from something that might be the gift of a lifetime."

Tears suddenly blinded her. She didn't know whether it was her mother's gentle touch or her soft voice or the fact that those same words had been whispering around inside her own head for days. But whatever the reason, she blinked them back stubbornly.

"Harding and I are...*friends.*" Somehow she just couldn't call him her lover to her mother's face. Thirty-two or not, some things one just didn't say to one's mom.

"Friends," Sally echoed sadly. "Is that all you want from him?"

"That's all there is," she said firmly.

"Lizzie honey, the sparks that fly when you two are near each other are bright enough to light up a city." She smiled tenderly. "Friends don't usually have that effect on each other."

"We're very *close* friends."

"Ahh..." Sally nodded, patted Elizabeth's cheek,

then let her hand fall away. "I thought as much. It's in your eyes, honey, how much you care for him."

"Mom..."

"Does he feel the same? Yes," she answered herself in the next breath. "Of course he does. Even your dad noticed."

"Don't make this into something it isn't, Mom," Elizabeth warned her. "In three weeks Harding's being deployed to Okinawa for six months, and that will be that."

"Will it?" Sally mumbled. "I wonder."

Nine

The groomsmen, all Marines, were wearing their dress blues uniforms. Only the groom himself wore a tuxedo, and Harding was the only person who seemed to notice Mike looking at the uniforms surrounding him just a bit wistfully.

But once he had gotten a look at his bride, that expression in his eyes faded to be replaced by a joy that was so strong, Harding had had to look away from it. It was either that, or be eaten by jealousy for his best friend's good fortune.

All through the short ceremony, Harding's gaze had continually shifted to Elizabeth standing just opposite him at the small altar. Beautiful in a silvery, lilac-colored, off-the-shoulder dress, all he could think was that it should have been the two of them standing in front of the preacher. It should have been *them* repeating those ancient words about love and loyalty and commitment.

He would never have believed it of himself. But the truth was hard to ignore—especially while staring into Elizabeth's eyes.

Lifting his bottle of beer to his lips, Harding looked around the reception hall, trying to find her without seeming obvious. He took a long drink as he casually noted the other Marines in the room, each of them surrounded by a cluster of women. Smiling to himself, he remembered plenty of times when he, too, had used the effect of dress blues on civilians to his best advantage.

Odd that only a week after meeting one particular woman he had no interest in any other. Odd, or fate? he wondered. Was it really fate taking a hand in things? Had he and Elizabeth been brought together by some karmic force?

He whistled low and soft, looked at his beer bottle suspiciously, then set it down on the table beside him. Apparently two beers was enough to kick his imagination into high gear.

Fate?

Karma?

No, what had happened between them was simple science. *Chemistry.*

Across the wide, crowded hall from him, he

finally caught a glimpse of the woman who had turned his brain into slush.

Busying herself around the cake table, she was making last-minute adjustments to the most-gorgeous-looking cake he had ever seen. Five layers, divided by white plastic columns, the wedding dessert had been lovingly decorated with lilac frosting flowers, silver stars and studded with real, live roses. Sterling silver rosebuds, fully bloomed lavender roses and white baby's breath, each blossom tucked into a tiny plastic bud vase then attached to the cake. Tendrils of ribbons streamed from the icing and lay in curled abandon at the base of the cake.

Elizabeth really *was* the Princess of Party Cooking.

Everyone who had seen the cake had paused to admire it. He had listened to their praise for the chef and taken great pride in every word.

"Beautiful, isn't she?" a voice from nearby asked him.

Startled out of his thoughts, Harding half turned to meet the steady gaze of Elizabeth's father. Marine Captain Harry Stone, retired, still looked as if he was ready to report to the parade ground.

At six foot one, Captain Stone stood tall and straight. A receding hairline, more gray than dark brown, and fine lines around his eyes and mouth were the only marks of age on the man.

Instinctively Harding straightened almost to attention. "Yes, sir," he said. "She is."

The captain's gaze shifted to his daughter, unaware of their regard. "You know, Lizzie always was the more hardheaded of my daughters. The one most like me, I guess."

"Sir?" Was he supposed to agree? Wouldn't that be insulting the man? Although he had to admit, Elizabeth was definitely a strong woman. One who knew her own mind and wasn't afraid to voice her opinion. It was one of the things he liked best about her.

"She's not fond of change, you know," her father was saying. "Never has been. Guess that's why she didn't like being raised in the Corps. Hated the moving. The deploying."

Harding nodded and wished for another beer. "My ex-wife felt the same way. Military marriages aren't the easiest thing in the world to maintain."

Captain Stone chuckled, shaking his head. "Never thought I'd hear a career Devil Dog complain about hard work."

Harding shot him a look. Hard work was a part of his life. He had never backed away from a challenge.

"Ease up, Sergeant Major," Elizabeth's father said softly, to avoid being overheard by the wandering guests. "I'm not trying to insult you—"

Harding nodded.

"I'm only trying to point out to you that the seemingly impossible is, most often, something we're afraid to try. Once tried, impossible becomes possible."

"Not always, Captain," Harding muttered, remembering the sense of failure he had experienced when his ex-wife left him, decrying the hard life of being married to the Corps.

"Call me Harry," the older man offered. "And no, Sergeant Major. There are no guarantees. But I can tell you from experience that a good marriage is a blessing." Unconsciously his gaze drifted from his daughter to his wife, chatting and laughing with several other women. His eyes softened, and his features gentled. "The right woman is more than a wife. She's a partner. A friend."

Harding shifted uncomfortably. What was this all about? Was the man actually trying to bring Elizabeth and him together? Hell, as her father, the captain should know better than anyone that his daughter was dead set against any kind of relationship with a career soldier.

Running one finger around the inside collar of his tunic, Harding had to wonder what this man would say if he knew that Elizabeth and he were lovers. Would he still be getting this speech about honor and commitment? Or would the captain be holding a noose?

Feeling distinctly uncomfortable with the conversation, Harding blurted, "If you'll excuse me, sir, I believe I'll go find your younger daughter and give her my condolences on marrying Mike."

The older man smiled. "Certainly, Marine. Go ahead."

Harding escaped immediately, blending into the crowd, losing himself amidst the mingle of voices, the snatches of laughter.

He didn't see the thoughtful expression on Captain Stone's face. Nor did he witness the meaningful glance the captain sent his smiling wife.

There was nothing left to do.

Elizabeth had managed to keep herself busy from the end of the ceremony until now. But she had worked herself out of a job. The buffet-style meal was being catered by a company entirely capable of managing their own help, and her masterpiece of a wedding cake was set up, awaiting its moment.

Clutching a glass of champagne, she wandered aimlessly at the edges of the crowd, smiling to friends and nodding pleasantly to strangers. Always, though, she kept one eye out for Harding.

Standing across the altar from him during the wedding, she had hardly heard the words of the ceremony. Instead, she had indulged silly daydreams—visions of Harding and her standing before a minister. Harding and her holding hands, exchanging rings and promises. Harding and her kissing before a gathering of friends and families, then listening to the applause erupt from the pews.

Silly, she told herself, and took another sip of champagne. No, more than silly. Ludicrous. She didn't even *want* to be married. Let alone to a Marine.

"Oh, Lizzie!"

She turned around in time to see her younger sister sweep down on her, veil flying, eyes sparkling. Terry enveloped her in a hug, then pulled back and grinned happily.

"Isn't this fabulous?"

"Yeah," Elizabeth said, unable to keep from returning Terry's smile. "It's wonderful."

"I actually cried at my own wedding," Terry said with a half laugh. "But it was so beautiful, I just couldn't help it."

"*You're* beautiful, kiddo."

She glanced down at her full-skirted, ivory lace wedding dress and nodded before looking back up at her sister. "You know, I think I am, today." She reached for one of Elizabeth's hands and gave it a squeeze. "The cake turned out so gorgeous. Thank you, Lizzie."

"You're welcome." Winking, she added, "And it tastes even better than it looks."

"Naturally," Terry huffed with pride.

Linking her arm through her sister's, Terry

started walking slowly. "Doesn't Harding look handsome in his uniform?"

Elizabeth narrowed her gaze and looked at her sister suspiciously. Her mother had already pointed out how well Harding filled out a set of dress blues. As if she hadn't noticed without any help from her family.

Deliberately she shrugged. "I never said he wasn't handsome."

Terry's lips twitched. "Has he told you how he got his nickname? Hard Case?"

Intrigued, Elizabeth said, "No." Of course, the only time she had actually *asked* for the information, he had been otherwise occupied. A ribbon of heat swirled through her body as she recalled exactly *what* he had been doing at the time.

"Well," Terry said, apparently not noticing her sister's momentary lapse of attention. "Mike told me. It started in boot camp. Mike says Harding refused to accept less than the best from himself. He pushed himself higher and harder than any of the others—which only earned his squad mates extra duty—because he would show them up so badly."

Elizabeth nodded. That sounded like what she would have expected from Harding Casey.

"When the guys called him on it, he only challenged them to improve." Terry shook her head and smiled. "Anyway, his stubbornness started the nickname there. But when he was sent to Grenada, some of his men were pinned down by enemy fire with no way out."

Immediately Elizabeth, the daughter of a soldier, envisioned the scene in her mind. She saw a small group of Marines, trapped, with bullets biting into the dust at their feet, zinging off rocks by their heads.

Terry continued. "Apparently, when no one else could think of what to do, Harding went in, under fire, and risked his own life to pull his men out— one by one. He went back time and again until they were all safe." She shrugged, stopped and faced her sister squarely. "He simply refused to give up. Refused to accept failure."

Her eyes teared at the mental picture of Harding risking his life repeatedly for the lives of his men. It was so clear to her, she could almost hear the bullets flying.

"Lizzie," Terry whispered urgently. "There's something between you two, isn't there?"

So much for keeping it a secret, Elizabeth thought as she nodded miserably.

"I knew it," Terry crowed. "I knew you two would be good together."

"Don't book the church," Elizabeth said, before her little sister could get up a full head of steam. "Whatever Harding and I have, it's not going to end in marriage."

"Lizzie…"

"Let it go, Terry." She looked directly into her sister's eyes. "Please. You know I never planned on getting married. And Harding is shipping out in less than three weeks."

"He'll be back, though."

Yes, he would be back. But would he be coming back to her? Or would the heat of the fire between them burn itself out while he was gone?

She didn't voice her thoughts, merely shook her head sadly.

Grabbing both of her hands, Terry bent in close and whispered fiercely. "Lizzie, don't blow this. Don't blow a chance to be happy."

"Stop, Terry. You don't know—"

"I know, I know. You hate the military."

"Not the military itself," she corrected. "It's the constant moving, never belonging I don't like. And the absences. Don't you remember all of those times when Dad was gone? All of the birthdays he missed? The Christmases?"

"Sure I do," Terry said. "But I remember everything else, too. I remember his homecomings and having him there, at home every night. I remember the love."

"So do I, Terry," Elizabeth said softly, "but—"

"No buts," her sister said. "I told you how stubborn Hard Case is, right?"

Elizabeth nodded.

"If he loves you, Lizzie, he won't stop. Just like

in Grenada, he'll keep coming back. He'll slip under any bullets you throw at him and keep coming back until you're convinced. As for the travel and deployment," she shrugged. "It wouldn't be hard, Lizzie. Not if you really love him."

She wanted to believe, which surprised her. A week ago she wouldn't have even entertained the notion of marriage at all. Now, here she was having a heart-to-heart with her baby sister about a Marine of all people.

Taking a deep breath, she gave her weary mind permission to shut down for a while. There was simply too much to think about. And now wasn't the time for it.

"I appreciate it, Terry," she said, leaning into her sister for a quick hug. "But Harding and I don't love each other." Not a lie, was it?

The blushing bride didn't look convinced.

"Look," Elizabeth said, "just enjoy your own wedding day, all right? Quit worrying about planning mine?"

"Okay," she finally answered. "But we'll talk about this again. When Mike and I get back from Jamaica?"

Elizabeth nodded, grateful for the respite. Hopefully, by the time the honeymooners were back, this firestorm with Harding would have fizzled out, and there would be nothing to talk about.

"There you are," Mike announced, coming up

behind his new wife and swinging her in a wide circle. "No one will dance with me."

"Well," Terry retorted, "we can't have that, can we?"

As the newlyweds started for the dance floor, arm in arm, Terry looked back over her shoulder. "Later?"

Elizabeth nodded, relieved to be alone again.

"Dance with me?" A familiar, deep voice rumbled from behind her and she slowly turned around. Her heartbeat thundered in her ears, her blood raced through her veins and her knees wobbled unsteadily.

Would she always react like this to him? she wondered. Would his voice always sink to the base of her spine and send chills coursing up and down her back?

His clear blue eyes locked with hers, and Elizabeth felt herself drowning in their depths. She couldn't have looked away if her life had hung in the balance.

"Dance with me," he repeated, this time making it a command, not a request.

She nodded slightly and took the hand he offered her. Sizzles of heat snaked up her arm from their joined hands as she followed him to the dance floor. There, he turned, pulled her into his arms and began to lead her around the floor. Swaying, their bodies touching, she let her mind wander, giving herself over to the sensation of being held by him.

Remembering that in less than three weeks he would be gone from her life.

Harding clenched his jaw tight and somehow managed to keep his grasp on her gentle. "Nice wedding," he said.

"It was, wasn't it?"

"They look happy."

She turned her head and looked at the happy couple. He did too. Mike and Terry were lost in each other. Joy radiated from them like warmth from the sun.

"What were you and your sister talking about?" he asked quietly. He had come up on them too late to overhear anything, but from the expression on Elizabeth's features, she hadn't been any too pleased with the conversation.

Elizabeth shifted her gaze to meet his. He studied those soft brown eyes for a long moment, but whatever she was thinking, she was managing to conceal it from him.

"Nothing, really," she said, and he knew she was lying.

The only reason she would have to lie was if she had been talking about him. Damn, he wondered what she had said.

"You've made quite an impression on my parents," Elizabeth said and moved with him through a slow turn.

"They're nice people." Lord, it was as if they were strangers. This polite conversation was tearing at him.

"I saw you and Dad talking together earlier," she commented.

He stiffened slightly. He wasn't about to let her know that he and his father were discussing her. She would immediately want to know what had been said—and the truth was, he wasn't very sure of that himself.

"Anything you want to tell me about?" she asked.

"No," he said, avoiding her gaze. Just like her, he was lying. Now he was convinced she and Terry had been talking about him. "Just two old Marines exchanging war stories."

She looked up at him, her eyes delving deeply into his. He would never get tired of staring into her eyes.

"My parents will be leaving tomorrow."

"So soon?" he asked, despite the fact that this seemed like the longest weekend of his life. Not being able to be with her was harder on him than boot camp had ever been.

She smiled wryly as if reading his mind. "Yes. Dad's anxious to get back to his cronies and the golf course, and Mom's sure that the volunteer staff at the local hospital can't get along without her."

Her smile didn't falter, but he could see that the thought of her parents leaving made her sad. "You'll miss them."

"Yeah, I will." Elizabeth inhaled sharply. "We don't get together often enough. But, ever since Dad retired, they're almost never home. Always off on some little trip or other."

"So even though he left the Corps, they still travel a lot."

She nodded. "I hadn't thought of it like that, but yes. Sometimes," she added wistfully, "compared to them I feel like a stick-in-the-mud."

He frowned slightly and pulled her closer against him. He inhaled the soft, sweet scent of the fresh lavender and sterling rosebuds that made up the wreath encircling her head. Harding concentrated on that scent, trying to memorize it, so that when he was alone, in Okinawa, thousands of miles from her, he would be able to draw on that memory and bring her close.

She laid her head down on his shoulder, apparently deciding to ignore whoever might be watching them. His right hand smoothed up and down her back, caressing the silk covering her flesh.

Silent now, they danced together with controlled, yet fluid movements. The intimacy of their dance announcing that they were more than polite strangers. He felt her soft sigh, and all he wanted to do was pick her up, carry her to the Mustang outside and drive like a shot to her condo.

But he couldn't. Not with her parents in residence.

Memories of the past few days filled him, making his body tight and hard and filling his mind with erotic images of Elizabeth.

He saw her as he made love to her, looking into her eyes as a climax took her. He saw her smile and reach for him. He saw her naked in her kitchen, scrambling eggs for the two of them at one in the morning.

His right hand slipped lower on her back, riding just above the swell of her behind. His fingers itched to touch her. The crowd of dancers swirled around them, but for him, it was as if they were alone in the room. All he saw was her. All he felt was her.

All he wanted was her.

A warning jolt shot through him. For all of his care, all of his noble intentions of keeping his distance, he wanted Elizabeth. Not just for the few short weeks he had remaining stateside, but for a lifetime.

But a lifetime of Elizabeth meant marriage.

The truth shocked him.

The depths of his feelings rattled around inside him like a sword in a scabbard.

He loved her. More than he had ever imagined

it possible to love a woman, he loved Elizabeth Stone.

Yet that simple fact was met and challenged by another.

She didn't want a husband. And even if she did, he had already tried marriage…and failed miserably.

Ten

Two weeks slipped by with almost eerie speed.

Elizabeth tried not to notice the calendar. She made every effort to not think beyond the moment. Daily, while working in her kitchen, testing new recipes, she had to focus to keep her mind on the work at hand. And still her gaze drifted to the clock on the wall, slowly counting down the hours until Harding would arrive.

She turned the water on, sending clouds of steam rushing up into her face. Squirting liquid soap into the sink, she absently watched bubbles froth and blossom on the surface of the wash water. Somewhere in the back of her mind, she noticed that the Beethoven CD had ended, but she didn't move to replace it. Instead, as she picked up a dishcloth and began to work, she indulged herself in thoughts of Harding.

They had eased into a familiar routine over the past two weeks. He reported for duty at the base every morning, then as soon as his shift was finished, he drove to her condo. They had dinner, rented movies and sometimes went for walks on the beach.

And they loved.

Elizabeth shivered as she washed a cherished ceramic bowl and set it in the dish drainer. She rarely used the dishwasher, since most of her equipment was too treasured to trust to machinery. Besides, washing dishes freed her mind, and she had thought up some of her best recipes while her hands were buried in soapsuds.

As she turned off the water, she reached for a fresh towel and began drying the mountain of mixing bowls and utensils. While she worked, her mind wandered back to the subject that seemed to fascinate it most.

Harding Casey.

Images raced through her brain. Erotic images. Loving images. Together they had christened nearly every room in her condo. There wasn't a place in her home where she could go and not be reminded of him. His touch. His kisses. His deep voice and the whispered words of passion that had been ingrained in her memory.

All night, every night, they lay in each other's arms, talking of their pasts, because any mention of a future would only destroy their present. And every morning at dawn he rose from her bed, showered and dressed. Then he left her to return to the base.

And every morning when he was gone, she moved over on her queen-size mattress to lie where he had lain. The still-warm sheets comforted her, his pillow rested beneath her head, and she dreamed of that night, when he would come again.

But the few short days they had left were quickly passing. In no time she would be alone again.

What would she do when he was gone?

Mechanically she walked around the kitchen, returning her equipment to its proper places. Soon, he would be leaving. Six long months when she wouldn't see him...be held by him.

And there was no guarantee that she would see him again when he returned, either. She stopped short, caught by that thought. Did she *want* a guarantee? Wasn't she the one who had insisted from the start that she wasn't looking for a long-term relationship? Hadn't she insisted that marriage wasn't in her plans?

Marriage? Where had that come from?

She almost laughed aloud at the pitiful attempt at self-delusion. Thoughts of marriage had been lurking near the edge of her consciousness for days. So far she hadn't let them get any further.

Tossing the damp towel down onto the butcher-block counter, Elizabeth stared around at the world she'd created for herself so painstakingly. Up-to-the-minute appliances. Plenty of workspace. Homey, yet modern. Everything she had wanted her home to be.

And yet...until meeting Harding Casey, she had never noticed just how *empty* it was. How the wind blowing across the shutters sounded like a soft sigh. Folding her arms over her chest, she leaned against the countertop, feeling the edge of the butcher block bite into the base of her spine.

Had the place *always* been this quiet? she wondered. Was that the reason she was constantly feeding the CD player or flipping on the TV? Or had she noticed the quiet now merely because the past three weeks she had rarely been alone?

Rubbing her face briskly with both hands, she then reached up and yanked her tortoiseshell headband off. Instantly a budding headache eased. She combed her fingers through her hair and tugged at the hem of her pale pink tank top.

Glancing down at herself, she wondered vaguely if she should change clothes before Harding arrived. A white splotch of flour and water had crusted over, in the center of her shirt between her breasts, and there was a grease stain on the right leg of her cutoff denim shorts.

Then she heard the front door open.

"Elizabeth?"

"In here," she called out, a familiar excitement already flooding her system. Her stomach muscles tightened, and every inch of her body went on red alert. Would she always feel this incredible surge of elation just at the sound of his voice?

He stepped through the kitchen doorway, a white paper bag resting in the curve of one arm. A familiar, somehow cloying, aroma filled the kitchen and Elizabeth swallowed heavily.

"Chinese?" she asked.

He shrugged and set the bag on the table. "I figured you might like takeout for a change."

Thoughtful. She loved Chinese food. Her stomach jumped again, but this time it wasn't as pleasant a sensation. Licking suddenly dry lips, she tried to ignore the flutter of uneasc rippling through her.

"Getting tired of my cooking?" she teased as she took a step closer to him.

"Nope," he assured her with a wink. "But I've got plans for you lady…and they don't include cooking."

Oh, Lord. Her knees turned to jelly, and damp heat rushed to her center. "What kind of plans?" she asked, after clearing her throat.

He pulled her up tight against him and wrapped

his arms around her. Elizabeth closed her eyes tight, wanting to always remember what it felt like to be held this close to him. There were six months of lonely nights ahead of her, and she would need every one of her memories to survive them.

She bent her head and buried her nose in his shoulder, hoping to avoid the almost overpowering odor of sweet-and-sour sauce.

Harding threaded his fingers through her hair, cupping the back of her head in his palm.

The need didn't ease. The hunger he felt for her only strengthened with each passing day. He kept telling himself that a passion as hot as theirs couldn't last. Couldn't sustain itself. But not only did it continue to burn, it continued to surpass itself.

She shuddered in his arms, and he told himself he was a lucky man. There weren't many men, he would wager, who had a woman as eager for him as he was for her. Smiling to himself, he looked down and eased her head back until he could see her clearly.

Eyes closed, her lips clamped tightly, she looked a bit paler than she had when he had walked in. As he watched her, she swallowed heavily, inhaled, then grimaced.

"Elizabeth?" he asked, sudden concern overriding his desire. "Are you all right?"

"I'm fine," she said through clenched teeth.

"Well, you don't *look* fine," he told her. As he

spoke he saw tiny beads of sweat break out on her forehead. Alarmed, he laid the back of his hand against her clammy skin to check for a fever.

She pushed back out of his arms. "I'm not sick, Harding," she said, her voice ringing with determination. "It's just that smell."

Frowning, he studied her. "What smell?"

Elizabeth waved one hand at the sack on the table. "That." She inhaled sharply again, scowled and took a few steps away from the food. "Can't you smell it?"

He sniffed the air appreciatively. "Yeah. It smells great."

She shook her head, lifting one hand to cover her mouth. "What did you get, anyway?"

"Your favorites," he said, really confused now. "Egg rolls, fried rice, cashew chicken and sweet-and-sour pork."

"That's the smell." Her lips pulled back from her teeth, and she nearly snarled at the cartoned food.

"What?" He reached into the sack, pulling out one of the small white cartons. "The pork?" he asked, opening the top and taking a step toward her. "It's the same stuff we had last week. You loved it."

She backed up like a vampire from a cross. "No. It's different. The sweet-and-sour sauce. Must be bad."

He inhaled deeply, letting the mingle of spices

and seasonings rush into his lungs. Nothing wrong there, he told himself, and glanced at the woman still backpedaling out of the kitchen. If he wasn't mistaken, Elizabeth's features had taken on a decidedly green cast.

"Are you all right?"

"Yes," she said quickly, then shook her head. Her eyes wide, she mumbled, "No," just before she turned and ran out of the room.

Hot on her heels, Harding rounded the corner to the bathroom in time to hold her head as she was thoroughly sick. Several minutes later he offered her a damp washcloth and led her to the living room. There, he sat her on the couch and eased down onto the coffee table directly opposite her.

"How long have you been sick?" he asked. He didn't want to think about her lying around the house all day, miserable and alone.

"I wasn't sick," she said. "Not until I got a whiff of that…" She shuddered and pointed at the kitchen.

"You mean the—"

She held one hand up. "Please. Don't even say it."

Reaching out, he touched her forehead again, pleased to note that she didn't seem quite so chilled and clammy anymore. "No fever."

Letting her head fall against the overstuffed

sofa back, she muttered thickly, "I told you. I'm not sick."

"Then why else would you—" He stopped dead. As far as he knew there was only one reason—other than the flu or food poisoning—for a woman to be sick to her stomach.

The same thought had apparently occurred to her. She lifted her head gingerly and looked at him. "This doesn't necessarily mean a thing."

"Yeah, right." He stood up, keeping his gaze locked with hers. "When were you due?"

"Excuse me?"

"Stow it, princess," he said softly. "When?"

"A few days ago." When he jerked her a nod and started for the front door, she added quickly, "But I've been late before."

"I'll be right back," he told her as he grabbed the doorknob and turned.

"Where are you going?" she asked.

"To the drugstore," he said simply. "It's time to find out one way or the other."

He actually purchased two different pregnancy test kits. Elizabeth stared at Harding as he paced aimlessly around her bedroom. When he returned from the pharmacy with the kits, he had told her that they shouldn't trust such a major test to one kit. She couldn't help wondering though if the real reason was he was hoping for two different responses so they could have another bit of breathing space.

Elizabeth didn't know *what* she was hoping for.

She'd gone over and over the options in her mind, but none of the other choices were valid ones for *her*. She couldn't give away her own child, only to perhaps have to one day face an eighteen-year-old adult angry about being abandoned. As for the other choice, she couldn't reconcile herself to that idea at all.

"Isn't it time, yet?" Harding asked.

She glanced over at him and sympathized. His solemn, almost-grim features echoed her own.

"No," she said. "The timer's set. It'll ring when the tests are finished."

He nodded, rubbed one hand over the back of his neck and stared down at the rose-colored carpet. "Five minutes never seemed so long before."

"I know." She wished time could stand still. She wished she could think of something brilliant—or comforting—to say.

A digital timer screeched suddenly, sending both of them into a dash for the doorway. Elizabeth beat him since she was a good three feet closer. Shutting off the ringing alarm, she took a deep breath, picked up the two plastic wands and looked down into the test squares.

"Well?" Harding asked from behind her. "What's the verdict?"

Her hands trembling, she inhaled sharply and forced a smile as she turned around to face him. "The verdict is mixed," she said.

"What do you mean?" He took a step closer. "One says yes, the other no?"

"Not quite," she told him as a wave of uneasiness washed over her. "According to these, I'm definitely pregnant."

Not a flicker of emotion showed on his face. "Then what's this 'mixed verdict' business about?"

"Well." She choked on a laugh. "One's pink, the other's blue. So I'm pregnant, we just don't know what it is, a boy or a girl."

"That's not very funny." If anything, his features had become even more solemn.

"Give me a minute, I'm new at this." She was babbling. She could feel it. She just couldn't stop it. "I know, it's twins. A boy *and* a girl."

"Elizabeth…"

"Or, no." She waved both wands in the air like a drunken conductor. "I know—with our luck, it's quadruplets!"

Harding stepped up close to her. Taking the test sticks from her hands, he glanced at the results, then laid them both down on the counter behind her.

Elizabeth shivered, suddenly cold right down to her bones. She was talking a mile a minute and he was too damned quiet.

A baby.

At thirty-two years old, she was going to have a baby.

A sheen of tears filled her eyes, and her vision blurred. Dropping one hand to her flat abdomen, she laid her palm gently atop her nesting child as if to apologize for ever wishing it away.

Harding saw the movement and immediately covered her hand with his. She looked up at him, and he was struck to the core by the unexpected film of tears shimmering in her eyes.

"Good heavens, Harding," she whispered, her voice catching on a strangled sob. "We actually made a baby."

His throat too tight to speak, he simply pulled her into the circle of his arms. Nestling her head beneath his chin, he gently stroked her back with long, caressing movements in an attempt to calm and comfort her.

A baby.

At thirty-eight he was going to be a father.

Something inside his chest tightened around his heart until he thought that organ might burst. Most of his life, he'd been alone. He hadn't had a family since he was a kid. And except for his one glaring failure at marriage, he had never *tried* to create a family of his own.

The Corps had always been enough.

Until now.

"I suppose," she said, her voice muffled against his chest, "you want to talk about it right this minute."

He smiled briefly. She knew him well. "Yeah," he said, dropping a kiss onto the top of her head. "I do."

She pulled in one long, shuddering breath and nodded before stepping away from him. "Okay, but let's go into the kitchen, huh? I could use some coffee."

He frowned as she stepped past him and made her way down the hall. "Do you think you should be drinking caffeine?"

"Oh." Elizabeth's steps faltered slightly. "I don't know. I guess not, though. Okay, I'll settle for herbal tea."

Following after her, he took a seat at the kitchen table and waited for her to settle herself. Strange, how well he had gotten to know her in the past three weeks. He knew that she needed to be moving when her mind was busy. He also knew that until she sat down with her cup of tea in hand, she wasn't going to be listening to him.

As she moved around the room, he let his mind drift. In less than a week, he would be shipping out for Okinawa. He wouldn't be here to help her through the next several months. He wouldn't be able to hold her head for her when she was sick or to comfort her when she was worried.

Harding leaned back in his chair and reached up to undo his collar button and yank his tie off. She sat down on the opposite side of the table, cupped her mug between her palms and took a long, slow sip of tea. Only then did she look at him.

"You haven't said much," she accused gently.

That was only one of the differences between them, he thought. When her emotions ran high, so did her tongue. He, on the other hand, had a tendency to keep quiet until he had his thoughts together.

"I want to make sure I say what I have to say right."

Her gaze flicked away from his, then back again. She looked to be steeling herself. "What do you have to say, Harding? Just spit it out. Lord knows, I did."

"All right," he said. Reaching across the table separating them, he took her mug and set it aside. Then he covered both of her hands with his. There was really only one thing to say, and he had to get it right. Everything depended on it. Inhaling sharply, deeply, he said on a rush, "I want you to marry me before I ship out, Elizabeth."

She drew her hands out from under his. Staring straight into his eyes, she said softly, "Somehow, I knew that's what you were going to say."

"That's not an answer," he reminded her.

"You're right," she agreed and nodded absently. "But this is. My answer is no, Harding. I *won't* marry you. I can't."

Eleven

"Why the hell not?"

She winced inwardly. That short, sharp question came out in a voice rough with undisguised frustration. Elizabeth could understand how he felt, and she really didn't enjoy turning down a marriage proposal from the father of her newly discovered child. But she wasn't about to sacrifice the lives of three people on the altar of *propriety*.

Preparing herself for what she knew would be a fierce battle, she deliberately kept her voice even and calm as she said, "Because you don't love me, Harding. You're proposing for the wrong reason."

He jumped to his feet, sending his chair clattering to the floor. Stopping, he bent, righted the chair again, then strode to the sink where he turned around to look at her again. "How do you know I *don't* love you? Maybe I've loved you all along and was too stupid—or too wary to say so."

Something inside her leaped at that notion, and she deliberately quashed the budding eagerness. She knew Harding Casey well. He was an honorable man to whom doing the right thing came as second nature. Of course he would lie and proclaim his love. He didn't want to ship out on deployment leaving behind his pregnant lover without *trying* to help.

"No, Harding," she said firmly. "You never would have asked me to marry you if I weren't pregnant."

"We'll never know that for sure, will we?"

No, they wouldn't. A small spear of regret shivered through her. How strange life was, she told herself. A month ago she would have sworn that she wasn't the slightest bit interested in marriage. She had long since buried her old dreams of children and resigned herself to the knowledge that she would never be a mother.

Now, four weeks later, she was pregnant and refusing the proposal of a man she loved.

Love. She breathed slowly, deeply as the acknowledgment settled into her bones. She loved Harding Casey. Career Marine. That elusive emotion had sneaked up on her when she wasn't looking, and now things were too complicated for her to surrender to a love that might be all one-sided.

"You wouldn't have proposed, Harding," she insisted. He'd made it perfectly clear from the beginning of their relationship that he wasn't looking for a wife, any more than she wanted a husband.

"Oh," he said, slipping into sarcasm, "so now you're the *Psychic* Princess of Party Cooking?"

"You said yourself that you had already tried marriage once and weren't interested in trying again."

"That was then. Things are different now."

She nodded sadly. "I know. The baby."

He inhaled sharply and curled his fingers tightly around the edge of the countertop. "Yes, the baby. This changes things. But dammit, Elizabeth, I cared about you before the baby, and you know it."

"Caring and wanting to marry someone are two entirely different things." Elizabeth folded her hands in her lap and tried to rein in her rising temper. "There's no reason for us to fight about this, Harding."

"There's plenty of reason, princess," he countered and crossed her kitchen floor in a few long, angry strides. Glaring down at her, he went on. "In less than a week, I'm out of here. I'll be thousands of miles away for six damn months."

"Harding—" She tried to interrupt.

"And you'll be here, pregnant with *my* baby. Alone."

She stood up, folded her arms across her chest and met his glare with one of her own. "I've lived alone for quite a while now, you know. I've managed to take care of myself quite nicely so far without the help of a certain Sergeant Major."

"Yeah, well up to now you haven't been pregnant, have you?"

No, she hadn't. A momentary thread of worry unwound within her. Oh, she didn't doubt that she could handle the pregnancy on her own. But once the baby was here, then what?

She paused mentally and almost sighed in relief. Apparently she had already made the most important decision. There would *definitely* be a baby.

Already Elizabeth felt the first stirrings of a long-denied maternal urge. She could no more rid herself of this baby than she could stop breathing. But answering one question only posed more.

What would her fairly liberal parents have to say about their unmarried, oldest daughter giving birth to their first grandchild? Could she handle the incredible responsibility of raising a child? And most important, was she capable of giving a child enough love so that it wouldn't miss having a live-in father? Or would she louse things up so badly her child would one day tell a doctor that "it's all my mother's fault"?

"Elizabeth?"

She dismissed her wandering thoughts and focused her attention on the man standing so close to her. "I'm sorry, Harding."

He grabbed her upper arms and pulled her closer. Staring into her eyes, looking for reassurance, he asked, "Are you going to—"

"No," she said. "I'm not going to end the pregnancy."

He exhaled heavily, clearly relieved.

"In fact," she said and forced a half smile. "I want to thank you."

"For what?"

"For the baby."

Harding shook his head briskly as if he couldn't believe what he was hearing. "Thank me?"

"Yes. I had given up on the hope of having children. So thank you."

"Oh." He released her and took a long step back. "You're welcome. Anytime."

She stiffened slightly, and Harding was sure his sarcastic comment had struck home. Dammit, she was shutting him out as completely as if he had already left the country. He felt like a sperm donor. Thanks so much, goodbye now. Have a nice life. Well, she wasn't going to get rid of him so easily.

Reaching up, he smoothed both hands along the

sides of his head. How was he supposed to convince her to marry him if he couldn't convince her that he loved her?

Blast it, he should have said something at the wedding. Or any time during the past two weeks. Why hadn't he asked her to marry him sooner? Before the baby. Hell, he knew why. Because he'd been a husband once before…and done a poor job of it, too. He hadn't wanted to risk hurting Elizabeth *or* himself with another failure.

Even now the thought of marriage terrified him. But the thought of living without her paralyzed him. And now there was his child to consider, too. His child. A well of emotion rose up in his chest. He wanted to be a part of his kid's life. Not a part-time parent every other weekend and three weeks in the summer.

He wanted it all. A home. Elizabeth. The baby. But even if she believed he loved her, would she marry him? Or would his being in the Corps stand in their way? What would he do then? Was he willing to give up his career? The only life he'd ever known? The Corps was more than a job to him. It was his life. It was a matter of pride. And honor. And duty. Could he stop being a Marine? Even if it meant having Elizabeth?

"You want me to resign, Elizabeth?" he asked suddenly, steeling himself for her answer.

She took a step toward him. "I would never ask you to give up who you are for me."

"You hate the military."

"I hate the absences. The moving around."

"That's part of it."

"I know," she said. "But, Harding, your leaving the Corps wouldn't change the fact that you proposed for the sake of your child."

"I didn't, though," he retorted, and reached for her again. He felt her tremble beneath his hands and lowered his voice. "I love you. Dammit, I never thought I'd be saying those words, Elizabeth. But I am, and I mean them."

"Harding," she started.

"No." He pulled her tightly to him, wrapping his arms around her and holding on for dear life. "I *love* you." Staring down into her soft brown eyes, he willed her to read the truth in his. But all he saw shining up at him was a deep sadness. "You're a hardheaded woman, Elizabeth, but I don't give up easily."

"You should, Harding," she said. "For both our sakes."

"I can't," he told her solemnly. "For that very reason."

She laid her palms against his chest and pushed out of his arms. The ache inside him blossomed as she tried to distance herself from him. He saw her close herself off as effectively as if she had stepped into a tiny room and shut the door behind her.

"Elizabeth," he said softly, already feeling her loss. "I won't be pushed away. Not from you and not from my child."

She threw a quick glance at him. "I would never try to keep you from your child."

"You are. Now."

"No, I'm just refusing to marry you."

"It's the same thing."

"No, it isn't," she replied hotly. "Lots of people share custody of their children. The kids grow up fine."

"Most do," he admitted. It was all slipping away from him. He felt it go and was powerless to stop it. "But if those kids had a choice, I figure most of them would want their mom and dad living in the same house. They'd rather be together."

"Sometimes we don't get a choice."

"And sometimes we do—we just make the wrong one," he countered quickly. "Don't do that, Elizabeth. Don't make a choice we'll all be sorry for. I don't want to be a visitor in my kid's life." He paused a moment, then added, "Or yours."

Her bottom lip trembled slightly, but she lifted her chin and fought through whatever she was feeling. "This will all work out, Harding. You'll see."

"All I see is that you're willing to turn your back on me and what we've found together."

She crossed her arms over her chest and rubbed her hands up and down her arms. "What we found was just what we both wanted, Harding. A few weeks together. A temporary affair enjoyed by two adults."

And they called *him* Hard Case. Stepping up close to her, he cupped her face in his hands and held her still when she would have moved away. "That's how it started, princess. I don't deny that we weren't *looking* for love. But whether we wanted it or not, it's here."

She shook her head and closed her eyes against his piercing gaze.

"It's here, princess. And it's the real thing. I think it always was, despite what we told ourselves. Trust me on this. I know." He smiled sadly, remembering the one other time in his life when he had thought himself in love. That puny emotion wasn't a tenth of what he had found with Elizabeth. Damn, why hadn't he had the courage to face that one simple fact before now? When he might have had a chance. "If we throw it away, not only will we miss an opportunity to be happy...our baby will be cheated out of a family."

"Stop, Harding," she whispered, still keeping her eyes closed. "Please stop."

"I'll never stop, Elizabeth." He stroked her cheekbones with the pads of his thumbs, wiping away a solitary tear that had seeped from the corner of her eye. "I don't quit. Even when it might be less painful to walk away, I don't." He bent his head and planted a series of soft, gentle kisses along her brow. "You can't get rid of me, and the only way you can convince me to stop asking you to marry me is to tell me you don't love me."

She opened her mouth to speak, and he had to smile at her stubbornness. Covering her lips with his fingertips, he added, "Say it and *mean* it."

She closed her mouth and opened her eyes. He was heartened to see a sheen of tears filming over their deep brown color. She loved him. She was simply too afraid to take a chance. He understood fear. But cowering in a corner trying to avoid it only made fear a stronger, more terrifying opponent. He had to make her see that the only way to defeat the fear was to stand against it.

Together. "This isn't over," he whispered. "Not by a long shot."

Two days later Elizabeth stared at her most recent culinary disaster.

"Why did no one ever tell me that pregnant women can't bake?" she muttered. Grabbing her cow-shaped hot pads, she picked up the torte pan and carried it to the trash can. There she dumped the charred pastry and glared in disgust at the mess.

It wasn't being pregnant that was ruining her

ability to cook. It was thoughts of Harding. Blast him, she hadn't been able to think about anything but him since he'd left her house two nights before.

And the situation wasn't being helped by the fact that she hadn't heard so much as a word from him in that time, either. What happened to all of his talk about not quitting? Not giving up on her? Was this some bizarre backward way of asking a woman to marry you? By ignoring her until she lost her mind, then sweeping in and overpowering her?

Setting the still-hot pan onto a folded-up, blue-checked towel, she plopped down into a chair. Resting her elbow on the tabletop, she propped her chin on her knuckles and glanced at the clock on the opposite wall.

Only one in the afternoon. She still had way too much daylight left before she could go to bed. Not that she could even look forward to sleep these days. Her dreams were filled with Harding, and memories of the past few weeks. The images tore at her, preventing sleep. Last night she had even dreamed about her child—only her unborn baby had been about six in her dream. Six and angry. Angry that his daddy wasn't around and furious that she wasn't doing anything about it.

Elizabeth yawned, then frowned when the phone rang, interrupting her perfectly good self-pity party.

Pushing herself to her feet, she walked across the room, leaned her back against the wall and snatched the receiver from its cradle.

"Yes?"

"Elizabeth Stone?" a deep voice asked.

A ridiculous flutter of excitement rippled through her body before she realized that the voice was unfamiliar.

"Yes? Who is this?" She straightened up from the wall.

"This is Captain Haynes at Camp Pendleton."

Dread settled in her chest. Her stomach took a nosedive, and she had to swallow past a hard knot in her throat. Danger to a soldier didn't solely exist on a battlefield. There were training accidents all the time. Her heartbeat unsteady, she forced herself to ask, "What is it? Is Harding all right? Was he hurt?"

"No, ma'am, the Sergeant Major is fine," the voice said. "In fact, I'm actually calling on his behalf."

Relief rushed in to replace the dread. "What do you mean?"

"I'd like to offer myself as a character witness for Sergeant Major Casey," the captain said.

"I'm sorry?" She frowned at the phone in her hand.

"I've known Sergeant Major Casey for several

years now. I find him to be an exemplary Marine and an honorable man."

Elizabeth crossed the room to the sink, stretching out the phone cord to its limits. Turning on the tap, she poured herself a glass of cold water, took a quick sip and said, "That's very nice to hear, Captain. But I don't understand why you would call me to—"

"I owe Harding Casey," the man said, effectively cutting her off. "If I can help him straighten things out with his fiancée, I'm happy to help."

She inhaled sharply, set the glass down and walked back to the phone cradle. Fiancée. Varied emotions scattered through her like fallen leaves caught in a whirlwind. Amusement, anger, frustration, sympathy and love all warred within her, battling for supremacy. Finally she gathered her wits and told him very politely, "I appreciate your thoughtfulness, Captain." She wasn't going to tell the man that she wasn't engaged to Harding. It would be the same as calling him a liar, and that she wasn't prepared to do. Especially to his commanding officer.

"Not a problem at all, Ms. Stone," he said, and his voice sounded as though he was pleased with the results of his call. "If there's anything else I can do, please feel free to contact me here at the base."

"Thank you," she managed to say, "but I think you've done enough."

After he hung up, Elizabeth slammed the

phone back into its base and glared at it. What was Harding up to now? Was he going to have every officer he knew call her to vouch for him? Did he really think that other people's opinions would be enough to sway her decision?

She shook her head and wished there were more time. More time for Harding and her to know each other. To get used to the idea of a baby. But she was out of time and she knew it. In just a few more days he would be leaving.

The doorbell rang and she jumped, startled. Tossing a glance from the now-silent phone to the front door, she wondered briefly if she should even answer the thing. For all she knew, the Marine Corps marching band might be standing in her front yard.

She laughed at her own exaggeration, determinedly went to the front door and threw it open wide. On her porch stood two women about her age, a blonde and a brunette, each of them with a toddler by the hand. "Can I help you?" she asked hesitantly.

"Are you Elizabeth Stone?" one of the women asked.

Wary now, she answered slowly. "Yeesss..."

They smiled at her. "Thank goodness," the blonde said. "We've been driving around this condominium complex for twenty minutes. They all look alike!"

Foolishly Elizabeth felt she should apologize for their troubles. She didn't. "Do I know you?"

"Nope," the brunette assured her as she picked up her little girl who'd begun to whine and slung her on one hip. "We're here because of Hard Case."

A sinking sensation started in the middle of her chest and slowly drifted down her body until it came to rest in the pit of her stomach. Apparently Harding wasn't finished "convincing" her yet.

"Let me guess," she said wryly. "Character witnesses?"

"Heck, no," the blonde replied. "Harding doesn't need a character witness. Anyone who knows him will tell you that."

The brunette spoke up, her voice drowning out her friend's defensive, squeaky tone. "Harding told us you were engaged, but that you were a little leery about marrying into the Corps."

Perfect. She swallowed back a groan of frustration. These women weren't at fault. This was all Harding's doing.

"He thought it might help if we talked to you," the brunette finished.

Trapped, Elizabeth's good manners kicked in. Her mother would have been proud. "Would you like to come in?"

"No, thanks," the blonde said as she bent to scoop up her son. "Tony's tired and we want to get back home for nap time. We only stopped by because we were up here shopping and—"

"It doesn't matter why we stopped," the brunette cut in again. "We only wanted to tell you that we can understand how you feel." She glanced at her friend. "Neither one of us was real crazy about marrying a Marine, either."

"Yeah," the blonde said. "I never figured me to be the military type." She shrugged and smiled. "But you can't plan who you'll fall in love with. Besides, it worked out fine." She grinned at her friend, then looked back at Elizabeth. "For both of us."

"Marines aren't always the easiest men to live with," the brunette continued as she gently pressed her daughter's head into her shoulder where the child promptly fell asleep. "But they are definitely the best."

Elizabeth felt she should say *something* in her own defense, so she blurted, "My father is a retired captain. I know about life in the Corps."

Rather than getting approval from one Marine family to another, she received a frosty glare from the brunette.

"If you're Marine, what's the problem? You should already know what life in the Corps is like."

"I *do* know. That's the problem." She couldn't believe she was having such a conversation with strangers! Just wait until she saw Harding Casey again. "Look, I've done my share of suitcase living. It's not something I enjoy. Surely you can understand that."

The blonde shook her head slowly as if sorry for Elizabeth. The brunette was a tad more direct. "My husband risks his *life* for his country," she said solemnly, yet with a spark of defiance. "All he asks of me is that I risk moving to a new neighborhood every few years."

Elizabeth hadn't really thought of it like that, and she felt slightly ashamed of herself. Her lifelong complaint sounded suddenly petty and childish. Still, she had to ask. "What about your kids? Don't you worry about dragging them all over the world?"

"My kids will see places most children won't," the brunette told her. "And they'll be proud that their daddy served his country." Half turning to her friend, she said quietly, "Come on, Sharon. We better get the kids home."

The blonde smiled a goodbye, then started for their car. The brunette stayed a minute longer.

"My husband is a Staff Sergeant," she said. "We've known Harding Casey off and on for years. They don't come any better than him."

"I know," Elizabeth whispered and felt the truth of that statement down to her soul. If she could only be sure of his love. But she couldn't. If she surrendered to her own fears of being a single mother and married him now, she would never know if he had proposed because he loved her—or because of the baby.

The brunette stared at her for a long minute and apparently approved of what she saw. When she finally nodded, she smiled and said, "Good. If you know that much, any problem can be worked out." She stepped off the porch and onto the walk.

Elizabeth opened the door and called out, "Hey, I don't even know your name."

Stopping, the brunette turned around and grinned. "Sorry. I'm Tess Macguire." She jerked her head toward the car. "That's Sharon Trask." In a lower voice she added, "Her husband's still a corporal, but he's up for promotion."

"Thanks for stopping by," Elizabeth said automatically. Her manners were really excellent, she thought, as she realized she had just thanked two strangers for butting into her life.

The two women waved as their car pulled out from the curb. Before the sound of their engine had died away, a florist's van came to a stop in front of her house. As she watched, a young man leaped out of the van, walked around to the back and opened the doors. He reached inside and came back out with the biggest bouquet Elizabeth had ever seen.

Roses. Roses of every color and scent. Packed tightly together and tied with a pale blue ribbon attached to a mylar balloon that read Marry Me in bright red letters.

Dumbfounded, she took the flowers from the delivery boy, snatched a small white envelope from the cluster of blossoms and opened it. As the van drove off, her gaze scanned the brief message. "Elizabeth, I love you. Marry me. Harding."

She inhaled sharply, unwittingly drawing the mingled scents of the roses deep inside her lungs. Biting her lip, she clutched the bouquet tightly and stepped back inside the house. She hurriedly closed the door on the world, just in case a general happened by.

When the phone rang again, she wasn't even surprised.

It had to be Harding. Unwilling to set the flowers down, she held them to her chest and snatched up the cordless phone closest to her.

Before she could even say hello, she heard her mother's voice demand, "Why didn't you tell us you were getting married?"

Twelve

She spent nearly a half hour soothing her mother and assuring her that she would be invited to the wedding—if there ever was one. Thank God Harding had had the sense not to mention the baby when he had made his call. But no sooner had she hung up with her mother than the phone rang again. Elizabeth spent the next hour fielding phone calls from everyone Harding Casey had ever known.

Finally, in desperation, she took the phone off the hook.

With her drapes drawn, door closed and locked, the phone beeping and metallically cursing at her, Elizabeth plopped down onto the couch. She felt like a prisoner in her own home. She was being outflanked by a professional soldier and didn't have the slightest idea how to fight back.

Turning her head, she glanced at the lead crystal vase, sitting in the center of the coffee table. She glared at the bouquet of roses and told herself she should throw them out or, better yet, send them back. But it was too late for the latter, and she couldn't quite bring herself to toss them into the trash.

She felt as though she was being bombarded from all sides. She couldn't think straight anymore. All she was sure of was that she couldn't afford to surrender to Harding's campaign. If she made a mistake, her baby would have to pay the price. And that, she wasn't willing to risk.

The doorbell rang, and her gaze shot to the closed door.

A moment later three brisk knocks sounded in the stillness. What now? she wondered. A parade? Groaning slightly, she pushed up from the couch and walked quietly to the door. There, she peered through the peephole and saw a thoroughly bored-looking teenage girl clutching a clipboard of all things. Looking past the gum-chewing redhead, Elizabeth studied her empty yard as if expecting an assault team to leap up from behind the rows of pansies and storm her house. A long minute passed before she decided the coast was clear.

She opened the door, faced the girl and asked, "Yes?"

"You Elizabeth Stone?" The redhead squinted at her.

Though she was beginning to seriously consider changing her name, she had to say, "Yes, I am. What is it?"

The teenager held up the clipboard and gave it a wave. "Got a telegram for you." She unhooked a small, yellow envelope, then held out the clipboard toward Elizabeth. "Gotta sign for it."

Sighing, Elizabeth edged the screen door open, scrawled her name across line nineteen, then took the envelope.

"You should get your phone checked, lady," the girl said. "They tried to call the telegram in, but something's wrong with the line."

"Thanks," she said, having no intention of putting that phone back on the hook. She reached for her purse, lying on the entry table. Grabbing for her wallet, she pulled a dollar bill free and handed it to the girl.

"Hey, thanks, lady," the teenager said with a grin.

Elizabeth nodded absently, then stepped back and closed the door. Leaning against it, she tore open the envelope and read the all-too-brief message inside. "Six o'clock tonight. Be ready. We have to talk. Harding."

Unbelievable.

She stared at the telegram a moment longer, then slowly, completely, crumpled it in one fist. He ignores her for two days, tells everyone he knows that they're engaged and sends them to plead his case for him, then has the nerve to order her around? Elizabeth pushed away from the door, stalked her way to the kitchen and unceremoniously tossed his precious telegram into the trash can. Who did he think he was, anyway? The man had even had the nerve to lie to *her* parents about them.

"Oh," she said with a tight smile, "I'll be ready, Harding Casey. I only hope you are."

Harding watched the limousine pull up and park. He tugged at the hem of his dress blue tunic and tried to ignore the rush of nerves sweeping through him. Hell, he'd been in battle. He'd crawled to safety under withering enemy fire.

Why was it that facing this one woman could bring him to his knees?

Because, he told himself, the object of war was to simply stay alive. To keep existing. The object of this crusade with Elizabeth was *life*. Not just existing. But really and truly living for the first time. If he lost this skirmish, he'd have nothing.

The limo driver opened the back door, and she stepped out. Just looking at her took his breath away. She straightened up, smoothed her black skirt and glanced around for a minute before she saw him. Then her eyes widened and her jaw dropped visibly.

Good. He'd gone to a lot of trouble to ensure just that reaction. As she looked around, he followed her gaze, seeing it through her eyes.

Alongside one of the fire rings set up for barbecues at the Huntington Beach pier, a small table was set up…with a white linen tablecloth, fine china and crystal glassware. A solitary candle burned brightly within the safe haven of a hurricane lamp. Standing a discreet distance away, a couple of Marines were stationed to keep other people from wandering in too close. For what he needed to say, he wanted privacy.

But he also had wanted the atmosphere of the beach. He was hoping the memory of their walk on the sand that night they met would help his cause.

Bending slightly to one side, Harding punched a button on a nearly hidden tape recorder, and immediately the soft, delicate strains of Beethoven lifted into the cool, summer air.

He thought he saw a smile flit briefly across her face, but he couldn't be sure, because it vanished almost instantly. Then she was walking toward him, and it was all he could do to keep from going to her, drawing her close and kissing her senseless.

"What is going on, Harding?" she asked when she was within a few steps of him.

"Dinner," he said, and walked around to her side of the table. "And the chance to talk."

"You haven't been very interested in talking during the past couple of days," she said, her gaze locked on his.

It had about killed him to stay away from her. But he'd forced himself to. To give her a little time. To think. To realize that they belonged together.

Damn, why did he have to be shipping out now? Never once had being deployed bothered him. Not in the twenty years since he had signed up. Until now. Now, he couldn't bear the thought of leaving her. Of not being there to watch her body grow and swell with their child.

"Or maybe," she was saying, "you were too busy talking to everyone else to bother with talking to me directly."

He winced inwardly at her tone. All right, so he probably shouldn't have had his friends talk to her. Obviously they hadn't accomplished what he had hoped they would.

"I'm sorry," he said softly, and reached for her unsuccessfully. She backed up, keeping a wary distance between them. "Maybe I shouldn't have, but you didn't leave me much choice, Elizabeth. I'm out of time. I had to try whatever ammunition I could come up with."

"You called my *parents!*"

"That, I'm not going to apologize for. I had to

talk to your father, man to man. I'm in love with his daughter and I had to get his blessing on our marriage." That's how things were done. Couldn't she see that?

Elizabeth glared at him. "My mother called me and read me the riot act for a solid half hour because I hadn't confided in her about our 'engagement.'"

"Elizabeth—"

"I'm only surprised you didn't tell them about the—" she tossed a quick look at the two Marines, standing with their backs to them "—baby," she finished in a much quieter voice.

"I wouldn't do that without you." This was not working out as he had hoped. "Don't you get it? I *love* you."

"Stop it."

"I can't stop. And I wouldn't if I could."

She shook her head firmly. "You're only doing all of this because you're leaving. You're feeling guilty about leaving me alone and pregnant."

"You're damn right, I do!" He covered the steps separating them in two quick strides and grabbed both of her arms fiercely. "Can't you see what it's doing to me? Knowing I won't be here with you? Taking care of you?"

Her head fell back on her neck. "I told you, you don't have to worry. I'll be fine."

"But I won't." He stared into her eyes, feeling the same, swift punch to the gut he always felt when looking into their depths. "I'll be thousands of miles away from the one person I want more than my next breath."

Her features tightened, and she chewed at her bottom lip furiously. Indecision shone in her eyes, and he pressed his advantage ruthlessly.

"I want to marry you, Elizabeth. Now. Tonight. We can fly to Vegas and be back in the morning."

For one short, heart-stopping moment, he thought he had won. Then a shift of emotions clouded her eyes, and the moment was lost. Pulling away from him, she shook her head proudly.

"You can't bulldoze me into marriage, Harding."

"Elizabeth…"

"No. I won't be bullied into making such an important decision." Her heel caught in the sand, and she wobbled precariously for a minute. An ocean wind shot across the sand, lifting her hair into a wild, curly halo around her head. "You can't simply decide what's best for me and then steamroll me into agreeing with you. Marriage should be *our* decision, Harding. Not yours."

She headed for the limo. The chauffeur leaped out of the driver's seat and scurried for the back door. Opening it just seconds before she arrived, he stood back while she slid inside.

Harding was just a step behind her. Jerking his head at the driver, he waited until the man moved off before looking down at the woman he loved and had to leave. Tears filled her eyes, but stubborn determination was stamped on her features.

Bracing both hands on the door frame, he leaned down and met her gaze squarely, silently daring her to look away. She didn't.

"Whether you believe me or not, Elizabeth. I do love you. Not just the baby. *You*."

She didn't say a word, and he finally admitted to himself that he wasn't going to convince her. Not now. Not before he left. Pain stabbed at his heart until he thought he wouldn't be able to breathe. At last he finally understood what some of his married friends felt like when they were leaving behind all that they loved.

His fingers tightened helplessly on the cold metal. There was only one thing left to say.

"I want you to know," he said softly, "I've done what I can to protect you and the baby." He inhaled deeply, then told her, "I've named you my beneficiary and my next of kin. If anything should happen to me, you and the baby will be taken care of."

She gasped in surprise, then said, "You don't have to do that. I don't need financial help, Harding."

He scowled at her. She still didn't get it. "This isn't about money," he said firmly. "This is about honor. Love."

"I...don't know what to say." One tear spilled

from the corner of her eye and traced its way along her cheek.

"Say goodbye, Elizabeth. I leave tomorrow night."

"Tomorrow?" she said. "Already?"

He nodded. "Tell me you'll miss me. Even if it's a lie."

"Of course I'll miss you, Harding," she said as another tear traced its way down her cheek.

"Take care of yourself," he said softly.

She nodded jerkily. "You, too."

"This isn't the way I wanted to say goodbye to you, dammit," Harding growled, feeling a huge, black emptiness welling up within him. Time had run out on him. He had failed at the most important mission in his life. And now he would have to wait six long months before getting a second chance at winning her.

The months ahead stretched out in his mind, bleak and empty without her. He glanced at her trim figure and tried to imagine what she would look like, round with their child. Just the thought of all he would miss threatened to choke him. He had to go. Before he made a bigger mess than he had already.

But he couldn't leave without one last taste of her.

Bending down, he reached into the limo, cupped her face with his palms and pulled her head close.

Planting his lips firmly on hers, he gave her all he had, pouring his love and concern and sorrow into a kiss that seared them both to their souls.

At last he released her and straightened away from the car. Staring down at her, he knew that this tear-streaked image of her was the one that would haunt him for six lonely months. He had had everything in the palm of his hand. How had it all disappeared so quickly?

"I love you, Elizabeth," he said, then closed the door and rapped his knuckles on the roof. The driver reacted to his signal instantly and keyed the ignition. With a muffled purr the long, white car drove away, taking Harding's world with it.

Elizabeth stared out the tinted back window until she couldn't see him anymore. Slowly she sank down into the plush seat and curled up in a corner. She'd made the right decision, she knew. A rushed marriage to a man shipping out immediately afterward wasn't the answer to a surprise pregnancy.

But if it was right...why did it suddenly feel so wrong?

Three weeks later, the first letter arrived.

Elizabeth plucked it from the stack of junk mail and tossed the circulars into the trash. Carrying the letter into the living room, she sat down in the corner of the couch and stared at the envelope in her hand. Lightly she dusted her fingertips across Harding's handwriting as if she was touching the man himself.

Lord, she missed him. More than she had imagined she would. And every day for the past three weeks, she had asked herself the same questions. Had she done the right thing in not marrying him? Or had she made the biggest mistake of her life?

Steeling herself, Elizabeth opened the envelope and slowly drew out the single sheet of paper. As slowly as a hungry man enjoying a fine meal, she devoured every word.

Dear Elizabeth,
I'm lying in my bunk wishing I was there, beside you. I know I made a mess of things before I left and I want you to know how sorry I am.

She sucked in a gulp of air and paused in her reading. Sorry? Sorry he had proposed?

You were right. I shouldn't have tried to bulldoze you into marriage. My only excuse is that I love you. And our baby. But during these weeks without you, I've realized that you need time to think about us. I want you

*to know I'll wait. My love won't change and it
won't stop. Take care of both of you for me.
Yours, Harding*

She let go of the letter, and the single page floated
to her lap. Covering her mouth with one hand, she
curled her legs up beneath her, laid her head on the
sofa back and cried. For Harding. For herself. For
lost chances.

Two months later Elizabeth reported for her first
ultrasound. Her doctor had suggested the routine
test as a "precaution." Uncomfortable after the
seeming gallons of water she had had to drink, she
stretched out on the examining table and stared at
a blank TV screen.

A male technician, who looked about eighteen,
with his long, pulled-back ponytail, entered the
room and took a seat on the swivel stool beside
her.

"All set?" he asked and readied his equipment.

"I guess so," she said, sighing.

His eyebrows rose slightly. "Well, you're the most
unexcited mom I've had in here in a long time."

Mom. She shivered slightly. Even though she had
broken the news to her family and everyone was
now used to the idea of a baby coming, Elizabeth
herself still sometimes had trouble believing it.

"So," the tech asked, "where's Dad? How come he's not here to catch the show?"

She swallowed heavily before answering. "He's overseas. In the Marines."

The teasing glint in his eyes softened a bit. "Sorry. Must be hard on him, missing all the fun."

"Yes," she muttered. "It is." She thought about the stack of letters she had received from Harding over the weeks. Almost every other day another one arrived. Lately she had found herself standing on the front porch, watching for the mailman's arrival. She tossed a glance at her purse, where all of those letters were safely tucked away. She kept them with her at all times. Somehow it made her feel closer to him. Less alone. Less afraid.

She couldn't help wondering if he felt the same about the letters she had mailed him.

"Well," the man said as he pulled back her gown and squirted cold jelly onto her abdomen, "I knew just from looking at you that you were the kind of woman whose man would be here if he could."

"You did?" She looked at him, watching him pick up the ultrasound scanner and position it above her belly.

"Sure," he said. "You see enough pregnant women, you get to know which ones are unhappy and which ones are, well, *loved*."

Tears sprung up in her eyes. Elizabeth tried to

blink them back, but the salty film was too much to be denied. She swiped at the tears on her cheeks, trying to hide them from the man beside her.

"Don't worry about it," he said, and patted her hand. "In my line of work, I see crying women every day." Nodding, he assured her, "It's just the hormones."

He went about his work, smoothing the scanner up and down across her flesh, the machine making a series of soft clicking sounds as it took pictures of her womb.

Elizabeth thought about what he had said. Hormones. No, it wasn't just the changes her body was going through. It was love. And misery. The younger man had been right about Harding. He would have been here if he could. Nothing would have kept him away. She and the baby were loved. *Really* loved. How foolish of her not to have believed it before. And how stupid of her to risk losing everything because of her own fears and doubts.

"There you go," the tech said. "He-e-c-re's junior!"

Elizabeth stared at the TV screen at the tiny spot of life she and Harding had created together. Her eyes filled again even as she felt a ridiculous grin spread across her face.

"Oh, Harding," she whispered in a broken voice, "I wish you were here."

* * *

Harding pulled the grainy eight-by-ten photo out of the envelope and studied it. What the hell? In bright red ink, someone had circled a small blob of *something* in the photo. Holding the picture in one hand, he picked up Elizabeth's letter and read it, hoping for a clue.

In seconds he had dropped the letter to his bunk and was holding the photograph under the desk lamp. A slow smile curved his lips as his gaze locked on the circled blob.

His baby.

Turning around quickly, he snatched at the letter and finished reading it. As he read the last paragraph, his smile faded and a worried frown creased his features.

Harding, when you get back, I'd like for us to sit down together and talk about all of this. Surely after six months apart, we'll both be certain about what we want. And what we don't want. Take care of yourself. I miss you.

Elizabeth

Damn. What did that mean? He winced inwardly. He knew just what it meant. Hadn't he lived through this before? Hadn't his ex-wife left him while he was deployed? Why should he expect Elizabeth—who hadn't even wanted to marry him—to be waiting for him with open arms?

He glanced at his child's first picture again and felt the first stirrings of fear thread through him.

Elizabeth stood near the back of the crowd. Hundreds of wives, mothers, husbands and children were stretched out along the edge of the Camp Pendleton parade deck. Signs dotted the eager crowd. Hand-painted with more love than style, they read Ooo-rah! and Get Some! the battalion's motto. There were other, more personal signs being waved high in the air by family members counting the minutes until their loved one arrived.

Elizabeth's fingers curled over her own sign as she clutched it tightly directly in front of her rounded belly. Maybe she shouldn't have come. Maybe she should have waited for him to call her. That's what she had planned to do. But at the last minute she had decided that the best way for her to know how Harding truly felt about her was to watch his expression when he unexpectedly caught sight of her.

She only hoped she would see what she wanted to see. Smiling at the families around her, she remembered other times, other bases. She recalled clearly, running into her father's arms as he came home from duty, and the all-encompassing sense of love that would wrap around her when he picked her up and swung her in the air.

Home wasn't a building. Home was love. The love that lived within the boundaries of a family.

That's what she wanted. That sense of belonging. With Harding.

"Here they come!" someone shouted, and Elizabeth looked up in time to see the first bus from March Air Force Base drive onto the asphalt.

She took a deep breath and watched, her heart in her throat. Within fifteen or twenty minutes the troops were assembled at attention on the parade grounds. After a brief welcome-home speech, the order, "Dismissed!" was shouted and pandemonium reigned.

Jostled as people streamed past her, Elizabeth laid one hand on her swollen stomach as if to comfort her child. Then she focused her gaze on the sea of soldiers, searching for the one face she had so longed to see.

Harding stayed near the back of the crowd. He had always been the last man off the tarmac. There had never been anyone waiting for him at the end of deployment. And this time would be no different. Elizabeth had already written him that she wouldn't be there to greet him. She would be waiting at home for his call.

He stopped dead as a young private darted in front of him, beelining toward a heavily pregnant, grinning woman. Harding watched their reunion for a moment, then continued on, slower than before. Better than being trampled in the rush of men running to their wives and kids. Slowly he walked across the tarmac, trying to ignore his friends' happiness. All around him new babies were being admired, and the kisses being shared were hot enough to melt the pavement.

He closed his eyes to everything, determined not to torture himself unnecessarily. He didn't begrudge them their moments of joy. Blast it, he would have liked to be a part of it himself.

Shifting his duffel bag to his other shoulder, he continued to weave his way through the noisy crowd. In the distance he heard the base band strike up a tune, but he wasn't really listening. He slowed his steps, deliberately putting off the time when he would have to enter his empty quarters.

An aching loneliness settled in the pit of his stomach. What if he couldn't convince Elizabeth to marry him? What if he lost her and the child he already loved? He didn't know if he would be able to stand that kind of pain.

"Hey, Hard Case," someone close by shouted and he half turned to see Staff Sergeant Jack Macguire running up to him, hand outstretched. Grabbing Harding's right hand, Jack pumped it wildly for a minute before saying, "Congratulations, you old Devil Dog! Why didn't you tell me?"

"Tell you what?" Harding asked, but his question went unanswered as Jack spun around and raced back to his wife's impatient arms. He stared after his friend and mumbled, "Now what was that all about?"

Shaking his head, Harding started walking again. As he did, the crowd drifted away until he was looking directly at a lone woman standing at the edge of the tarmac. Her hair was longer than he remembered, but the lovely features, he recognized. Elizabeth. His gaze shifted to the sign she held in front of her. It read simply, "I love you."

Harding swallowed back a sudden, rushing tide of hope inside him. Dodging around his fellow Marines, he kept his gaze locked with hers as he made his way toward her, desperately afraid that she would disappear before he reached her side.

She was here. Waiting for him. Surely that meant something. He felt a grin blossom on his face and didn't even bother trying to hide it. As he came closer, he dropped his duffel bag to the ground and stopped just inches away from her.

"You're here," he said softly, and wished all of the people, and most especially the blasted band, away.

"I had to be here," she whispered, meeting his gaze squarely. "I love you."

Something lodged in his throat, but he spoke around it. "I love you, Elizabeth. I always have."

"I know that now," she told him. "I can see it in your eyes. That's why I had to come."

He sucked in a gulp of air and risked everything he had ever wanted on one question. "Will you marry me?"

"Yes," she said quickly, tears spilling from her eyes and coursing unchecked down her cheeks.

"Ooo-rah!" Harding shouted and laughed all at once, feeling months of worry and fear fall from his shoulders like an unwanted blanket. He reached for her, but Elizabeth was still clutching that sign of hers and showed no intention of letting it drop. "Honey," he said with a smile, "to get the kind of kiss we both need, you're gonna have to let go of that so we can move in close."

Grimacing slightly, she lowered the posterboard to reveal a very pregnant body. "I'm afraid *close* is a relative term, Harding."

Stunned, he stared at the mound of their child for a long minute before gently laying his palm atop it. She covered his hand with one of hers. The baby gave a solid kick, and Harding's eyes widened in disbelief. Finally, after too many years alone, he at last knew what it was to have a family.

"I'm fat," she whined with a half smile.

"Uh-uh, lady," he whispered as he bent to claim her lips, "you're gorgeous."

He tasted her tears and swallowed them, knowing them as the blessing they were. Love rose up around them as surely as the mounting applause from the surrounding soldiers and their families. Harding didn't care who was watching. Everything he had ever wanted was right there, held tight to his heart.

And he would never let them go.

Epilogue

Three months later.

"Ah, sweetheart," Harding whispered as he brushed her damp hair back off her forehead. "I swear to you, I'm going in for a vasectomy today."

Despite the pain, Elizabeth laughed and held his hand tightly. "Don't you dare," she told him. "I don't want junior to be an only child."

Eyes wild, he bent, kissed her forehead, then looked at her like she was crazy. "How can you even *think* about another baby now?"

The crushing pain ebbed slightly, and she lifted her gaze to her harried husband's worried features.

God, how she loved him. Every day she gave thanks for whatever fates had brought them together.

"Don't worry so much, Harding," she said, then gasped as the next pain rushed at her, "I'm not the first woman to have a baby."

Whatever he might have said was lost as the doctor announced, "All right, everybody, it's showtime! Harding, get behind your wife and prop her up."

As he moved to follow orders, Harding brushed a kiss on the top of her head and whispered, "I love you."

"Me, too," she said, concentrating entirely on the task at hand.

"Here we go, Elizabeth, bear down."

She did and in minutes, her son had entered the world, screaming his displeasure. Breathing deeply, Elizabeth lay back down and watched the doctor lift her baby so that she could get a good look at him before handing the newborn to his father.

Harding held the squirming infant confidently, as he did everything in his life. She smiled gently as she watched her bear of a Marine tenderly inspect his child with a loving touch and a soothing whisper of sound. At last he looked at her, his blue eyes brimming with unshed tears, his face touched with a smile of wonder.

"He's beautiful, Elizabeth," he said, and gently laid their son in the crook of his mother's arm.

Bending protectively over them, he planted a quick, gentle kiss at the corner of her mouth. "Thank you," he said in a tone meant only for her to hear. "Thank you for bringing me to life."

She reached up and caressed his cheek, wiping away a stray tear with her fingertips. Smiling up at him, she said, "I love you, Harding." Then she winked and promised, "And don't worry. I won't tell your little Marine friends that their 'Hard Case' should really be called 'Soft Touch.'"

* * * * *

THE OLDEST LIVING MARRIED VIRGIN

Maureen Child

To Jill Shalvis,
friend and fellow writer,
for long talks over cold plots,
shared laughter and huge
phone bills.
See you in Tahoe!

One

"Just let me die," Donna Candello muttered as she rolled onto her right side, opened her eyes, then closed them. A helpless moan trickled from her throat.

Sunlight came pouring into the hotel room through floor-to-ceiling windows. Why hadn't she closed the drapes the night before? Good Lord, what a hideous thing to wake up to. Especially when her head was pounding with the mother of all hangovers.

Opening her eyes, she tried to get used to the golden light splashing across the industrial-gray carpet and the impersonal furniture. When her head didn't explode, she sighed and lifted one hand to push her black hair back from her face.

Lord, what a night.

From now on she would definitely eat something before trying to find courage at the bottom of a pitcher of margaritas. Heck, the only thing she'd eaten yesterday was the rock salt rimming her glass.

She made a face and licked dry lips with her thick, cottony tongue. Bracing both hands on the mattress, she pushed herself into a sitting position and watched as the world rocked, tilted, then thankfully righted itself.

Absently she noted the loud buzzing in her head and hoped it would wear off soon.

The blanket pooled at her waist and she glanced down to see she was still wearing her bra and panties. But then, the condition she'd been in last night, she was lucky she had remembered to take off her shoes before climbing into bed.

Heck, she had been lucky to find her room.

Suddenly a twinge of memory tugged at the corner of her mind, as persistent and nagging as the continued buzzing in her ears. Concentrating, Donna seemed to remember a very nice security guard in a dark blue uniform escorting her upstairs. Without his help, she probably never would have made it.

Too bad she couldn't remember his name or face. She owed him a big thank-you.

Abruptly the buzzing noise stopped. Before she could thank whatever gods were responsible, though, she heard the distinct sound of a man softly singing. And the sound was coming from behind the closed door of what she guessed was the bathroom.

Good Lord, that was no *buzz* she'd been hearing. It had been the shower.

Frantically, she tried to put a face to the voice of the man in the other room. But what was left of her brain drew a complete blank.

Dear Lord, she prayed silently, please don't let this be what it looked like. Please don't let her have been so drunk she'd slept with a man she couldn't even remember.

Briefly she cupped her face in her palms, trying to block out the man's voice. But she couldn't. Perfect, she said to herself, letting her hands fall to her lap. She'd gone from being the world's oldest living virgin to a one-night stand in one drunken night.

Well, she wasn't just going to sit here to wait for whoever he was to step out of the bathroom wearing nothing but a smile.

Casting a wary glance at the still-closed door, Donna edged clumsily off the bed and staggered to her feet. Spinning and swaying, the walls and furniture twisted and writhed like the characters in a Salvador Dali print.

Her stomach lurched and she clamped one hand over her mouth. Maybe it would be easier to just stay to face the no-good fink, she thought, then disregarded the notion entirely. She'd never had any experience with morning-after conversations before. And it wouldn't be fair to expect too much from herself while in the grips of a hangover.

Still, she briefly entertained the idea of jumping back into the bed and hiding under the covers. No, that wouldn't work.

She dropped to her knees beside the bed. Tossing her hair out of bloodshot eyes, she told herself to be calm. To think. To remember. Who was in her room? But it was no use. The night before was one long, foggy blank. Heck, she couldn't even remember registering at the hotel to *get* a room.

Donna inhaled sharply. Good God. If she didn't have a room, then *whose* room was she in?

Briefly she let her head drop to the rumpled sheets. Muttering into the mattress, she whispered, "What did you *do*, Donna? And *who* did you do it with?"

Abruptly the man in the bathroom stopped singing.

Donna looked up. She was trapped. Half-dressed, in a hotel where most of the guests were marines and their families, in town to celebrate the birthday of the Corps. Even if she made a break for the door, she was sure to run into people she knew. People her *father* knew. And some of those folks would be delighted to be able to spread gossip about Donna Candello running around half-dressed through one of the biggest hotels in Laughlin, Nevada.

She groaned at the thought and told herself there had to be a way to salvage this situation. If only her brain wasn't still hazy with lingering traces of too many margaritas.

How would she ever face her father?

How would she ever be able to look *herself* in the mirror again?

"Stupid, stupid, stupid," she moaned, slamming her forehead into the mattress to punctuate each word.

The doorknob turned.

Donna looked up, frantic. Black hair fell across her eyes. She squinted as the door opened slowly. The only thing missing, she thought, was the telltale horror movie music—to let the audience know that the dummy heroine was about to meet her maker.

The man in the open doorway didn't *look* like your typical villain. But hadn't she read somewhere that most serial killers looked like the boy next door?

In the next instant she realized that this guy didn't match *that* description, either. She reached up, pushed her hair out of her eyes and looked into a disapproving gray stare. Dressed only in a pair of faded blue jeans, his feet and chest bare, he looked perfectly at ease. Except for those eyes of his.

"So, you're finally awake," he said.

"Who are you?" Her voice sounded creaky.

"Jack Harris," he told her, flipping the hand towel he held across one shoulder. Then he crossed his arms over an incredibly wide, muscular chest and leaned negligently against the doorjamb. "Like I told you last night."

Harris. Harris, she repeated mentally. Why did that name sound familiar? She silently vowed to never again visit a friendly bartender as a therapist.

Trying to recover some of her dignity, which wasn't easy in her bra and panties, Donna stood, telling herself that she wore less clothing on the beach. There was no reason to feel self-conscious. Still, she folded her arms over her breasts, each hand gripping a bare shoulder.

Clearing her throat, she admitted, "I'm afraid I don't really remember much about last night."

He snorted.

Her eyebrows arched.

"Not surprising," he said tightly. "You could hardly stand up by the time I found you."

"Which was *when* exactly?" she asked, throwing dignity to the wind. She wanted to know what happened.

"About twenty-two thirty hours last night. Trying to get into the Battalion Ball through the emergency exit."

Oh, Lord.

"I stopped you just before the alarm could go off."

Dimly, she thought she recalled standing in the darkness, tugging and yanking at a door that had stubbornly refused to budge.

Oh, this just kept getting better.

Unconsciously, she lifted one hand from her shoulder to rub at an aching throb settling just between her eyebrows. "Look, Mr. Harris—"

"First Sergeant Harris," he amended.

First Sergeant Harris. Of course. *That's* how she knew the name. Not a serial killer. Worse.

A marine.

Donna stared at him, horrified at the implications of having spent the night in his room. No, surely she hadn't been drunk enough to— She cut that thought off at the pass, turned around and plunked onto the edge of the bed.

But wouldn't that be truly ironic? The last living twenty-eight-year-old virgin finally does the deed and is too drunk to remember it?

What an idiot she was!

Shaking her head carefully, Donna muttered more to herself than him. "I don't remember much from last night, First Sergeant."

"Like I said," he remarked, "I'm not surprised."

She ignored his sarcasm. She was in no shape to fire back. "I *do* remember a security guard bringing me here. But I don't remember *your* arrival."

Shaking his head, Jack Harris straightened, threw his towel back into the bathroom, then stalked across the room to a closet. Opening it up, he talked as he pulled out her dress and a pale green polo shirt for himself.

She frowned slightly. Where did all of the men's clothes come from?

"A security guard?" he asked, tossing a scooped-necked, floor-length, red velvet gown at her. "That's what you remember?"

"Yes," she snapped, grabbing the dress and holding it close to her body, luxuriating in the feel of something familiar. "And, I might add, he was decidedly more polite than you have been so far this morning."

"That's wonderful," he muttered, and yanked his shirt over his head. She tried not to notice the play of muscles beneath his darkly tanned skin.

She was in enough trouble already. Besides, a great build didn't make up for a nasty manner. What did *he* have to be cranky about? *She* was the one with the hangover here. *She* was the one who had lost her virginity to a man who only seemed vaguely familiar.

She scowled to herself. Just what did it say about

this guy, anyway? Did he usually lurk around hotels hoping to find a drunk woman he could take advantage of? Getting angrier by the minute, she realized he had probably felt as though he'd hit the jackpot when he'd discovered she was a virgin!

Lifting her chin, and holding her dress in front of her like a shield, she said quite calmly, "I really think you should be going, Sergeant."

"First Sergeant."

Like that mattered *now*.

"Fine. First Sergeant. It's morning. You're dressed. Why don't you run along to your own room?"

He shoved the hem of his shirt into the waistband of his jeans. "You're really something, you know that?"

"What a lovely thing to say," she said stiffly, then winced as a sharp pain darted across her forehead. Groaning slightly, she added, "Do all of your women curl up their toes and swoon at that line?"

"It wasn't a compliment."

"My mistake. I thought you were striving toward politeness."

"You expect 'polite' from a man who just spent the night sleeping on the floor because his bed was being used by a self-indulgent drunk?"

She jumped to her feet and knew immediately that it had been a mistake. Pain exploded behind her eyes. Her stomach pitched and Jack Harris seemed to fade in and out as her eyes desperately tried to focus.

Donna felt herself falling forward, but before she could hit the floor, he was there. Grabbing her, holding her close. The rock-hard strength of his chest seemed like the only stable point in her universe at the moment, so she held on as if it meant her life.

After a few terrifying seconds, it was over.

"Thank you," she murmured and, almost regretfully, pushed away from him.

He nodded, watching her carefully as if he half expected her to keel over again.

"I'm all right," she said.

One dark eyebrow lifted over his left eye.

"Wait a minute," Donna said, inhaling slowly, deeply. "You said *your* bed? Are you trying to tell me this is *your* room?"

"That's right."

"Then—" She took a halting step backward. "Why would the security guard bring me here? To you?"

"That was no security guard, honey," he said. "That was me."

She stared at him. Bits and pieces of memory fluttered through her mind like autumn leaves in a whirlwind. Her gaze narrowed as she studied him, trying to fit his face with the half-remembered image of the guard who had been so kind.

Oh, Lord, she thought on an inward groan. He was right. It wasn't a dark blue security uniform she remembered. It was a Dress Blue uniform. Jack Harris had been formally dressed last night for the Battalion Ball.

Maybe they'd all be better off if she simply looked for an oven to stick her head into.

"This is mortifying," she finally mumbled. Drunk and rooming with a strange marine for the night. Waking up in only her underwear, in *his* bed, with no memory of how she got there.

Looking up at him, she forced herself to ask the fateful question. "Did we—" She jerked her head at the bed behind her. "You know…"

Jack felt his features tighten. Looking down into those deep brown eyes of hers, he clearly recalled having to strip off her gown and tuck her beneath the blankets. It hadn't been easy, turning his back on a gorgeous woman, even a drunk one. But, damn it, there were rules about some things. Whether he liked it or not. "No. We didn't 'you know….'"

Finding her drunk, trying to get into the ball, had been pure chance. If he hadn't stepped outside for a cigarette, he never would have seen her. Dressed as she was and as determined as she had been to get into the party, he had known that she belonged with some poor marine. It had seemed like his duty to keep the clearly toasted woman from embarrassing herself, and the damn fool who loved her, in front of his superior officers.

He had taken her to his room with the thought of sobering her up. But she'd fallen asleep almost immediately. Now he had to find out where she belonged and get her there.

Fast.

"Nothing happened last night, lady," he said stiffly, turning his back on her to walk across the room and pick up his shirt.

"Oh."

He glanced at her unreadable expression and didn't know whether she was relieved or disappointed. Either way, though, it didn't matter a damn to him.

"Now, why don't you tell me who I should call about you?" he asked, determined to get her the hell out of his life as quickly as possible. *Before* the rest of the hotel guests woke up and someone saw her leaving his room.

"In case you hadn't noticed," she said, gingerly stepping into her red velvet dress, "I am no longer drunk, so I don't need you to phone anyone about me."

Disgusted, he told her, "Honey, this hotel is crawling with marines. If you leave my room wearing last night's dress, somebody's going to notice and talk. Now, tell me who to call, so they can bring you something to wear."

She fumbled with the tiny seed-pearl buttons lining her dress from the low-cut bodice to mid-thigh. He closed his eyes, not really wanting to look again at the high, wide slit in the front of her gown that exposed slim, shapely thighs. No reason why he should torture himself.

Man, this was the last time he'd be a Good Samaritan. Next time some gorgeous brunette was trying to embarrass herself, he'd let her.

Impatiently, Jack waited for her to answer him. Just before she finished her task, someone knocked on the door.

She looked up at him, her eyes wide.

"Damn it," he whispered. He had wanted to get this woman settled and out of his room before anyone else had a chance to see her. Quickly, Jack checked his watch—0930 hours. After last night, who in the heck would be up this early pounding on his door?

"Who is it?" she asked in a hush.

"How the hell should I know?" he snapped, then frowned. He felt like a cheating husband in an old movie. Well, that was nuts. He hadn't done anything wrong. He was the good guy here. All he'd tried to do was help a lady in distress.

But then, what was that old saying? *No good deed goes unpunished?*

The knocking sounded out again. Louder this time. Insistent.

Jack started for the door, but stopped dead when he heard the angry voice on the other side of it.

"First Sergeant Harris?"

"Colonel Candello?" Jack asked.

"Daddy?" Donna groaned.

"Daddy?" Jack repeated, horrified.

TWO

Tearing his gaze from the woman in front of him, he shot a quick glance at the door before turning a malevolent glare on her again. "Colonel Candello is your *father?*"

"Yes," she whispered, frantically finger-combing her tousled hair. "How do I look?"

"Like hell," he muttered, and thought it appropriate since they were both standing in the middle of an inferno.

Damn it, why was the colonel here this early? Did the man already know about his daughter spending the night? And if he did, how? Jack hadn't thought even the marine wives could manage to spread gossip at light speed.

"First Sergeant Harris," the colonel said in a tightly controlled voice, "are you going to keep me standing in the hall?"

Jack ran one hand across the top of his high and tight haircut and tried to think. His room was on the eleventh floor, so there was no sneaking her out the French doors that opened onto the balcony. And the room was too damned small to hide her for long. No choice here, he told himself.

Turning a hard stare on the colonel's daughter, he asked, "You ready to face the music?"

No.

Even without a mirror, Donna knew what she must look like. Standing there in her stocking feet, her dress wrinkled, smudged mascara shadowing her eyes... She groaned inwardly. No doubt she looked as if she'd spent a hot, passionate night with a wildly attentive lover.

How ironic.

She was about to be caught, tried, and convicted for something she hadn't done.

Had *never* done.

Good God, she hadn't seen her father in four years because she'd been too embarrassed to face him. After today, she'd have to move to Outer Mongolia.

Grimly, she nodded, threw her shoulders back and tried to look nonchalant.

Jack moved to the door, unlocked it, and opened

it wide, silently inviting the colonel inside. "Good morning, Sir," he said as the man walked into the room.

"Is it?" the colonel asked.

Dressed in civilian clothes, Thomas Candello was still an imposing figure. In gray slacks and a pale blue, short-sleeved sport shirt, he looked younger than he did when in full uniform. But he was every inch as intimidating as usual.

Her father's gaze seemed to bore into Donna's and she flinched slightly at the disappointment she saw glittering in those brown eyes so like her own.

"Sir—" Jack started.

The colonel interrupted him. "Would you mind leaving my daughter and me alone for a few minutes, First Sergeant?"

Donna flicked a glance at her erstwhile host. She saw the hesitation on his features and knew that he desperately wanted to stay in the room to take his share of whatever the colonel had come to deliver. She also knew that he wouldn't think of disobeying even a nicely phrased "request" from her father.

"Aye, Sir," he said brusquely, and stepped into the hall, pulling the door closed behind him.

Donna wanted to run. But then, she'd run away four years ago and it hadn't done her any good. This time she'd stick it out. Amazing, she thought. Today, she had courage.

"Why didn't you tell me you were coming, Donna?"

She pushed her hair out of her eyes and wished to high heaven for three pots of hot, black coffee. How did everyone expect her to think when she had a hangover strong enough to kill a moose?

Inhaling sharply, she finally said, "I wanted to surprise you." Shrugging, she added helplessly, "Surprise!"

He didn't smile.

But she hadn't expected him to.

"Look, Daddy, this is all a big mistake," she said, moving away from the bed and all of its implications. "It's perfectly innocent, actually."

"'Innocent'?" He shook his head and she noticed absently that there were a few streaks of gray at his temples. "You spend the night with my First Sergeant, a man you've never met before, and you call it innocent?"

Why did she suddenly feel as though she were seventeen and late coming home from a date? She was twenty-eight years old. She'd been living on her own for years. She had a master's degree. As a sign language interpreter, her expertise was in demand everywhere from colleges to corporate battlegrounds.

Yet one look from her father had her dipping her head and mumbling answers.

"It's not what you think," she told him on a tired sigh. "The sergeant—"

"First sergeant," he cut in.

"Whatever." She waved one hand dismissively. "Jack was just trying to be helpful." Great. Now she'd been reduced to defending the man she'd wanted to kick only a few minutes ago.

But what choice did she have? The colonel was her father. The man wasn't going to stop loving her no matter how disappointed he was in her. He was also Jack Harris's commanding officer, and Jack didn't need to take career heat for her mistake.

The colonel walked over to the only chair in the room and sat. Leaning forward, his forearms on his thighs, he looked at her solemnly. "Do you know that at least four different people have already felt it was their 'duty' to come and tell me where my daughter spent the night?"

"Oh, Lord," she said on a sigh.

"Why, Donna?" he asked.

She walked to the French doors and opened them, bravely facing the sunshine just to breathe in the fresh, morning air. She stepped onto the narrow balcony and curled her fingers around the railing. "I had a couple of drinks at the airport when I landed."

"So, you were drunk, too."

She glanced at him and noted that a well-remembered muscle in his cheek was twitching.

When she was a kid, that had always been her signal that she'd pushed him too far. Oh, not that he'd ever raised a hand to her. But Tom Candello's silence was as bad as any other man's rage.

"I guess the alcohol affected me more than usual because I forgot to eat," she said.

"And that makes it all right?"

"No, but that's what happened."

"And what's your reason for wanting a drink before seeing me?"

"Because I couldn't face you," she admitted, coming back into the room.

Planting both hands on his knees, he pushed himself to his feet. Towering over her by a good six or seven inches, he met her gaze and held it. "Because I was right about Kyle? *That's* why you didn't want to face me?"

"Kyle's only a part of it and you know it," she said quickly, not wanting to get into a discussion about her ex-fiancé—or what had happened the last time she'd seen her father. "As long as we're on the subject, it's not easy having a father who's always right."

"Not always," he corrected, his mouth still a grim line of disapproval.

"Often enough to make me think my judgment stinks." And, to be honest, in the case of her ex-fiancé, it *had* stunk. Big time.

The colonel raised one dark eyebrow. "Apparently, it still does."

She mentally flinched at that one.

"We're straying from the point here, Donna."

"What *is* the point, Dad?" She was tired. And her head hurt. And her stomach felt as if there was an 8.1 earthquake rattling around inside it.

She needed a bath, some coffee and maybe, if it wouldn't kill her, a little food.

"The point is that half the battalion is already talking about you and First Sergeant Harris." He paused and frowned. "The other half will be as soon as they hear about it."

"I'm sorry," she said. "I didn't mean to create such a mess."

"Sorry doesn't cut it, Donna," he told her sternly.

"I don't know what you want me to do," she said, and pushed past him to sit in the chair he had vacated.

A quiet knock on the door interrupted whatever he would have said.

"Come in, First Sergeant," the colonel said. When the door opened, he added, "I'm sorry to have kept you out of your room so long."

"Not a problem, Sir," Jack said, closing the door quietly behind him. "But if you'll pardon me for saying so, Sir, there *is* a problem you should know about."

The colonel rubbed the back of his neck tiredly. "What is it?"

"Well, Sir…" Jack went on, clearly uncomfortable. "Major Collins's wife spoke to me in the hall just now."

"Great," the colonel muttered, and Donna flicked a quick, worried glance at him. "What'd she say?"

Jack came almost to attention. "Sir, she said she saw your daughter and me enter my room last night. She wanted to know when your daughter and I were getting married and why she wasn't invited."

"The old—" The colonel's voice trailed off into nothingness.

"Great," Donna muttered. "My sex life—" *or lack of one,* she added silently "—is the talk of the marines." She shifted uneasily in the chair. If she had just stayed in Maryland, none of this would be happening. She would still have a perfectly good phone relationship with her father and she wouldn't be sitting in the first sergeant's room with him looking at her as if she were the Three Stooges and Mata Hari all in one.

"It'll blow over, Dad," she said tentatively, and was rewarded with a black look from her father.

"You know how gossip spreads," he said simply. "It gets bigger, not smaller."

All her fault, she thought, disgusted with herself.

"Sir." Jack spoke up again, and Donna and her

father turned to look at him. "If I might make a suggestion?"

"First Sergeant," the colonel said wearily, "I could use a good one right about now."

"The only way to stop gossip is to make it less interesting," Jack said, still amazed that he was even considering saying what he was about to say. He glanced at the hungover woman mumbling to herself, then shifted his gaze back to her father.

The man he owed so much to.

"Your point, First Sergeant?"

"My point is this, Sir." He sucked in a gulp of air and said the rest of it in a rush, before he could change his mind. "If you agree, your daughter and I can get married this afternoon. If we're married, the gossips will have nothing to talk about."

"*Excuse* me?" Donna jumped up from her chair, wobbled a bit, then grabbed her father's arm for support. Jack only glanced at her before looking back at the colonel.

"We can tell people we got married last night. No one would have to know any different."

The other man was silent for a long, thoughtful minute.

Jack looked at the officer across the room from him. He had admired and respected Colonel Candello for years. Standing out in the hall, with nothing to do but think, Jack had realized that because of his actions, the colonel's reputation would be sullied.

It was then he'd come up with his plan. Sure, it was a sacrifice. But there was nothing Jack wouldn't do for the colonel.

"That's quite a suggestion, First Sergeant," the officer said.

"It's nuts, is what it is." Donna spoke up, but neither man was listening at the moment.

"We can drive to Vegas," Jack continued, ignoring her for the moment. "It's only an hour away. We'll find an out-of-the-way chapel, take care of business and be back here before most of the battalion is even awake."

"It might work," the colonel said.

"Maybe," Donna agreed, nodding her head at the two of them. "Except for one little detail."

"Ma'am?" Jack asked, only to be polite.

"What detail is that, darling?" the colonel asked.

"The fact that I'm *not* going to go through with it," Donna told them.

Her father's features tightened a bit. Jack saw it from across the room. As the Candellos faced each other, he waited silently. He'd seen the colonel in action and he didn't have a doubt as to who would win this silent competition.

"Daddy," she said so softly Jack almost couldn't hear her. "You can't be serious."

"Why not, honey?" he asked, reaching out and laying both hands on her shoulders.

"For one thing, I don't even know him."

"That didn't stop you last night."

Jack tensed.

"I *told* you, nothing happened," Donna insisted.

"No one will believe that," her father said.

True enough, Jack thought. No doubt the major's wife was already spreading her story from one end of Laughlin to the other.

"But, Dad, this is practically medieval."

"I can't force you to do anything," the colonel said, his hands still gripping his daughter's shoulders.

"I can't marry a stranger, for God's sake," she whined.

Jack hated whiny women.

"He's not a stranger," the colonel insisted. "I've known First Sergeant Harris over fifteen years."

She shot Harris a glare through mascara-smudged eyes, then looked back at her father. "Then *you* marry him."

"Donna…"

"No way." She shook her head.

"What was it you were just saying about your judgment?" the colonel asked.

"That was different."

"How?"

Jack frowned slightly. He didn't have a clue what they were talking about now.

"Do you trust me?" the colonel asked quietly.

"Of course," she answered. "This has nothing to do with trust, though."

The colonel's hands dropped from her shoulders. He stood for a long, quiet minute, staring into her eyes.

Jack had the distinct feeling that there was a silent message being passed from father to daughter. But he was in no position to know what it was.

"Well, then," the colonel said softly. "If you won't, you won't. But I *am* disappointed, Donna."

Three

"I do," Donna said, and extended her left ring finger toward her new husband. The thin gold band felt surprisingly heavy on her hand.

Shortest wedding ceremony on record, she thought numbly. Assembly line marriages, no waiting. The preacher kept talking, though to Donna, his words sounded like little more than a low hum of sound. She couldn't believe she was actually doing this. Maybe she wasn't, she thought desperately. Maybe this was all just a really bad dream.

"I do," Jack said from beside her. His voice rumbled along her spine, letting her know that this was no dream.

The Reverend Thistle, a man whose frowsy white hair and long, sticklike body made him strangely resemble the weed he was named for, quietly closed his worn, leather Bible and said, "I now pronounce you husband and wife." He beamed benevolently at First Sergeant Harris. "You may kiss the bride."

Donna looked up into his cold, expressionless eyes and wasn't the slightest bit surprised to hear him say, "Thanks, I'll pass."

Forcing a smile for the perplexed reverend, Donna made her way back up the aisle toward the puddle of sunshine outside. *Go toward the light,* she thought grimly. Except for her, when she reached that bright light, there would be no salvation. Just a short car ride back to the hotel in Laughlin, where her father waited.

She glanced down at the ring on her finger again. There hadn't been time to locate a jewelry store. The simple gold band had come straight from the Reverend Thistle's collection of wedding rings for unprepared couples.

Twenty-five dollars' worth of gold plating, a silk flower bouquet, and the only witnesses to her wedding, the next couple in line.

Tears stung her eyes, but she blinked them back determinedly. Her own father hadn't given her away. Her bottom lip quivered and she bit down on it hard. He had already scheduled a golf game with the general. If he'd broken the date, he would have needed to explain. And explanations were one of the things they were trying to avoid.

Donna stepped into the bright Vegas sun and immediately shielded her eyes with her hand. Even in November, the desert produced sunshine like nowhere else.

Rummaging one-handed in her purse, she looked for her sunglasses while waiting for Jack to come out of the chapel. When she found them, she slipped them on, grateful for the dark lenses. Turning around, she glanced at the front of the Chapel of the Desert. Palm trees, fake brick and a do-it-yourself stained-glass window above the front doors.

Well, this was a far cry from the wedding she had planned so meticulously four years ago. Then, she had reserved the church months ahead of time. She'd had six bridesmaids, two flower girls and a ring bearer. Not to mention a groom who had actually professed to love her.

She scowled slightly at that last thought. All right, so it hadn't been perfect.

"Are you okay?" Jack asked as he stepped out of the chapel to join her on the walk.

"Peachy," she muttered darkly.

"Yeah," he said, shifting his gaze to stare at the crowds of gamblers already clogging the city sidewalks in their hot pursuit of instant riches. "It's been a helluva day so far, huh?"

He was still wearing the pale green polo shirt

and faded jeans he'd put on a couple of hours ago. Hardly formal wear. But then, her simple blue cotton skirt and matching, short-sleeved sweater was hardly a cover picture for a bridal magazine.

He pulled sunglasses out of his shirt pocket and stared at her from behind the safety of darkness. "You ready to head back?"

"What?" she asked, and couldn't seem to stop the sarcasm dripping off her tongue. "No reception?"

One corner of his mouth lifted, then fell again. "Oh, we'll get a reception," he told her. "I'm just not sure what kind."

Ah, the perfect end to the perfect wedding, she thought, and grimly started after him as he headed for the car.

Under the shade of an umbrella table on the deck overlooking the Colorado River, Jack took a good long look at his new wife.

Wife.

He just managed to hide a shudder.

Even though this had been his idea, he still had a hard time dealing with the fact that he was actually married. To the colonel's daughter, no less.

Not that marrying into an officer's family would get him anywhere careerwise. The U.S. Marine Corps was probably the last bastion of antinepotism in the free world. If anything, he'd probably be the butt of all kinds of jokes from his friends.

Still, the deed was done now, and they'd just have to live with it. At least for a while. And that was what he wanted to talk to the "little woman" about.

"This doesn't have to be hard," he said firmly, noticing that she winced at the tone of his voice.

Rubbing her forehead with her fingertips, she said, "Do you have to speak so loudly?"

"Still feeling the effects of that hangover?" he asked unnecessarily. Lord, he'd never seen a woman less suited to drinking. He'd be willing to bet that there were people on their deathbeds feeling better than she was right at the moment.

"Yes," she muttered. "Is there any more coffee?"

He picked up the beige carafe from the center of the table and shook it. Nothing. "You drank it all."

"Get more," she said desperately. *"Please."*

"No problem." He looked up, caught the waitress's eye and hefted the carafe. She nodded. Turning back to his blushing bride, he said, "It's coming."

"Thank God." She pushed her uneaten lunch away from her, set her elbows on the glass-topped table and cupped her face in her hands.

Jack shook his head, leaned back in his chair and stretched his legs out in front of him, crossing them at the ankle. "You're a lousy drunk," he commented dryly.

She lifted her head long enough to glare at him. "I probably just need practice."

"Don't do this often?" he asked. Maybe it was a personal question. But they were married now, and he wanted to know if he'd saddled himself with a lush.

Her voice muffled by her palms, she asked, "Why would anyone want to do this *often?*"

That had always been his point of view, too. But there were plenty of folks more than willing to suffer the pain for the few hours of a pleasant buzz.

"I can't figure out that one myself," he said, keeping his voice low enough to not be painful to her. "But lots of people do. What I want to know is, are you one of them?"

Their waitress arrived, picked up the empty carafe and set a replenished one in its place. Donna sat up, reached for it, and poured herself what had to be her tenth cup of coffee.

Cupping the mug between her palms, she looked at her new husband over the rim, inhaled the rich steam and said plainly, "No, First Sergeant. I don't drink." She took a sip, shuddered and qualified that statement by adding, "Usually."

"Glad to hear it," he told her. "You don't seem to have a talent for it."

"Now *there's* an understatement."

He caught himself before he could actually smile.

Damn it, he didn't want to like her. He didn't want to feel anything for her.

"I think we should get a few things straight," he said.

"Shoot," she muttered. "Please."

Jack swallowed another reluctant smile. "See, I didn't plan on marrying you."

She snorted. "Well, *duh*."

He studied her for a long minute. "Are you always this sarcastic?"

"Always," she said after another sip. "But it's a lot pithier when I'm in pain."

"I'll keep that in mind."

"Probably safer."

Jack helplessly shook his head in admiration. Damn, he was going to have an uphill battle not getting real fond of her. Her chin-length black hair twisted in the breeze off the river. She wasn't wearing her sunglasses, so he got a good look at those brown eyes he'd noticed right away last night. Even blurred by the glassy haze of alcohol, they'd been remarkable. Now, offset as they were by the bloodshot whites of her eyes, the liquid chocolate brown seemed to shimmer with depths he didn't even want to consider. Delicate, black brows arched high on her forehead and her full lips were tight with the pain throbbing in her head.

Damn, she looked good.

"How old are you?" he asked suddenly.

One of those delicate brows lifted high over her right eye. "Awfully personal for our first date, don't you think?"

"Since our first date was also our wedding, no, I don't think so."

"Hmm," she said. "Point taken. All right, I'm twenty-eight."

His brain raced for a minute. "But the colonel's only forty-five."

She smiled and gave him a wink that quickly became a wince. "That's right. He really prefers it if people don't do the math."

"But that would have made him only—"

"Seventeen when I was born."

Jack whistled, low and long.

"Before you ask," she went on, her voice tight, "Mom was sixteen. Though the older I got, the younger my mother used to get, so it's hard to be sure."

"Must have been hard on them," he said more to himself than to her.

"I'm sure it was," she told him. "But selfishly speaking, I can't really be sorry, can I?"

"Suppose not."

"So," she said, pulling in a deep breath. "You said you wanted to talk about something. I'm guessing it's not about my parents and their rather embarrassing history."

"No, it's not." He cocked his head to look at her carefully. "You sure you're up to this right now?"

"Probably not," she admitted. "But this is as good as it's going to get for several hours."

"Okay…" He hesitated, suddenly unsure of just how to put this. "We got married for your father's reputation's sake, right?"

"Do we have to go there again?"

"No. What I want to talk about is the future, not what already happened."

"What future?"

"Ours," he said. "This marriage."

"Well," she said as she leaned back cautiously in her chair, "I think you pretty much covered that back at the chapel."

"What?" Maybe she wasn't feeling up to this conversation.

"'You may kiss the bride,'" she intoned in a pretty good imitation of Reverend Thistle. "'Thanks,'" she mocked pointedly. "'I'll pass.'"

Now it was his turn to wince. Hell, he hadn't meant anything by that. But what would have been the point of kissing her to seal a marriage they both knew was a fraud?

"What'd you expect?" he asked.

"Orange blossoms, organ music, crowds of people, my *father*," she said with a sniff.

Jack tensed. Here he'd been ready to like her and now she was going to cry on him.

"Let's not make this something it isn't," he said quickly, relieved when he saw her blink away the moisture in her eyes.

"Don't worry, Sergeant—"

"First Ser—"

"I know." She cut him off. "Look, I didn't want this any more than you did, okay? You're safe. I'm not going to become the little wifey and follow you around the base like a lost puppy."

"That's what I want to talk about," he said. "Just exactly what we both expect from this marriage."

She lifted one hand to rub her temple. When she didn't speak, Jack continued.

"We're married," he said, sitting up and leaning toward her. "But it doesn't have to stay that way."

Her hand dropped to her lap. She looked at him thoughtfully. "Go on," she prompted.

"If we play the part of a married couple for a few months, then quietly have a trial separation, no one will think anything of it."

"'Trial separation'?" she repeated.

"Sure. Then after a couple more months, we get a divorce. We're both free to do what we want to do."

"A divorce." She managed to keep from shuddering. He made it all sound so cut and dried. But it wasn't. At least not to her. Donna had always thought that once she was married, she'd *stay* married. But then, she'd always dreamed that she'd marry for love, too.

"You have a problem with that?"

"Call me dysfunctional," she said with a shrug she hoped would hide the dismay rushing through her. "My parents' divorce was a nightmare. I was only two years old, but I grew up listening to my mother complain about my father. I didn't even really get to know him until I was almost thirteen."

"That's different," Jack said. He was sorry to hear about the colonel's troubles, but that kind of thing wouldn't affect Donna and him. If he was honest, he wasn't a big supporter of easy divorces and broken marriages, either. But then, this wasn't a real marriage, was it? "We won't have kids to worry about upsetting."

"Not in three months," she assured him. "I'm good, but even Super Woman would require at least nine."

He sighed heavily. "I *meant* that we wouldn't be sleeping together, so there wouldn't be any complications."

"Ah," Donna said, carefully nodding as if her head was about to fall off. "A platonic marriage."

"Of course," he said. Crossing his arms over his chest, he looked at her as if he was waiting for her to applaud.

Well, isn't this a wonderful turn of events? she thought.

The oldest living virgin in the world had just become the oldest living *married* virgin.

Four

She forced another swallow of coffee down her throat. Why did things like this keep happening to her? She wasn't a bad person. She didn't go out of her way to hurt people. Heck, she even hated calling an exterminator to wipe out bug civilizations.

And still she managed to screw up her life on a regular basis.

Risking a still-bleary-eyed glance at her new husband, she could almost see what he was thinking. And it wasn't flattering.

"Fine, First Sergeant Harris," she said softly. "Platonic, it is. Your virtue is safe with me."

One corner of his mouth tilted up slightly, then flattened out again. He'd done that move several times already that morning. Either she amused him greatly or he had a serious facial tic. It must be the latter, she thought. What he could find entertaining about a sexless marriage between strangers was completely beyond her.

Then that tic flickered again.

"What's so funny?" she asked, despite the fact that his half smile was now gone.

"Trust me, Princess," he said. "I don't think there's *anything* funny in all this."

"Then why'd you do it?"

"Do it?"

"Marry me."

His long fingers curled through the handle of his coffee cup. "For your father."

"I figured that much out for myself," she said, suddenly exhausted with the morning's activities. Getting married could really take a toll on a person.

He nodded. "Let's just say I owe the man."

"Enough to marry his daughter?" One eyebrow lifted. "Must be quite a debt."

"I think so."

Intrigued, and more curious than she cared to admit, even to herself, she stared at him for a long moment before asking, "I don't suppose you'd care to share that information with me?"

Again that corner of his mouth tilted up briefly. "No, I wouldn't."

She tried a shrug and was immensely grateful when her head didn't roll off her shoulders.

"How about you?" he asked.

"What about me?"

"Why'd *you* agree to the wedding?"

Now there was a loaded question. One she wasn't prepared to discuss with a man she hardly knew, even if he *was* her husband. Old embarrassing memories rose up in her mind and she deliberately pushed them all to the back of her still-foggy brain.

"Let's just say *I* owed him, too."

"No sharing?"

A distinct twinkle shone at her from his gray eyes. The first sergeant? Teasing? "I think I'll pass," she said, not even realizing that she was throwing his earlier words back at him. The twinkle dissolved in a heartbeat.

"Look, Donna," he said, "for better or worse, we're married."

"For richer or poorer," she intoned solemnly. "In sickness and in health—"

"At least for now," he interrupted. "We may as well try to get along."

A romantic speech designed to bring flutters of happiness to any girl's heart, she muttered to herself as she rubbed at that spot between her eyes again, hoping to ease the throbbing ache. Nothing.

Squinting at him, she felt her stomach drop, as it

did every time she rode a roller coaster. Ridiculous for a man's face to have that effect on her. Especially when it wasn't even a classically *handsome* face. Jack Harris was far too rugged and honed-looking to be called handsome. Attractive, sure, she supposed, in a rough-and-tumble sort of way. Her stomach pitched again and this time she ignored it.

He *did* have a point.

For the next few months at least, they would be married. Living together. So they wouldn't be sleeping together. Was that really so important?

Once again, she was on the roller coaster. The hangover, she told herself. It was just the hangover.

All right, they wouldn't be lovers. They would be *friends.* Or if not friends, noncombative opponents.

Good Lord, she sounded as marine-oriented as her new husband.

Taking a deep, steadying breath in the hopes of jumping off that stomach-lurching ride, she said, "Okay, First Sergeant—"

"Jack," he interrupted. "Call me Jack."

She nodded slowly. "Jack it is." Inhaling sharply, she sucked in the still cool air off the river before extending her hand in a gesture of peace. As he took her hand in his and shook it, she heard herself ask, "So, husband, do you snore?"

* * *

That night at dinner, Jack looked across the table at his wife and told himself to remember that this was, for all intents and purposes, a *pretend* marriage. But it wasn't easy.

She looked gorgeous. Amazing what the lack of a hangover could do for a woman. She wore a short, sunshine-yellow dress that hugged her curves, defining her many assets to perfection. The color of the dress deepened a honey-colored tan and somehow shifted the brown of her eyes to a shade of gold that drew his attention over and over again.

Sitting at the colonel's table was nerve-racking for Jack, but his new wife was completely at home. Of course, why wouldn't she be? Colonel Candello was her father. Raised by an officer, around officers, she actually *belonged* at that table.

As for him, Jack kept waiting for someone to leap up, point at him and shout. "This man's an impostor. He's not one of us. Get him out of here!" He grimaced slightly and told himself that the night was almost over. All he had to do was survive dessert. After that, he could go to his room and— Wait a minute. Not *his* room any longer. Now he shared it with a wife.

Mental images raced through his mind. Donna, tossing her newly purchased clothes and the bags they'd come in all over his hotel room. There had been no way to avoid her staying with him. A newly married couple wouldn't very well have separate rooms, after all.

So there wouldn't be any relaxation for him after dinner, either. Perfect. Why in the hell hadn't he just let her embarrass herself and the colonel the night before? Would it really have been so bad if the colonel's daughter had turned up drunk at the Battalion Ball?

Yeah, he thought. It would have. At least for the colonel.

"Jack?" that man asked in a tone of voice that clearly said he'd asked before and been ignored.

"Sir," Jack responded, unconsciously stiffening in his seat. "Sorry, Sir, daydreaming, I guess." Or, to be more accurate, nightmaring.

"Relax, Jack," his new father-in-law said, "you're not on parade, here. This is just an informal, family dinner."

Family. Him? And the colonel? Lord help him.

"Of course, Sir," he said, no more at ease than he had been a moment ago.

The colonel shook his head, but asked out of the blue, "Do you play any golf?"

Golf? Jack stared for a long minute at the man he most admired in the world, thinking how little they really had in common. Where *he'd* grown up, there were no golf courses. That game was for rich people. People with too much time and money on their hands. The folks in Jack's neighborhood had been too busy trying to find work and buy food to go out and chase some little white ball around a well-tended lawn. But he couldn't very well voice that opinion to his superior officer, so he said only, "No, Sir, I don't."

"Too bad," the colonel said. "I think you'd like it. Donna's pretty good, you know."

Now why didn't that surprise him? His gaze shifted back to the pretty woman across from him. Of course the spoiled, only child of an important man would play golf. "Really?"

"I haven't played in years," Donna admitted. The first sentence she'd uttered since sitting at the table an hour ago.

"Maybe you could teach Jack," her father said.

"That's probably not a bad idea," she conceded with a quick look at her husband.

Her gaze barely rested on him an instant before she pointedly looked away again. So much for their hastily made bargain to try to be friendly. Hell, now that she was stone-cold sober, maybe she was regretting their quickie marriage.

Now *that* he could understand.

Damn, this was going to be harder than he'd thought, Jack told himself. He let his own gaze wander the crowded restaurant. He recognized several of the other diners as marines and even caught a couple of them throwing curious looks his way.

He shifted uncomfortably in his chair. Jack

never had liked being the center of attention in any situation. Being a marine fed into that nicely. On base, he was simply one of thousands of soldiers. Now, though, he'd managed to step into the limelight, and he didn't care for it one bit.

"Would you two excuse me?" the colonel asked.

Jack turned to look at the other man. But the colonel's gaze was riveted on a spot at the far side of the room. As the older man pushed away from the table, he said, "I see someone I'd like a moment with."

He was gone before either of them could say a word.

"Well," Donna muttered as she followed her father's progress across the room. "I wonder what that's all about?"

"I don't know," Jack said, "but it's none of my business, either."

Both of her finely arched eyebrows lifted as she turned those brown eyes on him. "Feeling a little cranky, are we?"

"Cranky?" Stunned, he stared at her for a long minute. "*I'm* not the one who hasn't said a damn thing all night."

She winced. "Okay, so I haven't exactly been holding up my end of the conversation."

"You don't even *have* an end."

Those incredible golden eyes of hers narrowed

slightly. "You know, I don't much like pushy husbands."

Amazing. He'd almost found himself liking her earlier. Wouldn't you know his new wife would be at her *most* likable when she had been suffering from a hangover?

"And I don't much like whiny wives."

"Whiny?" She sat straighter in her chair. "Who's whining? You just said yourself that I haven't even been talking."

"You can whine by intent, too."

"How do you know what I intended or not?"

"I can tell what you're thinking just by looking at your face."

"Oo-oh, a mind reader. How fascinating."

"Knock it off, Donna."

"Knock what off exactly, Jack?" she asked, leaning one elbow on the table. Cupping her chin in her hand, she batted her eyelashes at him wildly. "I thought you wanted me to talk."

Disgusted with himself, her, and the whole damned situation, he snapped, "Forget it. I changed my mind."

"How like a man. Never sure what he wants."

"What's that supposed to mean?"

The humorous glint in her eyes was gone. "Never mind."

"Well, well," a booming deep voice announced from nearby, startling both of them into turning their heads toward the man just stopping at their table.

Immediately Jack jumped to his feet and came to attention. "General Stratton, Sir. Good evening."

The older man, dressed in a dove-gray suit, carried himself as if wearing a full dress uniform. "As you were, First Sergeant."

Jack relaxed only slightly, shifting into an "at ease" stance, arms behind his back.

"How's my favorite goddaughter and her new husband tonight?" the general asked, smiling down at Donna.

She stood slowly and rose up to kiss the older man on the cheek. "We're fine, Uncle Harry," she said.

General Stratton? Beads of sweat broke out on Jack's forehead. Uncle Harry? Good God, what had he gotten himself into here? By trying to save his colonel's reputation, he'd jumped headfirst into a pool he had no business trying to swim in. Generals. Colonels. Hell, he was drowning already and he hadn't been in the water for a whole day yet.

"You two should have waited," the general was saying as Jack focused on the conversation. "Had a big wedding on base, where we could all have been there."

Jack's mouth was very dry. He looked at his wife and in stupefied amazement, watched her smile at him as though she meant it before turning back to the general.

"Oh, Uncle Harry," she practically sighed, "it was so much more romantic this way."

Romantic? Memories of their less than perfect wedding flashed across his mind and Jack didn't know whether to be relieved or worried that his wife seemed to be such a good liar.

General Stratton bent, kissed her forehead, then straightened. "I suppose I can remember what young love is like," he said with a slow shake of his head. "Vaguely." Turning to face Jack, the general went on sternly. "You treat our girl right now, First Sergeant, or you'll answer to me."

Perfect.

"Yes, Sir," Jack said, his voice as stiff as his body.

Nodding, the older man gave Donna's shoulder a pat, then said, "You two enjoy yourselves. I've got to go find my wife before some young major runs off with her." His gaze already scanning the crowded dining room, he wandered away.

Jack and Donna, still standing at opposite ends of the table, stared at each other for a long minute. "Uncle Harry?" he asked.

She shrugged.

"Oh, man," he whispered, his rigid stance slumping a bit now that the general had moved on.

"What happened to the stalwart marine who rode

so bravely to the rescue this morning when facing my dragon father?" she asked quietly.

"He's in shock." Along with what friends of his had already heard about his hurried marriage. Only a few more people to tell, he thought, not looking forward to seeing their astonished faces or hearing the gasps of "Donna who?"

"Maybe he needs a little exercise."

"Huh?" Jack looked at her blankly.

She shook her head and he tried not to notice how her soft, black hair caressed her cheeks with the movement.

"Dance with me, First Sergeant."

He gave the crowded dance floor a wary glance. Already, the small band was shifting into a slow song and couples were beginning to sway in time with the beat.

Donna came around the table and stood right in front of him. Cocking her head to one side, she looked up into his eyes. "Dance? You know, moving around a floor while music plays?"

"I know what it is," he told her, and didn't add that he usually avoided dance floors at all costs.

"Well, good," she said, and took his hand before he could object. Threading her way through the hundreds of small tables scattered around the room, she pulled him along in her wake.

Once among the other couples, she turned and stepped into his arms. Automatically, Jack held her, his right arm sliding around her narrow waist, his left hand cupping her right. She smiled up at him and something hot and heavy settled in the pit of Jack's stomach.

He ignored the curious glances from the other dancers and stared into her eyes. Shadow and light played in their depths, captivating him. Her breasts pressed against his chest and he fancied that he could feel her heart beating in time with his own. His body stirred, responding to the warm nearness of her. He inhaled the soft, floral scent of her perfume and felt it slip into his soul.

"Jack?" she whispered.

"Hmm?" His right hand splayed open on her back, as if trying to hold more of her—*all* of her.

"Are you okay?"

"Yeah," he said, his gaze moving over her features as if he was seeing her for the first time.

"You're sure?"

One corner of his mouth tilted. "Why?"

She glanced from side to side, then back up into his eyes. Smiling, she answered him. "Because we're in the middle of the dance floor, standing still."

"I don't dance."

Shaking her head, she said, "Well, now's a fine time to tell me."

Another couple swung past them, bumping into Jack's back. He tightened his grip on her reflexively.

Her hips came into contact with his. No doubt she felt his body's reaction, since her eyes widened.

"Maybe we should go back to the table," she said.

"Nope." Maybe he was just plain nuts, Jack thought. But for the moment, all he wanted to do was continue to hold her. "You can teach me to dance. Now."

"Now?" she echoed. "Here?"

"Here."

After a momentary pause, she smiled again. "It's been a day of firsts, huh? Married in the morning, dancing lessons in the evening…" Her voice trailed off.

"And we still have the whole night ahead of us," Jack told her. "Who knows what *other* firsts are in store for us?"

Her eyes got even bigger and if he hadn't known better, Jack might have thought that Donna Candello Harris was worried about something. Maybe even… *scared.*

Five

This is no roller coaster, she thought wildly. This is the *grandfather* of all roller coasters. Her heartbeat skittered into overdrive and her hand trembled in his. Donna stared up into his gray eyes and watched each of their fine resolutions about a platonic marriage shatter.

Tiny sparks of electricity shimmered throughout her body. Her limbs felt as heavy and tingly as if she'd been asleep for years and was just now waking up. As that thought raced across her mind, Donna inhaled sharply, tugged her hand free of Jack's, and took a step backward.

"Donna?" His voice just carried to her over the sound of the band. "What's wrong?"

"This," she whispered, knowing he couldn't hear her. Knowing, too, that she had to keep her distance from him. It would go away, she told herself firmly. This odd, heated response to his slightest touch. This was only the first day of their marriage. Surely in another week or two, she would be used to him. Probably sick and tired of him.

With any luck.

"Donna?" he asked again, moving in closer. "Are you all right?"

"No," she said, loud enough to be heard. "I'm pretty tired, Jack. I think I'll go up to the room."

His features tightened. His gray eyes cooled until they were the color of an ocean fog—and they held just as much warmth.

He cupped her elbow with one hand. "All right, I'll see you to the room."

Tingles. Sparks of heat. Desire sputtering into life.

Donna gulped in air and jerked free of his hold. "No need," she said haltingly as she tried to steady her racing heartbeat. "You stay. Have fun. I'll be fine."

Without giving him a chance to argue, she hurried off the dance floor. She paused only long enough to snatch up her handbag from the table before running for the exit as though he was chasing her.

She needn't have bothered.

Jack stood where she'd left him. Alone in a crowd of smiling couples.

* * *

The room was dark and quiet when Jack let himself in a couple of hours later. Exhausted, he told himself that maybe it hadn't been such a great idea to walk up and down the river boardwalk for two hours. But he hadn't been ready to face his new bride until now. He'd needed to cool off. Time for some quiet thinking. An hour or two to himself, where he could make up ridiculous reasons to excuse the rush of need that had filled him the moment Donna Candello had stepped into his arms.

And he'd come up with some beauties. Everything from overtiredness to uncontrollable chemistry with a gorgeous woman. Hell, it wasn't the first time he'd been attracted to someone he hardly knew. He was a man. Human. He was turned on by a knockout female just like any other guy.

But all of his reasoning fell flat. He knew it. He just didn't want to admit it. Because at no other time in his entire life had he felt so completely...*alive* as he had when he'd held Donna on that crowded dance floor. Just the memory of those few seconds was enough to send blood rushing to an area of his body that had already plagued him enough for one evening.

He stepped into the shrouded darkness and quietly closed and locked the door behind him. Toeing off his shoes, he pushed them up against the wall, out of the way. In the blackness, he couldn't see a thing, but he turned his head in the direction of the bed, knowing she was there. So close and yet so completely out of reach.

If he closed his eyes, he could still see her expression as she'd backed away from him earlier. She had looked horrified. Confused. Worried. He blinked away the image in favor of a more preferable one.

He saw her as he had the night before. Sprawled across his sheets, her black hair gleaming against the white pillowcase. Only, in his mind, she was sober. And waiting for him. She looked up at him, lifted her arms and smiled softly.

Jack took one instinctive step forward and the darkness exploded into a starburst of pain. He allowed one surprised grunt to escape his throat before clamping his lips tightly together. There was no need to frighten her out of a sound sleep just because he'd just broken his foot.

Bending, he grabbed the toe he had just slammed into something and rubbed it until the throbbing eased somewhat.

What the hell had he kicked? he wondered absently. As his eyes slowly became more accustomed to the darkness, shadows began to take shape. He noted the lighter rectangle on the wall that was the draperies, closed against the neon glitter of the night sky. He swiveled his head toward the bed again, but this time he saw plainly that Donna wasn't there.

Standing straight, he turned back toward whatever had almost crippled him. "What the hell?" he muttered. The two easy chairs in the room had been pulled close together, their seats matched up to form a small, uncomfortable-looking bed.

And on that makeshift bed, the quilt tucked up to her chin and the pillow stuffed against a chair armrest, his blushing bride lay sound asleep.

In the dim, shadowy light, he studied her calm, peaceful features. He heard the soft whisper of her even breathing. She whimpered slightly, then scooted around, apparently looking for a more comfy position, before nestling her head deeper into the pillow.

Unexpected anger simmered in his gut.

Why hadn't she slept in the damn bed? What was this supposed to be proving? That she couldn't bear to be in the same bed with him? Hell, it was a wonder she hadn't set up camp in the hallway!

"And how can she sleep through me slamming my foot into her blasted bed and shouting about it afterward?" he asked out loud, hoping for a response from Sleeping Beauty.

Nothing.

Disgusted, he turned toward the bathroom, took a step and then stopped, swiveling his head back to look at the still-oblivious woman.

She was *humming* in her sleep.

Jack scowled.

Not only was she humming, he thought furiously. She was off-key.

Twenty minutes later he stretched out on the floor, still damp from his shower. Dragging a sheet over him, he stuffed a pillow behind his head and glared at Donna. He would be damned if *he* would sleep in that bed while *she* slept on a chair.

Then, grabbing up a third pillow, he pulled it down over his face and ears, trying, without success, to drown out the blasted humming.

Two days later, back at the base, things weren't running any more smoothly.

Donna gripped the receiver tightly and tried to keep her voice even. She'd learned long ago that in dealing with people, it never paid to lose your temper.

"Excuse me, Lieutenant Austin," she interrupted the man's apparently well-rehearsed speech. "You're saying that there *is* base housing available, but we can't have it?"

"Yes, ma'am," he said, approval in his tone. "That's it exactly."

Donna sank back into her father's burgundy leather desk chair. "Then what you're really saying is, nothing's available."

"No, ma'am." The faceless lieutenant sighed,

clearly disappointed in her. "We have a house for you and the first sergeant, but you can't have it for a day or two."

"And why is that again?"

"Like I told you before, ma'am," he said, "the house has to be cleaned, inspected and passed."

"Can't I *hire* someone to clean it?"

"No, ma'am, we have our own teams for that."

Donna picked up a pen from the desk in front of her and idly began doodling on a nearby tablet. "*When,* exactly, will it be ready, Lieutenant? Can you tell me that, at least?"

"No, ma'am," he told her.

She was really beginning to hate the word "ma'am." "How about a hint?" she asked, desperate now.

He chuckled.

Donna snarled silently.

"If I were you, I'd count on Wednesday."

Great. She couldn't move into Jack's apartment at the noncommissioned officers' barracks. Strictly for bachelors. *Her* apartment was in Maryland. Hardly a commuting distance.

She looked around her father's home office and muffled a sigh. Apparently they would be staying with the colonel a few days anyway. Since she and Jack were hardly talking, at least they would have her father as a buffer between them.

Images of the night before, their first night back

from Laughlin, swam in front of her eyes. They'd arrived late, with everyone tired from the long drive and even longer silences. Jack had gallantly carried hers and her father's bags into the colonel's house and then promptly disappeared into the night. Oh, he'd mumbled something about going back to the NCO barracks for his things, but Donna recognized an escape attempt when she saw one.

Still, he couldn't get away with staying at the barracks more than one night—not if he expected everyone on base to believe that they were the happily married newlyweds they were pretending to be.

Which brought her back to the problem at hand.

"That's the best you can do?" she asked the beleaguered man on the other end of the phone.

"That's it, ma'am."

Donna cringed. "Thanks very much."

"Yes, ma'am. Oh, and congratulations to you and the first sergeant, ma'am."

Donna hung up and glanced at the notepad. While talking to the lieutenant, her subconscious mind had doodled a gallows, complete with dangling noose and three steps to oblivion.

"Now *there's* a good sign," she muttered. Standing, she tore off the top sheet, crumpled it into a ball and tossed it into the trash can beside the desk.

* * *

"Married?" Gunnery Sergeant Tom Haley shook his head, slapped his ear as if he'd heard wrong, and said again, "Married?"

Jack shrugged off his friend's stunned surprise. Tom had been on leave, so hadn't yet heard all of the gossip. Jack figured it would take at least another day for the latest piece of news to sweep across the base. "Will you stop saying that?"

"Sorry," the other man said. "It's just that I never expected to hear you say those words."

"Yeah, well," Jack muttered, "neither did I."

"She must be something." Tom's blond eyebrows lifted high over blue eyes. "Who is she?"

Ah... Finally, the question he'd been dreading. He just knew that the minute his friends found out about him marrying the colonel's daughter, his life would become a living hell.

"Her name's Donna."

"Donna what?"

"Harris." He was stalling and he knew it.

Tom threw a pencil at him from across the room. It missed him, clattering on the linoleum floor. "I know that much. What was it *before* you married her?"

"Why do you care?"

"Is there a reason you don't want me to know her name?"

There was just no way out of this, Jack told himself, and the longer he stalled, the more interested Tom would become. Besides, what was the point? In another day or so, everyone in his world would know. He braced himself for the merciless ragging he was going to take. "Fine. Her name was Candello."

"Candello..." Tom leaned back in his chair, lifted both legs to the corner of his desk and crossed his ankles. Folding his hands atop his chest, he said the name again. "Candello. Now why does—" He stopped. His feet dropped to the floor with a thud and he sat up straight, a wild, disbelieving look in his eyes. "The colonel's daughter?" he finally said. "Are you nuts?"

Certifiable, Jack thought. "Nope," he said out loud. "Just married."

"You gotta be out of your mind, man." Tom jumped up from his chair and walked across the room. With both palms flat on Jack's desk, he leaned in toward his friend. "Don't you know the load of garbage you're gonna have to take because you married a *colonel's* daughter?"

Jack pushed one hand across the top of his head and leaned back in his chair. Staring up at Tom, he asked, "No, will I really?"

"I didn't even know you knew her," Tom went on.

"Yeah, well, I do."

"Sure, now. But when'd you meet her?"

"Does that—"

"Must have been years ago," Tom said more to himself than to Jack. "Didn't you serve with the colonel back in '90?"

"Yeah…" Of course, he'd never met Donna until a few days ago, but no one else needed to know that.

"Wow." Tom grinned, sat on the edge of Jack's desk and crossed his arms over his chest. "Imagine. *You.* And the colonel's daughter."

Jack frowned to himself. All right, it was unusual. And unexpected. But was it really so damn surprising that Donna Candello might actually find him marriageable?

Then he remembered that he and his blushing bride had agreed not to share a bed, and answered that silent question himself. Okay, the celibacy thing had been his idea. But she had sure agreed quickly enough.

"So?" Tom asked with a broad wink. "Think your daddy-in-law can pull some strings for you? Maybe get you your very own battalion?"

Jack shoved the man off his desk. "Shut up and get to work."

"Wow," Tom said between chuckles, "already, he has delusions of grandeur."

Perfect, he thought as Tom, still laughing, booted up his computer and got back to business. If this was any indication, he was going to have a real good time over the next few days. All because he'd gone outside for a cigarette.

The damn things really would be the death of him.

Donna hadn't been on base in four years.

She sucked in a deep breath, squared her shoulders and dug her fingers into the plush leather of her clutch purse.

Ridiculous to feel so quakey inside. She'd grown up on military bases—at least from the age of thirteen when she'd gone to live with her father. A brief smile crossed her lips and then faded. That had been a tough year, she remembered. Her father and she practically strangers, yet thrust on each other because her mother had suddenly gotten the urge to live in Paris and learn to paint. She'd died only a few years later.

But Donna and her father had gotten past the wary uneasiness. And together they'd found what they had both been missing. Family. Love. Trust.

Donna shuddered. If only she had trusted her father's judgment four years ago, she could have saved herself a truckload of embarrassment—not to mention this marriage that wasn't a marriage.

She lifted her chin and stared at the door not twenty feet from her. Just beyond that doorway, amid a bustle of marines, was her husband's office. Unfortunately, Jack's desk was depressingly close to her father's. Which meant by going inside, she would be forcing herself to face the scene of her grandest error in judgment.

It was right after her engagement had blown up in her face. She'd been feeling fragile and decidedly unwanted—a dangerous combination, as it turned out.

Inside that building was the very desk where she'd tried to seduce her father's assistant, only to have her dad unexpectedly interrupt her sad Mata Hari attempt.

She could still feel the heat of shame rushing into her cheeks. She saw the young corporal's wide, horrified eyes as he'd stared at his commanding officer, and in memory, she would always hear her father's quick intake of breath followed by the disappointed tone of his voice when he'd said her name.

Good Lord. She lifted one hand to shield her eyes as though it might block out the memory. How could she have been so stupid? And as if that wasn't enough, she hadn't even had the guts to stay and brave the situation out. No. Not Donna Candello. She'd jumped the first plane out of town and hadn't shown her face since.

Until now, when she was around just long enough to screw up again.

"Ma'am?" A deep voice came from just to her right.

Donna half turned and looked at the marine staring at her in obvious concern.

"You all right, ma'am?"

"Probably not," she said tiredly. "But thanks for asking."

"Can I help in some way?"

Kind. The lieutenant was just trying to be kind. She knew that. Unfortunately, that didn't change things.

"No, thank you," she said with a small, halfhearted smile. "If there's one thing I don't need at the moment, it's one more marine."

He blinked, surprised, but Donna ignored his confusion and started walking toward the doors. Determined to face her ghosts before she could chicken out again.

Six

Jack glanced up as Tom Haley leapt to his feet, his gaze locked squarely on the doorway. "Can I help you, ma'am?" he said in a tone that was more eager than polite.

"I'm here to see Sergeant Harris," a too familiar female voice answered.

Damn. Instantly it felt as though a lead weight had settled in the pit of Jack's stomach. Yet at the same time a lower portion of his anatomy experienced a far different reaction.

Slowly, he swiveled his head in her direction. "*First* Sergeant," he corrected automatically.

Twin black brows lifted slightly, arching over the dark brown eyes that haunted his sleep. What might have been a smile briefly crossed her lips before she said, "Right."

Damn, why'd she have to look so good? Her deep green blouse, open at the collar, was tucked into the narrow waistband of a short black skirt that skimmed her hips like a lover's hands only to flare out and swing about her thighs as she walked farther into the room. The tap of her high heels against the linoleum sounded like a heartbeat. Those legs of hers could be registered as weapons. As for her eyes...well, Jack didn't even want to *think* about them for the moment.

Tom cleared his throat dramatically, bringing Jack back from fantasies he shouldn't be indulging in anyway. Shooting his friend a frosty look, he scowled when Tom only grinned at him.

Apparently the man had no intention of going anywhere without an introduction. Standing, Jack said stiffly, "Donna, this is Gunnery Sergeant Haley—"

"Tom," the other man interrupted with a smile that looked entirely too friendly.

Frowning, Jack finished the introduction. "Tom, this is my *wife*. Donna."

All right, saying that word felt strange, but at the same time, he really didn't like the look in Tom Haley's eyes as the man studied Donna from head to toe. Though why all of a sudden Tom's charm with women should bother him, he didn't want to consider.

"It's a pleasure, Mrs. Harris," Tom said as he came out from behind his desk and crossed the room to her, one hand extended in welcome.

Donna placed her hand in his and said, "Please. Call me Donna."

Jack frowned to himself as his gaze landed on their joined hands. He couldn't help noticing that Tom held hers for just a bit longer than necessary.

His stomach churned and he knew it wasn't because of the rot-gut coffee he'd been pouring down his throat all morning. Damn it, wasn't it enough that he had to deal with Donna privately? Did she *have* to show up at his office, too?

But even as that thought crossed his mind, he had to admit that it wasn't just her presence that upset his peace of mind. It was her. Period. Ever since that first morning when she'd faced him down despite an obviously painful hangover, he'd been intrigued. Okay, he admitted silently, *more* than intrigued.

Sober, she was even more disturbing.

Gritting his teeth, he forced himself to ask calmly. "Is there a problem?"

Donna flicked him a quick look. One eyebrow lifted slightly. "Just because a wife comes to her *husband's* office, does there have to be a problem?"

"Yeah, Jack." Tom joined in, guiding her to a chair. "Lighten up. Maybe she just missed you."

"Yeah," Donna agreed. "Maybe that's why I'm here. I missed you."

Sure. Like she'd missed a toothache. But he couldn't very well say that in front of Tom. Not if they were going to keep up the pretense of being happy newlyweds.

She sat and crossed one incredible leg over the other. Her black stockings brushed against each other and the hem of her skirt fell back, displaying far more leg than Jack wanted Tom to see.

Turning to his friend, he snapped, "Don't you have somewhere you have to be?"

"Nope," Tom assured him, perching one hip on the edge of his desk.

Donna smiled at the man before turning her dark eyes back to Jack. He wasn't blind to the fact that her smile disappeared at the same instant.

"Look, Donna," he said, trying to keep his voice even and his gaze away from her upper thigh. "If it's not important, I've got work to take care of."

"Of course it's important," she said. Swinging her right foot gently, effectively drawing his gaze back to her legs, she went on. "I've been talking to base housing and—"

"You shouldn't have to do that," Tom cut in, reaching out to briefly stroke one of Donna's hands. "Jack, why don't you take care of all that for her?"

"Because," he said tightly, "I've got other things

to do." Silently he wondered how many bones in Tom's hand he could break with one quick move. Thankfully, the other man retreated, so it wasn't put to the test.

Donna stiffened slightly. "And I don't, you mean?"

"I didn't say that," he countered, meeting her dark eyes evenly. "It's just that I have a job to do and—"

"And I'm unemployed?" she finished for him.

Hell, he didn't even *know* if she had a job or not.

"It wasn't an accusation," he said.

"I happen to have a very good job," she told him, squaring her shoulders and lifting her chin just a bit higher.

"Really?" Tom interjected, pulling those eyes of hers to him. "Where do you work?"

She paused for a long minute, bit her lip, then answered, "Maryland."

"Kind of a long commute," Jack said.

Her gaze flicked to him instantly. Then, as if remembering Tom's presence, she plastered a smile on her face and cooed, "Naturally, I'll have to resign. I hadn't expected to spend my vacation being swept away by passion."

Passion. The only thing she'd been swept away by was a pitcher of margaritas…which they were both paying for.

"I'm sure you'll find another job soon," Tom assured her soothingly, managing to irritate Jack at the same time.

A long silence filled the passing moments until finally, Tom pushed up from the desk, smiled at Donna and completely ignored his longtime friend. "I still say, if I had a wife as pretty as yours, Jack, I'd be doing everything I could to help her get settled in on base."

And the chances of Tom Haley *ever* settling down with one woman were slimmer than Jack's chances of being an astronaut.

"Thank you, Tom," Donna said, giving him a wide, bright smile. One, Jack thought, she hadn't seen fit to bestow on the man who'd saved her reputation and her father's.

"You need anything, you just give me a call," Tom told her before gathering up a stack of papers from the edge of his desk. "And now, if you'll excuse me, maybe there *are* a few things I should be doing."

Once he was gone, Jack turned to her. "What the hell was that all about?"

"What?" She shrugged, her foot swinging at a bit faster pace. "Your friend was just being nice. So was I."

"Any nicer and he would have—" He interrupted himself, not wanting to go down that particular road.

"Jealous?" she asked.

That stung. "Now, why would I be jealous?"

"That's what I was wondering."

"Well, don't," he said quickly. "All I meant was, if we're supposed to be happily married, you shouldn't flirt with the biggest ladies' man on base."

"I wasn't flirting," she snapped.

"What do you call crossing your legs and swinging your foot like that?"

She shook her head. "I call it crossing my legs and swinging my foot."

He rubbed one hand over his face and fought for control. Ridiculous. He knew he was overreacting and still he couldn't seem to stop himself. But, damn it, watching Tom Haley watching Donna had been... unsettling.

Why that was, he didn't want to explore.

"Fine," he finally said. "Let's just forget it, shall we?"

She gave him a slow, thoughtful nod.

"What are you doing here, anyway?"

"We have to talk about our living arrangements."

"Now?"

"Yes, now." She stood and crossed the room to him. "I've been on the phone with Base Housing most of the morning. They say there's a house available but we can't have it for another two or three days."

Perfect. Just three days until he and Donna were actually living together. Well, he'd better find a way to control his hormones before then. "Fine. What's the problem?"

"The problem is, you can't stay at your apartment in the NCO barracks until then."

No, he couldn't. He'd known the night before that it would be his last night in the place. And frankly, he wasn't going to miss it much. A small place, it wasn't exactly anyone's idea of home sweet home.

"Unless of course," she said hesitantly. "I can stay there with you."

"No. Bachelors only."

She shrugged and nodded as if she'd been expecting that answer. "So we're left with two options."

"Yeah?" He had a feeling he wasn't going to like either of them.

"We can go off base and stay in a motel, or we can stay with my father at his house."

Faced with those two choices, he made the obvious call. "I vote motel."

She smiled briefly. "Somehow, I thought you would. But then people would wonder why we weren't staying with Dad."

"So," he said, "let them wonder."

Cocking her head to one side, she looked up at him. "This marriage was *your* idea, Jack. To keep people from wondering. Talking. Remember?"

Yeah, he remembered. All too clearly. It had seemed like such a good idea at the time.

"Fine." He knew when he was beaten. "The colonel's house, it is."

"Relax, Jack," Donna told him. "Your virtue's safe with me. It's a four-bedroom house. We don't *have* to share a room."

He glanced at her and Donna tried to read the emotions glimmering in his gray eyes. But she couldn't. Either he was a master at masking his feelings, or she just didn't know him well enough yet. And what did *that* say about the situation? She didn't know him well enough to tell what he was thinking, but she *did* know him well enough to marry?

Good God.

"That was the deal," he reminded her. "A platonic marriage. Easier on both of us."

Well, on one of us, anyway, she thought, letting her gaze skim down her new husband's trim, muscular body. Speaking as a twenty-eight-year-old married virgin, sharing a bed might not be so bad.

Heat suddenly rushed to her cheeks. She could hardly believe what she was thinking. A few days ago she hadn't known this man from Adam. Now not only was she married to him, she was entertaining fantasies of midnight romps in the hay.

Sucking in a deep breath, she nodded. "Yeah. Easier."

"So is that all you wanted?" he asked.

Now there was a loaded question. But she ignored the opening and simply answered, "Yes. That's all."

"Okay, then," Jack said, rubbing the back of his neck, "I guess I'll—"

"Sure." She cut him off neatly. "I'll let you get back to work. Since you are the only one with a job."

"Look," he said. "I'm sorry about that. I didn't know about your job."

"What? You thought I was independently wealthy?" She shook her head. "Sorry to disappoint you, but you didn't marry an heiress."

"That's not what I meant."

"What did you mean, Jack?"

"Hell if I know."

She inhaled slowly, deeply, needing a minute or two to steady herself. For heaven's sake, why was she baiting the man? It wasn't *his* fault that they were in this mess. The only reason they were married at all was that she was too much of a coward to face her father after the mess she'd created four years before.

Now, instead of trying to make the best of an impossible situation, she was doing her utmost to be as difficult as possible. Real smart.

"Donna—"

"Jack—"

They spoke at the same time, then looked at each other for a long moment in sheepish silence.

"You want me to walk you out?" he finally asked.

"No, thanks. I know the way."

"Are you going to stop in and see your father?"

No way, she thought. She was not ready to walk past the desk where she'd once made a complete ass of herself.

She shook her head and dug her fingers into her purse. But neither did she want to explain her reasons to a husband who wouldn't be around for more than a few months. The fewer people who knew of that little episode, the better.

"I'll see him tonight," she said. "He's probably busy, anyway." Then she turned and headed for the door. With every step she took, Donna felt his gaze burning into her back. Heat snaked through her bloodstream, warming her from the inside out. Her knees trembled. Her high heels suddenly felt precarious. Just before she left the room, his voice stopped her.

"Donna?"

"Yes?" She half turned to face him, hoping he couldn't see the flush of heat no doubt staining her cheeks. That inscrutable look was on his face again and she wished heartily that she could read minds.

"This will all work out. All we have to do is settle in. We'll get used to each other."

Sure, she thought. All she had to do was train her heartbeat not to jump into double time when she saw him. And, if she could just keep reminding herself that sex hadn't been part of their deal, that would be a big help, too. In this case, she wasn't sure if being a virgin was a help or a hindrance. Never having been intimate with a man, she couldn't miss what she'd never had. On the other hand, her fantasies weren't based on reality, so her mind had free rein in coming up with wild imaginings designed to torture the lovelorn.

Lord, she was in trouble.

Donna gave him what she hoped was a carefree smile and lifted one hand in a brief wave. "Of course we'll get used to each other, Jack. It's just a matter of time."

He would never get used to this, Jack told himself as he lay wide awake in one of the colonel's guest bedrooms. Dinner had been a disaster, even though his superior officer had done everything to make him more comfortable. The colonel had made an issue of taking off his uniform blouse and telling Jack to do the same. Then, with both of them in plain white T-shirts, Colonel Candello had assured him that inside that house, there were no ranks.

Though Jack appreciated the gesture, he still hadn't been able to get comfortable. Not with Donna sitting directly across the table from him. Damn it, even in an old T-shirt and cutoffs, she looked good enough to stop his heart.

Grumbling to himself, he sat up, punched his pillow into shape and lay down again. Wide awake, he turned his head toward the window where a silver strand of moonlight poured through the half-open drapes.

His brain wandered aimlessly, conjuring up image after image of Donna. What the hell had he gotten himself into? And how was he ever going to survive a platonic marriage that was already making him nuts?

From the next room he heard the soft, unmistakable sound of Donna humming in her sleep. Apparently she wasn't having any problem at all adjusting to this frustrating situation.

Groaning, he yanked the pillow out from under his head, slammed it down over his face and prayed for sleep that wouldn't come.

"It's so small," Donna said, and heard the whine in her voice. But the house was so dismal, she couldn't help herself.

"It's big enough for us," Jack told her, strolling

across the eight-foot-wide living room into the tiny kitchen.

Donna followed him, hesitantly poking her head around the corner to inspect a kitchen almost too small for the appliances it held. "You're kidding," she muttered, her gaze landing on a refrigerator that looked to be an antique. "Does it require a block of ice to keep things cool?" she wondered out loud, only half kidding.

He slapped one palm against the short, scarred fridge. "It's not *that* old."

"It's beyond old. Closing in on 'archeological relic.'"

Jack slapped it again, as if to prove her wrong, and the machine groaned, gurgled and shook on its four metal feet.

"I think you killed it," Donna whispered, half expecting the blasted thing to explode.

"It's a marine refrigerator," Jack told her, taking one step back from the still-shaking appliance. "It's not dead. It's regrouping."

"Ooo-rah," she muttered, and let her gaze slide away from the quivering fridge to the two long cupboards, a stove that told her she'd be doing a lot of barbecuing, and a sink that had more gouges and scars ripped into its porcelain surface than most tanks saw in a lifetime. Wonderful, she thought, and glanced at the faded, drooping curtains over the one tiny window. The blue-and-white-checked gingham hung limply, its starch long gone, along with most of its color.

As she watched, Jack reached up and pushed the curtains back, allowing a narrow shaft of sunlight to slide through the glass. An instant later the curtain rod dropped from its hardware and clattered into the sink.

Donna jumped.

Jack's eyebrows lifted.

Stepping up behind him, she glanced down at the fallen curtains spilling over the rim of the sink, then up at Jack. "Nice," she said. "And to think, it passed inspection."

He frowned slightly, picked up the short rod and inspected it. "Not a problem. I can fix this."

A full-time handyman wouldn't be able to fix this place, she thought. Not without twenty years at his disposal.

"So, *First* Sergeant," Donna said thoughtfully, "this is the house your rank has earned you."

He slanted a look at her. "Actually, no. But this is all that was available, remember?"

True, Donna thought, her gaze sliding from his to roam over her temporary home. She suppressed a shudder. Every wall in the place was painted the same shade of eggshell white. Apparently, the corps painters lacked imagination. She reached out to touch one of the kitchen walls and wondered idly just how many layers of latex paint actually covered it.

And how many families had lived there? How many kids had scrawled their names on these walls in crayon only to have them painted over? A wistful smile crossed her face briefly as she recalled the years she'd spent growing up on military bases. It hadn't been easy, she thought, but at the same time, there had always been a sense of community.

Glancing at Jack, she fought a twinge of regret that their marriage was nothing more than pretense. She'd wanted a family of her own for so long. And now that she finally had a husband, it was only temporary.

"I know it's not much," he was saying, "but we won't need the place for long, anyway."

She nodded and walked off, headed for the incredibly short hallway that led to two bedrooms and the bathroom. Jack's footsteps sounded right behind her. But she hadn't had to hear him to know he was near. She felt his presence in every cell of her body. Which was probably not a good thing.

"Look, Donna," he said softly, and she half turned to face him. "I know this isn't quite up to what you're used to, but—"

"I know," she interrupted, "it's only temporary." Shifting her gaze again, she inspected the place slowly. "But je-ezz, Jack, how can the marine corps expect people to live in shacks like this?"

He stiffened a bit at the slur on the corps, but to

give him his due, he shrugged and nodded. "They don't, really." Lifting his gaze to the patched, water-stained ceiling, he went on. "All of these old places are scheduled for demolition in the next couple of years."

An unexpected splinter of regret shot through her. Lord knew the house was in sad shape. Still, the little place had sheltered hundreds of families. Didn't that count for something, too? Silly, but she felt the sting of tears tickle the backs of her eyes. To cover up her sudden twist of emotion, she said, "If they don't fall down first."

Jack's features tightened briefly before relaxing. "Yeah, I guess. So, which room do you want?"

It didn't matter, so Donna waved one hand to the room on the right. "This one will be fine."

"Okay, then," Jack said. "I'll bring in my stuff, then we'll go to your father's house and pick up the rest."

Until her things arrived from Maryland, Donna's father was loaning them an extra bed and a few of his furnishings.

Leaning up against the wall, Donna asked, "So what do you think the neighbors will say when they watch us carry in two beds?"

He rubbed the back of his neck, a habit Donna had already noticed.

"Probably nothing. They'll just assume one of the rooms is for a guest room."

He was right, she thought. After all, who would ever guess that happily married newlyweds weren't even sharing a bedroom?

Seven

Donna stood on the front porch of the colonel's residence and watched Jack load furniture into the back of a borrowed pickup. Two of her father's lamps, a box spring and mattress, a dresser, and one small coffee table filled the compact truck bed.

She inhaled sharply, blew all of the air out, and deliberately fixed her gaze on her husband. The pale blue T-shirt he'd tucked into faded blue jeans stretched and pulled across his muscular chest and shoulders. He placed a hand on the edge of the truck bed and in one fluid motion, jumped inside to secure their cargo.

Shaking her head, she told herself not to notice the curve of his behind as he bent to straighten something. He'd made it clear from the beginning that he wasn't interested in pursuing anything other than a platonic relationship with her. The least she could do was stop drooling over him and save herself from any further embarrassment.

"You okay?" her father asked as he stepped up behind her on the porch.

"Sure," she said, forcing a brightness she didn't feel into her voice. "Why wouldn't I be?"

"The First Sergeant's a good man, Donna."

She half turned to look up at him, saw the gentleness in his eyes and looked away again, before she could cry. "I really screwed up big time, didn't I?"

Easing one hip against the porch railing, he lifted a hand to smooth the hair back from her face. Donna risked a quick glance at him and saw the same love and understanding she'd always found in his eyes.

As she watched him, he smiled briefly. "Let's just say, this was one of your more memorable achievements."

Donna groaned quietly. "And to think all of this started because I was too embarrassed to face you."

"Now, that," he said, "I don't understand. Why would you feel like that, Donna?"

Why? Because she could still see the look on his face when he had walked in on the most embarrassing moment of her life.

"I've missed seeing you," he said softly.

Her heart twisted and the backs of her eyes stung as she walked into her father's arms. She felt the warm, solid strength of him as he held her just as he had so many times during her adolescence. "Oh, Daddy, I've missed you, too. Three or four phone calls a week just isn't enough, I guess."

"Then why didn't you ever come home?" He pulled back and looked down at her. "God knows, I begged for a visit often enough."

"I just couldn't bring myself to face you." She sniffed and took a step back. "News flash. Big Strong Marine Has Coward For Daughter."

"You're not a coward, Donna."

"What would you call it?"

"Impetuous?" he suggested with a grin.

She wiped her eyes and gave him a small smile.

"Don't you know I love you?"

"Of course I do," she said, though silently she admitted that it was good to hear him confirm it. "But even Job had limits. Didn't he?"

Tom Candello chuckled and shook his head. "No father has limits. Not where his little girl's concerned."

She took a deep breath and looked at him. Donna had missed seeing him. Visiting him. But in four years she'd never been able to work up the nerve to look him in the eye. "Not even when he walks into his office to find his daughter trying desperately to seduce a corporal, who in turn was trying desperately to escape?"

His smile faded, but the light in his eyes didn't dim a fraction. "Not even then."

Relief poured through her. She'd been so ashamed. So humiliated. *Why* hadn't she gone to him that night at the ball instead of looking for courage at the bottom of a margarita pitcher? If only she'd used her brain, she wouldn't have traded one mess for another, bigger one.

"God," she muttered, disgusted with herself. "I'm an idiot."

Her father laughed gently. "You *do* have some interesting moments."

"Interesting. That's one word for them."

"Don't be so hard on yourself, honey."

"Why not?" she asked. "Not only did I screw things up for myself this time, but I dragged Jack along with me."

The colonel turned his head to look at the other man. "Jack's a big boy. He knew what he was doing."

"Did he, Daddy?" Donna waited until her father's gaze had shifted back to her. "The man *married* me, for God's sake."

"It was his idea."

"Yeah," she agreed. "One I'm sure he's regretted every moment since."

Her father frowned slightly. "Has he said so?"

"No," she said quickly, not wanting her father to think Jack was being anything less than damned nice about this whole thing. "Actually, he seems fine with the situation." Except of course, she added silently, for the fact that he wants nothing physical to do with his temporary wife.

"Then why don't you relax?" her father asked.

"How am I supposed to do that?" she demanded.

"Just try not to make everything so hard. It doesn't have to be."

"Easy for you to say," she muttered, glancing back at her husband's tush as he backed his way out of the truck.

The colonel reached up, grabbed a lock of her hair and gave it a gentle tug. She looked at him.

"Donna, give yourself—and Jack—a chance. Who knows? You two might end up *enjoying* being married."

"Sure and what color blue do you think the sun will be tomorrow?"

He shook his head and stood beside her. "All I'm saying is, as long as you're married—make the best of the situation. You didn't trap Jack into a marriage. He volunteered for this mission."

"Yeah," she said on a sigh. "And him without a bazooka."

"Cut it out," her father snapped, and her gaze

shot to his. "Make the best of this, Donna. Don't throw away what might turn out to be a blessing because you're too proud, or stubborn, or whatever, to admit that you actually *like* Jack Harris."

"Don't you get it, Dad?" she countered quickly. "It doesn't matter if I like him or not. He's not interested. Hell, I'm not even sure *I* am."

"He's not Kyle."

"No, he's not," Donna said, tossing another glance at the man she'd married only days before. "Jack didn't sleep with my maid of honor two days before the wedding. Heck, he doesn't even want to sleep with—" She broke off quickly. Heat rushed to her cheeks as she realized that she was talking to her *father* about her lack of a sex life. Lord, when would she learn to shut up?

Thankfully, her father let that statement go, apparently just as eager to avoid such a talk as she was.

"Donna," he said, taking her by the shoulders and turning her to face him. "Sometimes, life's little surprises turn out to be the best thing that you could hope for."

"And sometimes, it's just another screwup by Donna Candello."

"Donna Harris."

She groaned.

Her father shook his head and pulled her close for a brief, hard hug. When she stepped back, she looked up at him hopefully. "I don't suppose you'd be interested in coming over for dinner tonight? Kind of help ease us into this moving-in-together thing?"

"Sorry," he said. "I can't. I think I may have a date."

Her eyebrows lifted. Her father had hardly *ever* dated. "You 'think' you 'may' have a date?"

He nodded as his gaze moved past her to stare out into the side yard. "It's a little iffy right now."

"Who is she?"

He shook his head, meeting her eyes briefly. "I'll tell you that if I can actually convince her to go out with me."

"Why wouldn't she?" Donna demanded. "You're smart, handsome, funny, kind—"

"Thanks for the vote of confidence," her father interrupted, laughing. "But why don't you let me handle my love life and you concentrate on your own?"

"Yours would be easier."

"What was that you said about cowardice?"

"Guilty."

The colonel turned his head slightly. "Looks like Jack's ready to go."

Donna looked up to see her husband moving toward them, and told herself once again not to notice how well those jeans fit his long legs. Oh, she was in deep water here, and there was no one around to throw her a life preserver.

She started reluctantly for the steps, then stopped suddenly as if something had occurred to her. "Dad?"

"Yes?"

"What ever happened to the corporal?"

Thankfully, he knew instantly who she was referring to. "You scared the poor kid to death. He requested a transfer almost immediately."

Donna grimaced. "To where?"

"Greenland. I think he wanted to get as far away from here as possible."

"You mean," she clarified unnecessarily, "from me."

"Donna..."

"Some seductress," she muttered more to herself than her father. "Come on to a man and he runs thousands of miles in the opposite direction."

As she walked down the sidewalk, she met Jack's gaze and felt another flutter of awareness streak through her. He waved to the colonel, then took her arm to escort her to the truck. And Donna couldn't help but wonder if her husband would scare off as easily as that corporal had.

More important, did she have the nerve to find out?

Jack dismissed the private he'd enlisted to help move furniture, then stood back and surveyed his new bedroom. Donna was right. The place was small. And old. And falling apart. But it had one definite plus. It wasn't in the NCO barracks.

"Jack," Donna called from the other room.

On the down side, he was living with a wife he wasn't allowed to touch. "Yeah?"

"Can you come here for a minute?"

Steeling himself against the sight of Donna's bare legs and nicely rounded butt, Jack headed for her bedroom. Evidently it didn't matter how prepared he was. One look at her and his body tightened like an overtuned guitar string.

He stood in the doorway, watching her as she struggled and yanked at one of two windows. Half bent over in her effort to shove the window open, her cutoffs crept high on her thighs, the worn fabric stretching dangerously thin across her curves. The midriff-length T-shirt she wore rode up on her back, displaying even more of her deliciously smooth, ivory skin.

His teeth ground together as he struggled to hold on to what little self-control he had left. "What do you need?" he asked.

She shot him a harried look over her shoulder and blew a lock of dark hair out of her eyes. "Help."

He chuckled despite the pain in his lower body.

"This isn't funny," she told him, narrowing the one eye she had locked on him. "Somebody must have nailed this darn thing shut." She grunted for good measure as she gave the window another shove. Nothing.

Sighing heavily, she straightened and glared at the closed window, while idly rubbing a spot on her lower back.

Before he could do something stupid like offer to massage her strained muscles, he walked around the edge of her bed and straight to the window. Slowly, he inspected the wooden frame, giving himself time to adjust to the nearness of her. Damn. What kind of woman wore perfume to move furniture?

Obviously, he told himself as he breathed in the soft, floral scent, *this* one.

Keep centered, he warned himself. Mind on the job.

"It's not nailed shut," he said over his shoulder. "It's just been painted over."

"Perfect."

"If you'll get me a knife, I'll open it for you."

"Deal."

Brushing up against him, she mumbled, "Sorry," as she squeezed past and headed for the kitchen.

That incredibly brief touch shouldn't have been enough to start a wildfire in his blood. But it had. Setting both hands flat on either side of the window, Jack let his head fall forward until his chin hit his neck. Closing his eyes, he concentrated the iron will he was known for to defeat this completely irrational hormonal attraction for his wife.

Hell, he didn't even like her much. Well, all right, he liked her more than he had thought he would. But she still managed to give the impression that she was visiting royalty and he was a lucky, though unworthy, peasant to be allowed in her presence.

Just her attitude about this house was enough to underline all of the differences between them. He could tell by looking at her that she was disgusted to have to live in the place.

He lifted his head and looked out the window to the backyard. Knee-high, burned brown grass covered the lot, but there was a single, scrawny tree in the far corner and plenty of possibilities. He was willing to admit that the little house wasn't much, but it was the first *home* he'd lived in since his parents had died when he was a kid.

The aunt and uncle he'd stayed with after the car accident had lived in an apartment and hadn't exactly been the Ward and June Cleaver types. They hadn't abused him or anything, though. In fact, they'd hardly noticed him at all until he'd turned sixteen and landed a part-time job. And even then, they'd only really been interested in his pathetically small paycheck.

Gritting his teeth, he pushed all of those memories to the deepest, darkest corner of his mind. That was over. That life was so far behind him, even the memories usually couldn't catch him. But he'd been doing too much thinking lately. And that was her fault.

"Sorry it took me so long," she said as she came back into the room.

Jack dismissed the past and focused on his present. "No problem."

"I couldn't find a sharp knife," she went on as if he hadn't spoken, and didn't stop walking until she was right beside him. "Will this one be all right?"

A butter knife with a bent blade wasn't exactly a precision tool, but he'd make do. He wanted to pry up the window and get the hell out of her bedroom as quickly as possible. "Yeah, it's fine."

His fingers closed over the knife handle, brushing against hers as she handed it to him. He swore he actually *saw* bright blue sparks rise from where they touched. He damn sure *felt* the sizzle. Right down to the soles of his feet.

Before he could blatantly ignore it, though, Donna took one long step back from him and put her hands behind her back for good measure.

His grip on the knife tightened as he deliberately turned to the task at hand. Running the blade along the painted-over seam, he cracked away the latest layer of white paint until the sash was free. Then he gave a hard shove and pushed the window open.

Instantly, a cold wind rushed in, carrying the scent of the sea. Donna inhaled sharply and smiled. "Isn't that great?"

"Yeah. But cold."

She grinned up at him. "Cold, yes. But not freezing. I talked to my old roommate this morning and she told me Baltimore got hit by a blizzard last night."

The weather, he thought. They were actually discussing the weather.

Trying for a different subject, he asked, "So, was your roommate mad about you getting married and skipping out on your share of the rent?"

She shook her head. "Mad? No. Surprised? Yes. But it's working out all right. She had wanted her boyfriend to move in anyway."

"Handy," he said for lack of anything better.

"Yeah," Donna agreed with a ridiculously overbright smile. "All's well that ends well."

A long moment of silence stretched out between them.

She shivered slightly in the blast of cold air coming in the window. Jack lowered it several inches.

"Uh, do you want me to do the other window, too?"

Her smile faded as she shook her head. "No, one window's enough for today. I would like it if you could find the switch on that refrigerator and turn it on. Though I'm still not sure it actually works with electricity."

"No problem," he told her, already moving, grateful for a reason to escape the too close confines of her bedroom.

"You always say that, you know."

"Say what?"

"No problem. Isn't anything a problem for you, Jack?"

He only had one at the moment. Keeping his hands off his wife. But all he said was, "Any problem can be handled." He hoped.

"Before you go—" Her voice stopped him just inches from a clean getaway. He turned in the doorway and waited. "What is that?" she asked, pointing to the ceiling.

His gaze followed hers, then narrowed on an odd-shaped plaster bubble. Why hadn't he noticed that earlier? he wondered, then knew the answer. He'd been keeping his gaze down, trying to avoid staring at Donna. He took a step closer, tilted his head to one side and studied the plaster oddity for a long minute before admitting, "I don't know."

"It's right over my bed," she observed unnecessarily.

He tossed her a glance. "You want to switch rooms?"

She looked around at the few things she'd already unpacked and he could tell she didn't want to move any of it again. To reassure her, he took another look at the warped ceiling. "It's probably just that the plaster's gotten damp over the years. Most likely, the repair crews just keep slapping more plaster on it every year until it looks like a blister."

"A blister," she mused thoughtfully. "Yeah. That's exactly what it looks like. Or maybe a pimple."

"So, you're okay with this?"

She glanced at him and nodded. "Sure. I mean, if it's been this way for years, what are the chances it's going to pop on me?"

He jerked her a brief nod, then said, "I'll go get the fridge going."

He only hoped the old appliance would be as adept at running as he was quickly becoming.

After sharing a frozen pizza and a cheap bottle of wine they'd picked up at the commissary, Donna and Jack retreated to their own bedrooms.

Lying wide awake in the moon-washed darkness, Donna stared blankly up at the plaster pimple on her ceiling. Her father's words kept repeating over and over again in her mind.

It was tempting, she thought. The idea of treating this pretend marriage like a real one. After all, she was twenty-eight years old. If she was ever going to have a husband and kids, she'd have to start sometime soon. And Jack seemed like a nice guy. Hadn't he leaped into the fray to rescue her father's reputation? Wasn't he being a good sport about living in this miserable little hut?

And...didn't she get goose pimples just watching him walk across a room?

Sighing, Donna resettled more deeply into her pillow. None of this mattered, she told herself. Because Jack had already made it painfully clear that he wasn't interested in anything more than a temporary marriage. So it was pointless for her to daydream about other, more pleasant possibilities.

Wasn't it?

These thoughts were getting her nowhere. And now she had the extra added bonus of a deep, unsettling ache building slowly inside her.

Her gaze locked on the stupid pimple hanging over her bed. How hard would it have been for the contractors employed by the corps to just *fix* the ceiling?

Scowling and muttering darkly to herself, Donna stood on the mattress, directly under the giant pimple. Tilting her head back, she examined the darn thing as closely as she could. Finally she reached up and gingerly poked at the white, crinkly plaster.

Instantly the ceiling exploded.

What must have been oceans of water and tons of wet plaster dropped on her.

She screamed and ducked.

Jack bolted out of bed as if he'd been shot. Donna! He took the pitifully few steps that separated their bedrooms and threw her door open. Stunned at the disaster in front of him, he raced barefoot across the chunks of wet plaster and absently noted the sound of the rug squishing beneath his feet.

Bracing one knee on the waterlogged bed, he grabbed Donna and yanked her off the mattress. Holding her tightly, he demanded, "Are you all right?"

Slowly she lifted her head, then reached up and pushed her soaking wet hair off her forehead. Plucking a piece of plaster off her lips, she nodded. "I think so."

"What happened?" he asked, even though he could see for himself that the damn ceiling had come down on top of her. He never should have let her take that room. He should have insisted on sleeping in there himself. She could have been killed.

"I popped the pimple," Donna said, half turning in his arms to survey the damage.

"You popped it?"

"I swear. All I did was touch it. And *boom!* Just touched it. That's all," she said, her voice sounding faint, as if coming from a distance.

His heart racing, Jack pulled her closely to him. His arms closed around her and he ran his hands up and down her body, telling himself he was simply checking her for injuries. But she seemed all too healthy.

"Honestly," she was saying. "I don't know what happened. One minute everything was fine and the next minute, the world blew up."

"It's okay," he told her. "I'll call base housing in the morning. See about getting it repaired."

She pulled back in his arms and looked up at him. Bits of plaster clung to her wet hair like an abstract crown, and her face was pale. "Guess our two-bedroom apartment just became a one-bedroom, huh?"

Jack stared at her, admiration rising in his chest. She was amazing. Her ceiling blows up in her face and there's no hysterics. No crying. Damn it, he didn't want to like her. He really didn't. He could deal with wanting her and not having her. But blast everything, if he liked her, too, it would be too much.

His gaze slipped over her quickly. And just as quickly, he wished he hadn't looked. Her nightgown, God help him, was soaked through, outlining and defining every one of her curves. His body reacted immediately and he took a half step back. Standing there wearing nothing more than his military-issue boxers and his dog tags, he suddenly felt every bit as exposed as she must.

Running one hand over the back of his neck, he shifted his gaze to the wreckage that was her room. "We'll deal with this tomorrow. For tonight, you'll sleep with me."

He glanced at her in time to see one dark eyebrow lift into a high arch.

"I'm not suggesting anything more than sleep," he said, determined that she not think he was using this situation to his own benefit. "We're adults. We can share a bed without sharing anything else."

"I suppose so," she said quietly, picking her sodden nightgown off her chest with her fingertips. Stepping past him into the hall, she added, so quietly he almost missed it, "Seems like a waste of a good bed, though."

Eight

It was more than a waste, Jack thought much later. It was damned torture.

Donna hummed tunelessly as she slipped into a deeper sleep. He turned his head on the pillow to glare at her. How in the hell could she sleep when only inches of mattress separated them?

But as that thought shot through his brain, he realized the answer. She wasn't bothered by his nearness because she simply didn't want him the way he wanted her. Hot. Sweaty. Moaning.

He threw one arm across his eyes and tried to wipe that particular image out of his brain. Hell, he'd never get to sleep otherwise. Scooting over a bit more, he clung to the edge of the mattress, trying to keep as much space between them as possible without actually falling off the bed.

If he had known that this temporary marriage was going to be so blasted hard, he never would have offered to go through with it. He snorted a muffled laugh. Who was he trying to kid? He would have married her, anyway. So what kind of a nut did that make him?

A nut destined for long, frustrating nights. Because he could admit, if only to himself, that from the moment he'd laid eyes on Donna Candello trying to sneak into the ball, he'd wanted her as he'd never wanted anything else in his life.

Two days later Jack was still telling himself that he must have heard her wrong. No way would Donna Candello be interested in him. Okay, fine, she had married him. But that was different. That had been desperation talking. And guilt screaming.

He glanced across the room to where Donna sat curled up on one end of the couch, thumbing through a magazine. She licked her forefinger before turning the page and Jack's insides tightened. His gaze locked on her mouth. He found himself hoping she'd do it again. Breath held, he waited while she perused the page, then slowly lifted her right hand to her lips.

Her tongue darted out and smoothed across her fingertip in an unconsciously seductive manner.

Jack swallowed heavily, closed his eyes and tried to ignore a throbbing ache low in his body with which he was becoming all too familiar.

What if she *had* said what he'd thought she'd said—about wasting a perfectly good bed? She couldn't have meant anything about him specifically. He was not the kind of man she would be interested in. They had absolutely nothing in common. So why did he want her so badly? And where did that leave him? Was he supposed to be the one to go back on their agreement? Hell, it had been his idea to make this a platonic marriage. He couldn't just up and announce that he'd changed his mind, could he?

"Change your mind, Jack?" Donna asked.

"Huh?" He blinked, startled at her mind reading abilities. Just to be sure, though, he asked, "About what?"

She waved one hand at the file folder on the coffee table in front of him. "I thought you said you were going to get those reports done tonight."

That had been the plan. Unfortunately, he couldn't keep his mind on any figures other than hers.

"Nah. Do 'em in the morning."

She frowned at him. "Are you all right?"

Dandy, he thought. "Yeah. Fine."

She didn't look convinced. "Something is wrong," she said. "Still getting ribbed about marrying the colonel's daughter?"

"Not too much," he told her, and didn't add that

he was never ribbed by the same man twice. Once some joker faced Jack's steely gray stare, he seemed reluctant to try it again. In general, the hoo-hah was dying down, just as he had predicted it would.

Of course, if he and Donna hadn't gotten married so quickly, the gossip would never have eased off.

And, if they hadn't gotten married, he might be a well-rested man right now. Certainly, he wouldn't be questioning his own sanity.

"You know," she said quietly, "you never did tell me what debt you owed my father that required such a huge payback as marrying me."

Now it was his turn to frown. "Yeah, I know."

Donna studied him for a long minute. This husband of hers was a study in contrasts. Tough, rule-following marine by day. Touchy, skittish husband by night. They'd managed to live together for nearly a week now without killing each other and she was quite sure she was the only one suffering from bouts of near fatal attraction. Little by little, she was coming to know him and yet she knew that there was a big part of himself that he kept hidden… tucked away.

She wanted to reach that part of him and didn't even bother to ask herself why it was so important to her.

"So?" she prompted. "Aren't you going to tell me?"

"Hadn't planned on it," he admitted, standing and

walking to the window that overlooked the street. Planting both hands on the wall at either side of the window, he stared quietly out at the darkness.

"Jack," she said, half turning to look at his broad back and rigid stance.

"You want to know why?" he muttered thickly, his voice rough and harsh as it grated over clearly unpleasant memories. "All right, I'll tell you."

Donna almost stopped him. Almost. She didn't like the way he was holding his shoulders. Stiff, yet hunched, as if expecting a blow. But her instinct was to draw him out. To find out more about the man she had married in such a hurry.

"I got in some trouble when I was a kid," he stated flatly.

"What kind of trouble?"

He snorted a choked laugh that died almost immediately. "*All* kinds. My folks died in a car wreck when I was eight. Went to live with an aunt and uncle."

"How awful," she whispered.

"They weren't real thrilled with becoming instant parents, so I pretty much raised myself after that."

"But you were just a kid," she said, sympathy for the boy he had been welling within her.

"No, I wasn't," he said quietly, stiffly. "My childhood ended in that car accident."

She could see the tension in his body from across the room. What a lonely life he'd led, she thought sadly. Although her parents hadn't been together, she had always known she was loved. Her gaze moved over Jack and a part of her ached to go to him, ease years-old pain. But Donna knew that he wouldn't appreciate sympathy, so she didn't move. Instead, she held her breath and waited for him to continue.

"Anyway," he said, his voice tight, "the trouble I found escalated the older I got. My aunt and uncle couldn't be bothered to deal with me. So, when I was eighteen, a judge gave me a choice. The corps or jail."

Donna blinked. She never would have believed that Jack had, at one time, been faced with jail.

He seemed to sense her surprise, or maybe he had simply been ready for it. Turning, he stood straight, shoulders squared, as if someone had planted him against a wall for a firing squad. Not meeting her gaze, he stared straight ahead as he went on. "Not being a dummy, I chose the corps." A sliver of a self-mocking smile tilted one side of his mouth briefly. "But I almost screwed that up, too."

"How?" she whispered, her gaze locked on her husband's stoic, grim features.

"A bad attitude and a big mouth." That smile that wasn't a smile chased across his lips again. "A deadly combination anywhere. But in the corps, a one-way ticket to disaster."

It was hard to imagine First Sergeant Harris as a big-mouthed private, but she tried.

He rubbed the back of his neck, a sure sign that he wasn't happy. "Anyway, the colonel—your father—was a lieutenant back then."

She nodded.

"One day he'd had his fill of my attitude and took me aside for a private lesson in the chain of command."

Frowning, Donna asked, "What do you mean?"

"I mean," Jack said, looking directly at her for the first time, "he took off his lieutenant's bars and offered me the chance to back up my mouth with my fists."

"He *fought* you?"

A different smile briefly appeared on his face then. A smile of admiration. "No, ma'am," he countered. "He beat the hell out of me." At her horrified expression, he added, "In a fair fight."

"I don't believe it," she muttered, trying to imagine her loving, patient father as a brawler.

"Believe it. He convinced me." Jack moved away from the wall and stalked across the small room. "After that," he said while pacing like a caged lion, "he requested me as his radioman. I got to know him. Respect him." He stopped suddenly, his gaze shooting to hers. "He saved my miserable life. I owe him everything."

"So you married his daughter," she said, vaguely surprised that her voice sounded so hollow.

"Yeah."

Ridiculous to feel this pang of disappointment. After all, she'd known that he had only proposed marriage in an attempt to help her father. Why should hearing him say it now affect her in the slightest?

She knew darn well why. Because she had been hoping that maybe he was hiding a small kernel of interest in her. At least now, she knew. That was a good thing, wasn't it?

"Well," she said, deliberately forcing a brightness she didn't feel into her tone, "I guess the debt is paid in full now, huh?"

"I'll never be able to repay him completely," Jack assured her stiffly.

"Jeez, Jack, why don't you just offer to throw yourself on a grenade?" she snapped as a headache leaped into life.

"What?"

"It would be quicker and a lot less painful than having to pretend to love me. To like being married to me." Shut up, she thought. Close your mouth and leave the room. But her feet wouldn't cooperate. She wished she could say the same for her mouth.

"How much of your life are you willing to lay down on the altar of Colonel Thomas Candello?" she asked tightly.

"What the hell are you so mad about?" he demanded.

"I don't know," she shouted right back, throwing her hands high in the air. "I guess, even knowing why we got married, I just don't like the idea of being the poison pill you were forced to swallow for the good of your country."

"What's that supposed to mean?"

"You know," she snapped, "'Close your eyes and think of England.'"

"Huh?"

"You figure it out," she told him as the headache between her eyes began to throb with an insistent, ugly regularity.

"Donna."

"No." She held up one hand, effectively silencing him. "It's okay. I only gave up my apartment, my job, and my roommate. *You* sacrificed your life for the good of your commanding officer."

He took a step closer, but she backed up.

"I'm sure my father appreciates your loyal service, Marine."

"This is nuts," he told her. "Why are we fighting about this now?"

She laughed, more at herself than anything else. "I guess the honeymoon's over, First Sergeant."

"We've been getting along all right so far, haven't we?" Jack asked, apparently determined to smooth things over. Though she couldn't imagine why.

What possible difference could it make now?

"Sure," she said, shrugging in what she hoped conveyed nonchalance.

"Then why can't we just leave it at that?"

"Because we're people, Jack. People talk. People fight."

"What's the point?"

She drew her head back and stared at him as if he'd slapped her. Emotionally, he had. Heck, he wasn't even willing to *fight* with her. She wasn't worth a good argument. "You're right. This whole situation is only temporary. What *is* the point?"

"That's not what I meant."

"Maybe not, but it's the truth."

"Donna—"

Jack looked hard at her and tried to figure out where this had all gone wrong. He'd thought he was giving her what she wanted. A small enough piece of his past to prove to her that they didn't belong together. The reasons behind his loyalty to her father.

Hell, he'd had no idea she would react this way. If he didn't know better, he'd swear she looked as if she were about to cry or something. Over *him?*

That didn't make sense at all.

"What are you so mad about?" he asked finally.

She shook her head slowly. "I'm not mad," she said, but her tone was unconvincing. "I'm just... tired."

Okay, that he understood. He hadn't had a good night's sleep since they'd started sharing a bed. Hoping to help, he offered, "Look, I'll sleep on the couch tonight. Let you get some rest."

She snorted a laugh. "Perfect. You're even willing to sleep on a couch that's two feet too short for you. Heck, Jack, you shouldn't be a marine. You should be a saint."

Anger began to simmer in the pit of his stomach, boiling with other, just as strong emotions to blend into a dangerous mixture. "Why don't you just tell me what you want from me, Donna?"

She opened her mouth as if to speak, then shook her head, more firmly this time. "No. I think it's best if we just forget this whole night ever happened. How about that?"

Forget it? He couldn't even make sense of it. But for the sake of peace and because he didn't want to get any deeper into the mess he'd somehow created for himself, he agreed. "Deal."

"Good." She inhaled sharply, unconsciously drawing his gaze to the swell of her breasts beneath the dark blue T-shirt she wore. "Now. I'm going to bed. Good night, Jack."

"Good night, Donna," he returned as evenly as possible.

She walked away, headed for the bathroom, and he took a deep, unsteady breath. It was going to be a long night. He wasn't sure how many more nights he was going to be able to survive lying beside her and not touching her.

At that thought, he spoke up suddenly. "Did you talk to housing about fixing the ceiling?"

She stopped in the doorway and turned to look at him.

"Yeah," she said tiredly, "for all the good it did me."

"What'd they say?" he asked, even knowing, from long, painful experience, what the answer to his question would be.

"Let's see…" She tilted her head to one side and tapped her chin with the tip of one finger. "I want to get this right. Oh, yeah." She smiled tightly. "'Mrs. Harris,'" she mimicked in a deep, slow, Southern drawl, "'of course we'll get on out there just as soon as we can. But it could take some time.'" She dragged the word "time" out to be three syllables long.

Naturally, Jack thought. The corps didn't do anything in a hurry. Except go into battle. *Then* everybody snapped to and got their jobs done in record time. But as far as getting repairs made, he'd probably have his next duty assignment before that ceiling got fixed.

Great.

"Anyway," Donna said, her voice deliberately more cheerful than necessary, "the guy told me how fortunate we were that it was just our 'guest' room that had been ruined. So I don't think they're going to be in any big hurry to get to us."

"I suppose not." Absently, Jack wondered if he could figure out how to fix the damn ceiling himself.

"You coming?" Donna asked before heading for the bedroom again.

Not likely, he thought grimly. Out loud, he said only, "In a minute."

"Okay, then, good night." Then she added. "I'm sorry about—"

"Me, too. 'Night." As she left, his chin dropped to his chest. How could she be so relaxed about the very sleeping arrangements that had him walking around like a zombie for lack of rest?

Easy, he told himself. She obviously didn't want him. So, there was the answer to the problem of whether or not to break his own word about sexless marriages. If the bride wasn't interested, the groom really had nowhere to go.

Jack straightened and looked toward the bedroom. He couldn't help wondering just what kind of horrible karmic debt he was paying off.

They each started out on the edges of the mattress. Lying on either side of an invisible but nonetheless impenetrable brick wall.

As always, though, after a few tense minutes, Donna's breathing deepened and the first, soft sound of humming reached him.

Jack turned his head to look at his wife. Black hair fanned across the pillow, her expression unguarded, Donna's lips curved slightly as if she were enjoying a dream. Well, he was glad one of them had something to smile about.

Donna lay on her side, facing him, one hand stretched out across the mattress as if reaching for him in her sleep. He smiled to himself at the idea. Man, she really was something, Jack thought. Strong, gorgeous, intelligent and funny. Not afraid to face him down in an argument, giving as good as she got. Everything he had ever dreamed of finding in a woman.

A wife.

He shifted his gaze to stare at the ceiling in the dark. Wouldn't his aunt and uncle laugh at him if they could see him now? They'd always told him he was worthless. That no woman would ever love him.

Oh, yeah, he thought grimly. They'd get a real kick out of knowing that the only way he could get a woman to marry him was by swearing that he wouldn't touch her.

Memories rose up inside him, swirling around his mind until the images twisted together into a blinding mass of remembered pain. He'd tried to make them love him. After his parents had died, he'd done everything he could to show his new family that he was worthy of their love.

But they'd paid no more attention to him than they might a stray hound that had wandered into their home. So, just as an unwanted dog would, he had turned on them. It had been as if there'd been a devil on his shoulder, urging him, guiding him into trouble.

He closed his eyes against the old wounds. That Jack was gone, forgotten as he should be. Things were different now. He'd made his own life. He'd become a man to respect. To admire.

But still, just as his aunt and uncle had predicted so long ago, no one loved him.

Donna suddenly rolled up against him. Before he could ease to one side, she'd draped one arm across his chest and snuggled her head into the hollow of his shoulder.

Jack inhaled sharply. His body hardened instantly. He muffled a groan that might have awakened her, and tried to slip out from beneath her. But she only moved in closer, her soft humming becoming louder as she cuddled against him.

Insistent desire ebbed and was replaced by an emotion so tender, it caught him unaware. Lust gave way to the instinct to protect. To cherish. Briefly, he wondered what it might be like to spend the rest of his life like this. With Donna curled in beside him. An imagination he hadn't been aware of before, suddenly produced images of the two of them together, surrounded by kids and dogs. Happy. Laughing. Loving.

He closed his eyes, letting those visions fill his mind until his soul felt full, complete.

His right arm encircled her shoulders and he turned his head to breathe in the flowery scent of her hair. His heartbeat slowed and though the ache in his groin didn't ease one iota, the rest of his body relaxed and for the first time in his marriage, he slipped into a deep, dream-filled sleep.

"'What's married life like?'" Donna repeated her ex-roommate's question to stall for time. Her fingers tightened around the phone receiver. Swallowing the lump in her throat, she said brightly, "It's great. Why wouldn't it be?"

"You tell me," Kathy said, apparently unconvinced by Donna's answer.

Idly, Donna picked at the layers of paint covering the kitchen windowsill. There were dozens of tiny bumps, as if the wood had gotten cold and gooseflesh had hardened on the surface. Scraping her fingernail across one of the hard nubs, she was surprised when the eggshell-white paint peeled up.

"Donna," Kathy said, "something's going on

and you're not talking. Unusual, at best. At worst, frightening."

She grimaced and tugged at the loose piece of paint, hoping to flatten it out somewhat. Instead she peeled up a long strip of rubbery substance. Her eyes widened as she stared at the bare wood where paint used to be.

"There's just nothing to tell, Kat," she assured her friend, while trying to tear off the uneven edges of the multilayered paint strip. Another section tore off in her hand. She smothered a groan and tried again.

"You get married to a guy I've never heard of, want me to send you all of your things *and* quit your job for you, and you say there's nothing to talk about?"

"Uh-huh," Donna muttered, hiding a gasp as another, larger section of paint pulled away from the sill.

"What's he like?"

"Gorgeous," came the immediate response that surprised Donna as much as it did her old roommate.

"Well, well…" Kathy practically purred. "The plot thickens."

"What plot?"

"The one in this little mystery."

"Mystery?" Donna countered. "It's more like a romantic farce."

"Okay," Kathy demanded, impatience simmering over the wire. "Give."

"There's nothing to give. I got married. I'm living on basc in a reconstituted Quonset hut, I'm unemployed, and the only married virgin in the free world." Oops. She hadn't meant for that part to slip out.

"What?" Kathy's voice hit an all-time high. "Explain."

"What's to explain?" Donna asked, tearing off yet another strip of paint and adding it to the growing pile in front of her on the table. "My gorgeous husband has no interest in me."

"Bull."

"Thank you," Donna said, touched by the vote of confidence.

"Is he crazy?"

"No, just temporary."

"You're losing me here, Don..."

Donna sighed. She hadn't meant to tell anyone about the bizarre marriage she found herself in, but darn it, she had to talk to *somebody*. While she explained the entire situation, she peeled another strip of paint off the window, this time trying for length.

"That is the dumbest thing I've ever heard," Kathy said when she'd finished.

"I've always been an overachiever," Donna conceded, and grinned when the paint strip went all the way to the top of the window casement before snapping off like an old rubber band.

"What are you going to do?"

"What I've been doing," she said, tossing the strip of paint onto the table.

"Which is?"

"Pretend to be a happy little wife."

"What do you *want* to do?"

There's an easy question. She'd known the answer most of her life. She wanted to have a family. Kids. A nice little house somewhere. Two dogs, maybe a cat. But mostly she wanted a husband who loved her. Who wanted to make love with her.

But right now, all of the above boiled down to a single, overwhelming want. "I want to make love with my husband."

"Ahhh…"

"I mean, I'll never have a better opportunity to lose my virginity crown, will I?"

"True," Kathy agreed. "But if you've waited this long, why not wait until the big moment would be special?"

"It would be," Donna admitted, standing to get a better grip on the next strip of paint.

"Uh-oh," her friend said. "Sounds like love."

"Or a close facsimile." She smiled as the paint tore off in a lovely, straight line.

"I don't buy that," Kathy told her. "You've been

in lust before and not given in to temptation. What makes him different?"

Donna stopped, dropped the paint strip to hang like a flag on a windless day and stared silently out the window for a long moment. What made Jack different?

Only everything, she thought.

Gray eyes. Strong face. Gentle hands. That look in his eyes that said he didn't expect her to care for him.

So many little things that she wasn't even sure she could list them all.

"Don—"

His laugh, she thought. That was special. Arguing with him. My, she did enjoy their arguments. And just being in the same room with him was enough to raise her temperature by at least ten degrees. She smiled to herself, remembering how straight and proud he'd stood in front of the Reverend Thistle. How he'd promised to love, honor and cherish her.

A chill swept up her spine and Donna's smile faded as she slowly came to a stunningly undeniable conclusion. "Ohmigod," she whispered.

"What is it?" Kathy demanded.

Donna sat as her knees weakened and her head began to spin. The answer was so obvious. And so terrifying. How had this happened? she wondered frantically.

"I'm falling in love with him," she said softly.

"You're kidding!" her friend shouted loud enough to be heard from Maryland without benefit of the phone.

"No, I'm not," Donna whined. "I'm in love with the one man I shouldn't be. My husband."

Nine

After making that alarming discovery, Donna kept herself so busy over the next several days that she didn't have time to think about it.

Now as she sat back on her heels in the winter sunshine of a November day in California, she paused briefly to admire the bed of impatiens she'd just planted between the two still straggly bushes beneath the living room window. Then she turned her head to take in the rest of the front yard.

Amazing what a lawnmower and regular watering could do for a place, she told herself. Not to mention the regimentally straight row of petunias aligning the front walk. Idly, she wondered what sorts of flowers the previous owners had planted.

There was no way to be sure, since, true to marine tradition, once a family moved out of base housing, the neighbors came in and pillaged the flora—digging up whatever plants weren't original to the house and replanting them in their own yards.

While her mind was busy elsewhere, she didn't even notice Jack's truck pull up in front of the house. He was halfway up the walk when he asked, "Daydreaming?"

Donna jumped, clutched at her chest as if trying to hold her heart in place, and looked up at him. "You scared me."

He squatted beside her. "I have that effect on a lot of people."

Yeah, but he probably didn't affect many others the way he did her at this particular moment, Donna thought as a familiar, fluttering sensation started up in her stomach.

"Thought you'd be getting ready for your father's party."

She groaned inwardly. There was no way to avoid the small reception Tom Candello had arranged for his daughter and her new husband. When she'd tried to remind her dad that the whole marriage was a temporary situation, he'd insisted that they do everything they could to convince everyone that it was a real marriage in every sense.

Hard to argue with that. Though heaven knew, she'd wanted to try. She just didn't want to have to spend hours at her father's house pretending to the world that she loved her husband—while at the same time, pretending to him that she didn't.

"Looks nice," Jack said suddenly, snapping her attention back to him. She looked at him in time to see his gaze sweep across the yard.

"Thanks."

"Why are you doing it?" He turned his head to look at her, his gaze colliding with hers.

"Doing what, exactly?"

"This." He waved one hand at the greenery and the splashes of color.

"I like flowers?" she asked.

"No, I mean…" He shook his head. "I guess I mean that I never figured you for the Mother Earth type."

Intriguing. "And what type *did* you figure me for?"

"I don't know. Luncheons. Fundraisers. That sort of thing."

Dusting her grubby hands together, Donna folded them in her denim-clad lap, tilted her head to one side and very patiently asked, "What gave you that idea?"

He smiled and Donna's stomach turned completely over. At least, she thought it was her stomach. It might have been her heart. "I don't know, really. But planting flowers, stripping the wood in the house and refinishing it yourself…"

She cleared her throat uneasily and pushed herself to her feet. Well, she'd had to tell him *something* to explain why she'd peeled layer after layer of perfectly good paint off a windowsill.

"Since I remain unemployed," she said, following him with her gaze as he stood beside her, "I prefer to keep busy."

"That reminds me." Jack reached into the pocket of his camouflage uniform, pulled out a small piece of paper, and handed it to her.

Donna glanced at it. *Marie Talbot, 555-8776.* Lifting her gaze to his again, she asked, "What's this for?"

"She's a teacher at the base school." He smiled at her. "When she found out that you're a sign language interpreter, she asked me to give you her number. Said she could really use someone like you."

He'd found her a job? "And how did she hear about me in the first place?"

He rubbed the back of his neck and let his gaze slide from hers to focus on the new bed of impatiens. "I might have mentioned you to her."

A warm, curl of pleasure snaked through her. He'd been talking about her to other people. Thinking about her. He'd found her a *job*. Giving in to an undeniable impulse, Donna threw herself at him, wrapped her arms around his neck and squeezed, hard. Gazing up at him, she grinned. "You, First Sergeant, are one terrific husband."

His arms closed around her slowly, hesitantly. The restrained strength of his hug took her breath away as he pulled her tightly to him. Her hardened nipples tingled and a like sensation began to burn in the very core of her.

His gaze moved over her features lovingly, as if committing everything about her to memory. When he spoke again, his voice sounded strangled and so soft, she had to strain to hear him at all. "Am I?"

Something in his eyes, a glint of vulnerability, a hint of uncertainty, tore at her. She swallowed the knot of emotion in her throat and rose up onto her toes. Giving in to yet another impulse and unsure of his reaction, she very carefully, very deliberately, kissed him. Beneath her lips, she felt his mouth tighten, then slowly relax.

Nervous and so very hungry for the feel of him, Donna pulled in closer to him, giving herself over to the *rightness* of kissing Jack Harris.

When he groaned from deep in his chest and squeezed her so hard she thought her ribs might crack, she knew she'd reached him. Then he took control of their kiss.

He parted her lips with his tongue, taking her soft exhale of breath into his own lungs. He tasted her, stroked her, caressed her warmth until Donna's knees buckled and only the strength of his arms kept her upright.

Bright splashes of color flashed in front of her closed eyes. She felt as though sparklers were going off in her bloodstream. Though technically still a virgin, she hadn't exactly lived in a closet for twenty-eight years. She'd been kissed before. By men she would have classified as experts.

But *nothing* in her life had prepared her for this.

Explosions of desire rocketed through her. That indescribable ache she'd become accustomed to living with blossomed into a throbbing, demanding need. Her lungs strained for air but she was too busy to breathe. Her hands fisted on his shoulders, her fingers clutching at him.

This kiss was every romance novel she'd ever read, every late-night fantasy she'd ever entertained, and every dream she'd ever held in a safe, dark corner of her heart.

At last, when she was about to faint for lack of air and had ceased to care, he pulled his head back, breaking the almost magical connection that had bound them so completely to each other.

For a long moment their labored breathing was the only sounds she heard. The scent of a neighbor's barbecue drifted toward them and a cool wind wrapped itself around them, tugging at their clothing.

"Donna," Jack finally whispered, and his eyes shimmered with...regret.

Her mouth still tingling, her knees liquified permanently, she shook her head. She didn't want to hear it. She didn't want what had been an earth-shattering moment for her splintered by the sounds of "I'm sorry." Speaking up quickly, to stop him, she said, "So help me, if you apologize, I'll have you killed."

A slow, sexy smile curved his lips. The shadows left his gray eyes and they shone with amazing clarity. "You're a colonel's daughter. You could probably do it."

One hand slid from his shoulder to cup his cheek. Her thumb traced the high, defined ridge of his cheekbone as she said, "And don't you forget it, mister."

Jack wandered around the colonel's immaculately tended backyard, sticking to the edges of the crowd. His gaze moved over all of the familiar faces. Dozens of people had turned out to attend a spur of the moment barbecue in celebration of Donna's and his marriage.

The sizzle of steaks on the grill whispered above the drone of conversation. A soft breeze lifted the scent of mesquite into the air.

Jack's fingers tightened around the neck of the cold bottle of beer he held as he took a long drink.

Elsewhere in the country, people were battening down the hatches, already fighting off winter's cold grip. But in California, it was picnic weather.

As he walked past tight knots of people, his friends slapped him on the back and offered congratulations, while their wives sighed and smiled over the romance of it all.

Romance. He wondered what they'd all think if they knew the truth. Jack took another long pull at his beer. But it didn't do any good. He could still taste Donna. His jaw clenched at the memory that had been dogging him all afternoon. She'd fit into the circle of his arms as if made to be there.

And ever since he had released her, he'd felt empty.

When a master sergeant grabbed his arm and dragged him into a conversation, he went along, although he didn't hear a word any one was saying. Instead he looked for Donna. His wife.

Though there were no ranks visible—everyone was wearing civvies—invisible lines were drawn through the crowd anyway. It happened all the time. The noncommissioned officers and the enlisted men on one side—the officers on the other. And never the twain shall meet.

It was in the midst of the officers' wives that Jack finally located Donna. Her chin-length black hair shining in the afternoon sunshine, she wore a dark red T-shirt tucked into faded blue jeans that hugged her legs as he had dreamed of doing.

"Where's the bride, Harris?" someone close by asked.

Without taking his gaze off her, Jack nodded his head in her direction.

The man beside him grunted. "Well, she *is* a colonel's daughter. Guess it's only right that she hang with the officers."

True. Jack understood. He told himself that it made sense for her to talk to the people she knew. But that did nothing to the twinge of regret that pierced him. This was just another symbol of the differences between them. He was one side of the yard. She was the other.

Donna smiled at the captain's wife and tried to listen to Lieutenant Jorgensen's wife at the same time. But unerringly, her gaze kept drifting across the yard to Jack.

She'd tried, when they first arrived, to meet some of the enlisted men's spouses. But it was hard. She was so used to playing the role of the colonel's daughter and hostess at his parties, that she wasn't quite sure how to negotiate new waters.

She spotted him then, surrounded by his friends, and felt her heartbeat stagger slightly. In his marine green T-shirt and well-worn Levi's, he looked hard and strong and completely unignorable. But then she'd given up on ignoring him anyway. She figured it was pointless now, since she could still feel the kiss they'd shared.

"Donna?" someone asked. "You okay?"

"Yeah," she answered, keeping her gaze locked on Jack. "I'm fine."

Or, she would be as soon as she made her stand, she told herself. Ever since arriving at the party, she'd been torn between the old Donna and the new—if temporary—one. Should she be the colonel's daughter or the sergeant's wife?

Now, suddenly, she knew the answer and was disgusted with herself that it had taken her so long to realize it.

Suiting actions to the thought, she muttered, "Excuse me," to the ladies and started for her husband.

Jack had seen the indecision on her face. He'd been able to tell, even from across the yard that she wasn't sure what she was supposed to be doing. How to act. He knew his life would be a hell of a lot simpler if she simply stayed where she belonged. With the officers and their families. But, damn it, sometimes simpler wasn't better.

As she left the group of women and started toward him, a determined smile on her face, he felt a bright flash of pride and...*pleasure*. Maybe it was just for show, he told himself. Maybe it was all part of the plan they'd agreed on, to look like the happily married couple. But maybe, he found himself hoping, it was something more.

"Hi, First Sergeant," she said as she came up alongside him.

"Hi, yourself."

"Congratulations," someone said as Jack's friends melted away into the crowd, leaving the two of them alone.

"I didn't mean to scare everyone off," she said, looking after them for a minute before shifting her gaze to his.

He grinned briefly, unable to contain it. "They're marines," he told her in a whisper. "They don't scare."

She smiled and nodded. "Ah, yes, a strategic retreat, then?"

"Much better." God, she was beautiful. His gaze locked on her mouth and it was all he could do not to kiss her senseless in front of her father and everyone else in the yard.

"Hope you don't mind if I hang out with you for a while," she said, her voice carrying a twinge of doubt.

Mind? Hell, at the moment, he wanted to shout. For whatever reason, she'd chosen to come to him rather than stay with her father's friends.

"I think I can stand it," he said in the biggest understatement he'd ever made.

One dark eyebrow arched high on her forehead.

She pointed at his beer. "And do you think you might find another one of those, too?"

"Lady," he said, feeling suddenly, inexplicably happy, "I can find anything. I used to be Recon."

"Then get busy, Marine," she said quietly, and moved in close to him.

"Yes, ma'am." He draped his left arm around her shoulders and pulled her tightly to his side. He didn't even ask himself if it was for the benefit of everyone there—or if it was because he couldn't stand not touching her for another minute.

The reasons no longer mattered to him. All that counted now was holding her.

Tom Candello looked past the crowd to where his daughter and her husband stood staring into each other's eyes. A swell of pleasure rushed through him. Maybe it would all work out, he thought. Maybe the two of them would realize how good they could be together.

He'd seen his daughter hurt and humiliated by the wrong man. Now he'd like to see her find love with a man he knew would be good to her.

"What are you thinking?" A woman walked up beside him, dragging his attention away from Donna and Jack.

"Hmm?" He swiveled his head and caught himself smiling. Major Sally Taylor. Dedicated career officer, brilliant mind—and God help him, great legs. He scratched that thought immediately. A man couldn't be too careful these days.

"Oh," he said at last, after noticing the patient expression on her face, "I was just thinking what a nice-looking couple they make."

She followed his gaze and nodded. "Yes, they do. I hope everything works out well for them."

"You don't sound hopeful," he commented, reacting to the cynical note in her voice.

Sally chuckled and shook her head. "That's because I'm not, Colonel."

"We're off duty," he reminded her, "Call me Tom."

"All right, Tom. I'm Sally."

"Now that we have that settled," he said, glad to at least be on a first name-basis at last, "why so cynical?"

She lifted her glass of iced tea and took a sip before saying, "Because I'm all grown up now, Tom. And fairy-tale endings are for kids."

He blinked, not sure what to say to that. She smiled and moved off to talk to Lieutenant Jorgensen.

The sky was blanketed with stars when Jack and Donna started for home. With soft jazz pouring from the truck's CD player, they drove through the base slowly, as if neither of them was in any particular hurry to get home.

"Who was that woman talking to my father most of the night?" she asked finally, more to end the silence than anything else.

"Major Taylor," Jack said shortly. "She's new here. Hasn't been on Pendleton for more than a month or so."

"Dad sure seems interested in her."

"Does that bother you?" he asked, glancing at her briefly.

"I don't know," she admitted, not at all sure if she was comfortable with the idea of her father actually dating someone. It didn't matter if he was fairly young and handsome. Or even that he'd been alone for most of his life. It was just an odd sensation, thinking of your parents as having a private life. A love life. "I guess it feels a little strange," she said, "but I hope everything works out for him." Better, she added silently, than things had been working out for *her*.

Another minute or two of silence spun out before Jack said softly. "It was a nice party."

"Yes, it was."

"Everyone seemed to have a good time."

"Seemed to," she agreed.

"Did you?" he asked, glancing at her again.

Donna took a long moment before answering. She studied his profile in the dim, reflected glow of the dash lights. Strong, rugged, and completely, heart-stoppingly attractive.

When had this marriage stopped being a pretense to her? When had she begun to care for this man? And did it really matter?

"Yes," she said finally. "I did."

He shifted another look at her and gave her a small smile. "Me, too."

In another moment he was pulling up in front of their house and cutting the engine. When he shut off the headlights, dark fell down around them like a thick, new blanket.

Giving in to an impulse, Donna quickly unhooked her seat belt and slid across the bench seat toward him.

Jack inhaled sharply, half turning his head toward her. "Donna—"

"Jack." She lifted one hand to cover his mouth with her fingertips. "Don't say anything, okay?"

He caught her hand with his and said quietly, "I just don't think—"

"Good," she interrupted again. "Maybe it's time we both stopped thinking and started feeling."

Then she leaned in, tilted her head and kissed him.

After an instant's hesitation, he kissed her right back. As if picking up where they'd left off, passion burst into life, igniting the inside of the small pickup like a match set to gasoline.

Jack groaned and grabbed her to him, shifting in the seat to drag her across his lap. She wiggled her bottom, looking for a comfortable position, and unknowingly, torturing him further. His groin hard and ready, as it had been during each of the long, frustrating nights of their marriage, he groaned from the back of his throat as she settled in his lap.

She reached up, cupped his face with her hands and deepened their kiss. He parted her lips with his tongue and plundered her with all of the thoroughness of a marine landing in enemy territory.

Donna moaned gently and pressed her breasts against his chest. Even through the fabric of their shirts and the confinement of her bra, he felt the rigid tips of her nipples and had to touch them. Caress them. Taste them.

He pulled her T-shirt free of the waistband of her jeans and slid his hands up over the smooth, warm skin of her back. In seconds he had her bra clasp undone. His left hand skimmed around to cup one breast and his thumb rubbed her nipple until she arched into him, instinctively seeking more.

Reluctantly, he broke the kiss and bent his head to take that small, hard bud into his mouth. He felt her fingers cup the back of his head, holding him to her. And when he suckled her, she gasped and let her head fall back on her neck.

"Oh, Jack..." she whispered brokenly.

His lips and teeth teased her sensitive flesh until

he was crazy with want and need. His body felt as though it was about to explode, and every one of her quick intakes of breath only fanned flames that were threatening to engulf him completely.

Her hands moved to his shoulders, her fingers clutching at him, digging into his skin through the fabric of his T-shirt. Her hips bucked on his lap, she could feel that he was as hard as steel.

"Donna," he whispered as he lifted his head for another kiss, "I have to touch you. Feel you. All of you."

"Yes, Jack," she answered, her words tumbling from her in a rush. "I need that, too. Now. Please, now."

Already, his fingers were working at the button and zipper of her jeans. She twisted in his arms, trying to help but succeeding only in torturing him further.

At last the brass button popped free and the zipper slid down noiselessly, allowing him access to her body. To the secrets he'd been wanting to delve ever since that first night when he'd rescued her and then lain awake all night staring at her.

Sliding his fingers beneath the fragile elastic of her bikini underwear, he pushed onward, downward, until he felt the soft brush of curls covering her most intimate flesh.

She gasped again, louder this time, and lifted her hips slightly into his touch.

His heartbeat slowed, then seemed to stop altogether when he touched her damp heat for the first time. She sucked in a gulp of air and wiggled her hips, inviting him, silently asking him to explore her body.

His fingertips skimmed across the small, sensitive nub of flesh at the peak of her center and she shuddered in his arms. His left arm tightened around her, holding her securely while his right hand sent her spiraling out of control.

Fighting against the confines of the denim jeans, he dipped one finger into her liquid heat and sighed in satisfaction when she groaned.

It wasn't enough, he thought desperately. Not nearly enough. He wanted to have her naked beneath him. Open to his entry. He wanted to push his body into hers and feel her quivering response. He wanted to watch her reach that ultimate feeling of ecstasy just before emptying himself within her.

"Jack," she whispered, and shifted her hips again. "This feels…"

"Too confining?" he asked quietly, and leaned forward to press a kiss to the pulse point in her throat.

"Wonderful," she finished, and arched into his hand again.

"Let's go inside, Donna," he said, wanting to move now, while he could still walk.

"It's too far away," she argued.

"We need more room, Donna," he told her, reluctantly pulling his hand free of her jeans.

She groaned her disappointment, but lifted her head to look at him. "Room?" she repeated.

"To romp," he told her, already reaching for the door handle.

Ten

The short walk to the front door had never seemed so long before. They practically raced each other to the house.

Once inside, with the door closed and locked, they fell together, lips seeking, hands grasping. In a hushed symphony of whispered urgency, they stumbled across the living room to the bedroom where they had lain together yet apart since their marriage.

Tumbling down onto the mattress, Jack propped himself up on one elbow, staring down into her face as though he needed reassurance from her that she really did want him. One hand slid under the front of her T-shirt, then beneath her still-loosened bra to cup one of her breasts. As his fingers smoothed across her hardened nipple, she gasped, arching her back like a kitten demanding to be stroked.

"Donna," he asked quietly, "are you sure you want this?"

"Look at me," she answered, a soft, strained smile on her face. "My heart's racing, my legs couldn't support me if I tried to walk, and every time you touch me, I forget to breathe."

His throat tightened unexpectedly. Emotion rose up in him. Emotions that terrified him, yet filled him with pleasure.

His thumb caressed her nipple and she squeezed her eyes shut briefly.

"Yeah, Jack. I'm sure."

"Thank God," he murmured, and bent his head to claim a kiss. His lips brushed across hers gently. His teeth nipped at her lower lip and his tongue defined the shape of her mouth before slipping into her warmth and stoking the fires within into an inferno.

He tugged the hem of her shirt up and pushed the fine white lace bra aside. Breaking the kiss, Jack inhaled sharply and filled his gaze with the sight of the smooth, creamy flesh he'd dreamed of caressing. As he dragged the palm of his hand lightly across her chest, he felt her heartbeat thundering behind her rib cage.

He swallowed heavily and his own heartbeat

jumped into a matching rhythm. Dipping his head, he claimed first one nipple, then the other, flicking at the dark, rosy buds with the tip of his tongue until Donna twisted and writhed beneath him.

Her hands bunched in the fabric of his shirt and when she tried to pull it up so that she could caress his skin, he sat up, pulling her with him. "Too many clothes here," he whispered, and gently lifted her shirt up and over her head.

"Way too many," she agreed, reaching for the hem of his shirt, tugging it off, and tossing it to the floor.

He eased her bra straps down off her shoulders and along her arms until it, too, landed in a heap on the floor.

In seconds she was in his arms again, and the incredible sensation of his skin brushing against hers pushed him over the fine line he'd been walking.

Without words, they tore the rest of their clothing off, and turned to each other in a haze of desire so intense neither of them could have spoken if they'd tried. But there was no need for words. Not now. Now, there was only the need to touch. Taste. Discover.

Impatiently yanking the multicolored quilt off, Jack laid Donna down on the cool, flower-sprigged cotton sheets and leaned over her. He kissed her until his lungs were clamoring for air, and still he didn't want to stop. But there was so much more he wanted to do to her. With her. Tearing his mouth free of hers, he slid his lips along the line of her jaw to the column of her neck. His tongue traced a warm, damp course down the elegant column and he paused at the base of her throat to test the thrumming pulse point hidden there.

She moved against him, arching, twisting, holding his head to her as if afraid he would stop. As his mouth tormented her, his hands slid over her body, discovering and exploring every dip, every curve. His callused fingertips stroked her satiny skin with the delicate touch of a sculptor working with glass. Yet the hunger, the need, continued to build until he felt as though he could never feel enough of her...taste enough of her.

At last, his right hand skimmed over the curve of her hip and along her thigh. Caressing the inner flesh of her leg, his fingers dusted across her center in a promise of things to come.

She jerked in his arms and tipped her head back into the mattress. Her legs parted for him and he accepted her invitation. As his hand cupped her warmth, she shivered, her hips lifting from the bed, moving into his hand, instinctively searching for the completion they both needed so badly.

Raising his head, he stared down into her passion-glazed eyes, wanting to remember every second of this time with her. Every moment. He wasn't fool enough to think that this changed anything. That she would be with him forever. But that knowledge only made tonight more special. More wondrous. And in the years to come, he knew he would turn to this memory often.

Threads of moonlight pierced the room, sliding through the gaps in the curtains. Her lips parted as puffs of strangled breath escaped her lungs. A soft, cold breeze slipped beneath the partly opened window, scattering gooseflesh over her body.

"Cold?" he whispered.

She shook her head. "Not enough to stop to close the window." Cupping his face with one hand, she smoothed her fingertips across his cheekbone, sending spears of light and heat deep into the darkest corners of his soul. Corners he had been sure were closed off forever.

Any danger warnings coming from the back of his mind, though, were ignored. He couldn't have walked away from this woman if his life had depended on it.

Breathlessly, he slipped one finger into her passage, eager now to become a part of her. To touch her as deeply as she had him.

So tight, so warm. His heartbeat thundered in his ears as he stroked her inner flesh. She planted both feet firmly on the mattress and lifted her hips again and again, rocking with an ancient rhythm, silently pleading with him, demanding everything from him.

Groaning, he surrendered to the moment. Shifting position until he knelt between her updrawn legs, he withdrew his hand from her body despite her moan of disappointment.

Donna fought for a breath she couldn't catch. Every nerve in her body was sizzling with an inner fire so hot and wild, she was afraid it would never be quenched.

This was so much more than she'd ever imagined. Every touch of Jack's hands sent her skittering closer to the edge of a precipice she'd never even been near before.

She looked up at him as he moved to kneel in front of her. His gray eyes glittered in the moonlight. His broad muscular chest tapered to a narrow waist and hips. But it was the hard, solid length of him that made her eyes widen in both desire and apprehension. Ridiculous thing to have to admit at the ripe old age of twenty-eight, but she was a little scared. What if they didn't fit together? What if he was too—she looked again—big? What if she did something wrong and not only ruined her initiation into lovemaking but humiliated herself into the bargain?

What if she was disappointed?

No. What if *he* was disappointed?

Lord. Was it too late to stop? To change her

mind? To go to her grave a vestal virgin, untouched by any man?

His fingertips stroked her damp inner flesh again and the throbbing ache centered there tripled. She bit down hard on her bottom lip. Definitely too late to stop. She couldn't back out now. She had to know it all. And most importantly, she wanted Jack Harris to be the man who showed her all of the secrets she'd waited so long to learn. She wanted him to feel for her what she felt for him. She wanted this marriage to be a real one, damn it.

"Jack," she said brokenly, "I want—" Half sitting, she reached for him. He caught her hands, threading his fingers through hers. Still keeping their hands locked together, palm to palm, he loomed over her, bracing their entwined hands on the mattress at either side of her head.

He bent to kiss her briefly and then she felt the soft, hard tip of him as his body searched for the entry to hers. Instinctively she lifted her hips, moving into him, drawing him closer, deeper.

And then he was inside her, slowly pushing himself into her warmth. Her eyes widened at the unfamiliar yet completely wonderful sensation. She felt her body stretch to accommodate his presence and her breath caught in her throat at the utter beauty of the moment. Sweet tears stung the backs of her eyes, but she blinked them away. She didn't want him to see tears and think she was uncomfortable, and she doubted he would believe her if she told him that she was crying because he was simply too beautiful, too wonderful to be real.

The thick, rigid length of him pierced her body with a gentle insistence. She stared up into his eyes and saw him frown slightly, his brow furrowed in concentration.

"So tight," he whispered, bending his head for another brief kiss. "So small and tight."

She choked back a groan of misery. He *was* disappointed. "Is that bad?" she asked.

He smiled ruefully. "Not hardly," he said, and pushed himself all the way inside her.

Donna gasped, then clutched at his hands, still entwined with hers. Her fingernails dug into his flesh.

Jack went completely still, his body buried so deep within her, she was sure she could feel him touching her heart.

"You're a virgin," he said flatly.

"Not now," she told him with a pleased smile.

"Donna." His head dropped to his chest. "You should have told me."

"Why? Would it have changed things?"

"I don't know. Maybe."

She shook her head. "Then I'm glad I didn't tell you. Because I wouldn't change a thing."

He lifted his head again to stare down at her.

Their gazes locked and she tried to tell him with her eyes what she couldn't quite bring herself to say yet. That she loved him. That she wanted him more than her next breath. That she would die if he pulled away from her now.

She twisted her hips slightly as her discomfort eased and he sucked in a gulp of air at her movement. Smiling to herself, she repeated the maneuver and Jack's eyes closed.

"Jack," she whispered. "Don't stop. Please don't stop."

His eyes opened again and he looked down at her. "I won't stop, Donna. I won't ever stop."

Then he moved, rocking his hips against her, and the friction of that movement sent new tremors of expectation racing along her spine. She moaned gently, arching her head back into the mattress. Trying to mimic his actions, her hips moved, too, with him, into him, driving them both onward, pushing them toward the edge of completion that waited, shimmering, just out of reach.

Her heartbeat staggered. Her chest heaved with the effort to breathe. And none of it mattered. Every thought in her head was centered on the exquisite sensations rocketing through her body.

Jack set the rhythm of their dance and Donna matched him move for move. When at last he freed one of his hands and skimmed it down between their bodies, she was desperate with need. So completely caught in a web of passion and desire that she felt as though she would never be able to draw an easy breath again.

Then he touched her. His fingertips stroked one small, incredibly sensitive piece of flesh and stars exploded in the room. Her body jerked. Her legs locked around his hips, holding him to her. She shouted his name as tremors coursed through her limbs, making her feel both weak and energized at the same time.

A heartbeat later Jack's body stiffened, he threw his head back and, groaning her name, joined her in the sweet rush of fulfillment.

He collapsed on top of her and Donna smoothed her hands up and down his back, relishing the strong, warm feel of his flesh. His heavy weight felt comforting, right somehow. When he tried to roll off of her, she held him still. "No," she said softly. "Stay with me awhile longer."

"I'm too heavy," he argued, lifting his head to look down at her.

"No, you're not." She smiled and boldly slid her hands farther down his back to the curve of his rear. She explored his body with the same tender thoroughness that he had hers and watched his gray eyes shimmer with a renewed passion.

"Donna," he warned her, "it's too soon. You'll be sore enough as it is."

She shook her head against the sheets. "I want to

feel all of it again," she told him, her hands cupping his bottom and kneading his flesh. "And if I'm already sore, why not?"

"You're crazy, you know that?" he asked, dipping his head to plant a kiss at the corner of her mouth.

She turned her face into his, kissing him deeply, fully. Her tongue parted his lips and swept into his mouth, and his teasing manner instantly fell away, dissolving into a fresh storm of rising passion.

Deep within her, Donna felt his body tighten in response to her kiss and she felt the first stirrings of a delicious sense of power. Whatever he may claim to the contrary, Donna knew in that moment that he was far from feeling nothing toward her.

Unlike the first time, there were no soft murmurs, no lazy strokes and caresses. Now there was only a hunger to be fed. A desire to be quenched.

His mouth on hers became ferocious. Nipping with his teeth and grinding his lips against hers, Jack laid claim to her, body and soul. Donna groaned into his mouth and gave herself over to the tumultuous feelings swamping her. Clutching at his back, her fingernails dragged along his spine, as if branding his flesh the way she hoped she was branding his heart.

Drawing her legs up, she locked them tight around his hips, pulling him deeper, harder, inside her. When he began moving within her, she shuddered violently at his strength and gentleness.

His hips bucked against hers. She moved into him, knowing now what pleasure awaited her and desperately anxious to experience it again.

Small spirals of delight began to build at her core and she tightened her muscles, straining to reach that starburst of sensation.

His harsh breathing puffed against her ear. She felt the muscles of his back bunch and cord beneath her hands. His powerful thrusts inched her backward on the mattress and she held on to him as though he were the only stable point left in her universe.

And then, almost without warning, that world exploded again. In a bright swirl of color and light, she found not the same completion she had expected, but a deeper, more vibrant, more all-encompassing swell of delight. She rode the wave of pleasure as far as it would take her, and then gathered Jack to her tightly when he cried out, emptying himself into her depths.

Hours later she woke up, cradled in his arms.

Jack held her close when she would have moved, unwilling to give up the feel of her tucked safely beside him.

"Did I fall asleep?" she whispered, her warm breath brushing across his chest with a feather-light touch.

He chuckled. "No, ma'am," he said, his hands

stroking up and down the length of her back. "You fell unconscious."

Despite his tight hold on her, she managed to lift her head to look at him. Tossing her dark hair back out of her eyes, she said, "You shouldn't have let me sleep, Jack. I don't want to miss a minute of this night."

"Honey," he told her, smoothing back that stubborn lock of hair again, "you're new at this, remember? You've had enough for one night."

"No." She shook her head, tumbling her dark hair back into her eyes only to be swept aside again. She bent and kissed one of his flat, brown nipples, running her tongue across the pebbly surface.

He groaned as the sensation of her tongue on him swept down throughout his body. Amazing, he thought, but he was ready and raring to go. Again. It seemed that he couldn't get enough of this incredible woman. And maybe, at least for this one night, he shouldn't think beyond that thought.

There would be time enough for thinking in the morning. And the morning after that. Something inside him coiled tight and dark as he realized that very soon she would probably regret every moment they had shared in this tiny room. Shouldn't he take the opportunity to build enough memories to see him through the lonely years he would face without her?

"Donna…"

She smiled and lifted her head again. "I've waited a long time for this, Jack. I don't want to wait another minute."

"Baby," he said reluctantly, "if we go again this soon, you won't be able to walk tomorrow."

"Then we'll spend the day in bed." Her eyebrows wiggled and her smile broadened just a bit.

"Man, whatever happened to shy virgins?" he asked, though he was infinitely grateful that she obviously wanted him as badly as he did her.

"It's a myth," she told him, bending to taste that flat nipple of his again. The tip of her tongue traced across that piece of sensitive flesh and Jack's arm around her tightened further. Lifting her head again, she looked at him out of one eye. "Virgins aren't shy. They just don't know what they're missing. Once we find out—there's no stopping us."

"I'm convinced," he muttered thickly as her right hand began to stroke his belly and parts farther south.

"You know, Jack," she whispered between hasty kisses following the narrow trail of curls down the length of his chest, "I really think I'm getting the hang of this. There's really not a lot to learn, is there?"

He caught her head in his hands and brought her face to his. Sealing her lips closed with a mind-boggling kiss, he finally let her go long enough to assure her. "Baby, this class is just getting started. You're a *long* way from graduating."

Then, before she could say a word, Jack flipped her onto her back.

"Hey! What are you doing?"

"You'll find out," he said, his voice low and husky, filled with promises of long nights and careful loving.

"Jack..."

She reached for him but he pushed her hands aside then dipped his head to claim first one hard, rigid nipple then the other. Slowly, lavishly, he worshiped them, each in turn. His tongue swirled around the dark, pebbly buds and he nibbled at her with the edges of his teeth.

He felt her passion blossom beneath his touch. Pleasure tore through him as he realized that for the first time in his life, giving satisfaction was more important to him than finding it himself.

His hands swept up and down the length of her, his fingertips sliding into her warmth and then out again, leaving her breathless and tortured. She tossed her head from side to side on the pillow and small, inarticulate sounds erupted from her throat.

He smiled and slowly trailed kisses down her rib cage, across her abdomen and past the triangle of dark curls that hid her treasures from him.

She flinched and tried to move away. "Jack, what are you doing?"

He held her still, his big hands gentle but firm on her hips as he moved to kneel between her legs. Glancing into her eyes, he smiled and said, "I'm keeping you after school for an extra lesson."

"Jack—" She shook her head, one hand reaching toward him. "I don't think—"

"Good." He cut her off neatly. "Don't think. Feel."

Lifting her bottom from the mattress, he held her, suspended as he nudged first one of her legs, then the other, over his shoulders.

Her hands fisted in the sheets and her eyes held a glimmer of wary apprehension. Then his mouth covered her and she whimpered helplessly.

Jack sipped at her as though her body was a cup, containing the finest, most intoxicating brew. With his tongue, he stroked her most sensitive spot until she was trembling in his arms. Glancing at her again, he saw her eyes close as she trustingly gave herself to him, opening herself to whatever he chose to do to her—with her.

Her surrender fed his own passion and he deepened his touch, sliding one finger into her depths as he continued to lavish attention on her inner flesh.

Donna gasped, opened her eyes and looked at the man she loved as he caressed her more intimately than she had thought possible. She should be embarrassed, she knew. At the very least, she should close her eyes so that she wouldn't have to *see* what he was doing to her.

But she couldn't. Her gaze locked on him as her heartbeat accelerated until she thought it would burst from her chest. Intense spears of delight shot through her body, ricocheting off of each other until she was nothing more than a coil of anticipation, being wound tighter and tighter with every passing moment.

He stroked her with his tongue again and suckled gently at a spot that seemed to be directly linked to every nerve in her body. Tremors coursed through her. She heard herself whimper again and was powerless to stop it. As an internal tension built she was certain would kill her with its strength, she reached forward and cupped the back of his head, holding him to her.

And when the first incredible shudder shot through her, she held him tightly to her. She shouted, "Jack!" as her body exploded in his arms and kept him firmly locked to her until the last, lingering ripples of satisfaction faded away.

Finally spent, her hands fell to her sides and she lay limply in his strong hands. When she gathered the strength to open her eyes, she looked up and met his desire-filled gaze.

She didn't know what to say. What *could* she say to a man who had just done what he had?

Thankfully, Jack solved that problem for her. He gently set her back onto the bed, smiled and whispered, "Class dismissed."

Eleven

After a couple of hours of sleep, they awoke to the slivers of dawn poking through the gaps in the curtains.

Donna moaned quietly and stretched against him.

Jack's teeth ground together as he tried to halt his body's instantaneous reaction. But that, as he realized a moment later, was a losing battle. It seemed all she had to do was draw a breath and he was eager to become a part of her again. To feel her warmth surround him, pulling him inside her, where he wasn't alone. Where incredibly, after all of these lonely years, he had found peace.

But it was a temporary contentment and he knew

it. As if to remind himself of that fact, he swung his legs off the bed and stood.

"Where you going?" she murmured, her voice still husky, whether from sleep or renewed passion he didn't know—and couldn't afford to find out.

"Take a shower," he said abruptly. "Gotta get to work."

She pushed herself into a sitting position and the sheet dropped away, puddling in her lap. Instantly his gaze dropped to the swell of her breasts and his palms itched to cup them, caress them.

He inhaled sharply and told himself to get a grip.

Donna raked one hand through her tousled hair, shoving it back from her face with lazy grace. Slanting him a smile, she yawned, then said, "I guess I'd better get moving, too. Talk to Marie Talbot about that job."

He nodded but couldn't help wondering if she would be telling Ms. Talbot that she would only be on base temporarily. Or would she keep it a secret, continuing the charade of their marriage?

A marriage that, for last night anyway, had felt suddenly, and completely, real. Memories filled him, rushing through his mind like a strong gust of sea air. Images of her, open and trusting, reaching for him, crying his name, rose up in his brain and he wondered how he would ever live without her.

She absently rubbed her stomach as it grumbled noisily.

"Guess I worked up an appetite," she said, and gingerly moved to the edge of the bed.

"Sore?" he asked, even knowing the answer.

She shot him a quick, mischievous look. "It was worth it."

Like a bolt of lightning, sudden realization struck him with the force of a blow that threatened to knock him to his knees. She'd been a virgin. Jack's eyes widened as the implications of that fact raced home.

How stupid could one man be? he wondered frantically. Desire was no excuse. Passion no defense. He could only hope that she had been smarter than he.

Warily he asked, "Donna?"

"Uh-huh?" She eased up off the bed and stood facing him, naked and completely unself-conscious.

"I'm ashamed to admit it, but something only just now occurred to me."

"What's that?" she asked, taking a step toward him as if to comfort him.

"Last night..." he said, holding up one hand to ward her off long enough to let him keep his thoughts straight. "Please tell me you were safe."

She laughed and he felt a momentary respite from

the worry that had suddenly dropped over him like an early morning fog.

"Of course, I'm safe," she told him. "That's one good thing about a virgin, Jack. No worry about diseases." She paled then and looked at him. "You're not—"

"No," he assured her quickly. "I'm healthy. I'm not talking about diseases here, Donna. I'm trying to ask you if you're on the Pill."

She laughed again.

Incredible.

"Now why would a *virgin* be on the Pill?" she said, smiling and shaking her head at the notion.

The sinking sensation in the pit of his stomach was apparently contagious. He watched her face pale again and when she plopped down onto the bed behind her, he wasn't even surprised at her stunned expression. "Ohmigod," she whispered.

"You can say that again," he muttered as his temporary marriage suddenly began to look a lot more permanent.

All day Donna tried to dismiss the worries from her mind. After all, she told herself, it wouldn't do her a damn bit of good to get all wound up about it. She either was or wasn't pregnant. It was too late now to do anything about the situation one way or the other.

Instead she concentrated on her new job. Marie

Talbot, an older woman with gray hair and sparkling green eyes had hired her on the spot and immediately put her to work.

There was only one child in the base school who was hearing impaired. Dylan, a nine-year-old boy, had taken signing courses before, but his skills had weakened since he'd had no one to continue his lessons. The first time Donna signed to him, his eyes lit up with excitement.

And as the day went on, Donna was pleased to note that some of his classmates, intrigued with her flashing hands and Dylan's giggles, wandered over, expressing interest in learning.

Within an hour or so, Dylan was transformed from a shy, solitary child to an excited little boy, eager to make friends and teach them how to talk to him.

Her day flew past and Donna was thankful. It wasn't until she was driving home from work that she at last had time to think about the possible repercussions of her one wild night of lovemaking.

Hands tight on the steering wheel, she let her mind race from one blossoming thought to the next. No matter what happened, she resolved firmly, she wouldn't regret a moment of what she and Jack had shared. Already, those hours with him in the dark had taken on a misty, dreamlike quality, too perfect to be real.

She should have known it was too good to last.

But why couldn't it? she asked herself, stopping at a red light. As a trickle of cars streamed through the intersection, she stared blankly ahead.

Okay, her judgment was lousy. She could accept that. But she hadn't actually *chosen* Jack. Fate had. Surely that counted for something. On the other hand, knowing her judgment was so bad, was loving Jack a good thing? Or a bad thing?

The fact that her father approved of Jack was reassuring. Dad had *never* liked Kyle. Still, she had to admit that Jack had never shown any signs at all of wanting to *stay* married.

Her head hurt. A dull, throbbing headache pulsed behind her eyes and she leaned forward, resting her head on the cool, black steering wheel of the truck Jack had insisted she drive. Why was her life always so complicated? Why couldn't she do anything like a normal person? Fall in love, then get married, then have a baby?

Oh, no. Donna Candello Harris had to get married, make a baby, then fall in love.

One hand dropped to her flat abdomen on that thought. Was there a baby already growing inside her? She sucked in a gulp of air and told herself that she only had another week or so to find out. She'd always been as regular as clockwork. If she missed her next cycle, then she'd know.

Something warm and lovely settled in the pit of

her stomach. Jack's baby. *Their* baby. With her dark hair and his gray eyes. She smiled to herself and squeezed her eyes shut, the better to build an image of her maybe-baby.

And that image was suddenly so strong, she could almost feel her child lying safe in the crook of her arm. She could *see* the proud gleam in Jack's eyes and taste his kiss as he admired his daughter.

Oh, yes, she thought. It would be a girl. A girl who would wrap her daddy around her little finger as easily as she would wrap herself around his heart.

Donna caught herself as her fantasy blossomed to include three more children, a nice house and a flower-filled yard. This was ridiculous. She didn't even know if the man loved her or not. She thought he did, but God knew, she'd been wrong before.

A horn blasted into the silence, startling her.

Donna jerked upright, shot a glance into her rearview mirror at the irate man waving her on, then looked at the now green light. Obediently, she stepped on the gas.

"So help me," Tom Haley said stiffly, "you bark one more order at me and I'll borrow a tank and turn you into a spot on the road."

Jack glared at his longtime friend as the other man stomped out of their shared office. He couldn't blame Tom. Hell, if he had been in Tom's shoes, Jack would have punched himself senseless.

His frustration had been riding him all day and Tom had just been the most convenient person to dump on.

Jack set both hands on either side of his skull and squeezed, as if he could rid himself of his thoughts and the pounding headache accompanying them. But it didn't help. Visions of Donna still rose up in his brain, blinding him to work, friendship, *everything* else.

What if she was pregnant? What then?

The thought of Donna and him making a child together filled him with warring emotions. Pleasure, first and foremost, followed quickly by desperation and fear.

A helluva thing for a career marine to admit to.

But there it was. Jack rubbed one hand over his tired eyes and sank back into his chair. Staring up at the ceiling, he acknowledged that the coiled tension in his belly could only be fear.

Fear that when she eventually left him—and he didn't have a doubt that she would—he wouldn't be able to go on without her.

For most of his life, the corps had been everything to him. Father, mother, lover, wife. His sense of duty had been polished and honed like the sharpest of steel knives. Honor was as much a part of him as the color of his hair and eyes.

But how could he act in an honorable fashion—sticking to their temporary marriage vows—when everything inside him screamed to never let her go?

"Jack?"

He straightened and jumped to his feet at the sound of that familiar voice. "Colonel, Sir," he said, keeping his gaze from meeting that of his father-in-law's.

"How's everything?"

"Fine, Sir," Jack replied, his features frozen into the stony mask of a full attention stance.

"At ease, First Sergeant," the colonel told him.

Jack followed orders. He always followed orders. Finally, unable to avoid it any longer, he looked at the man in the doorway. For years he'd respected and admired Colonel Candello. He'd looked forward to the times when they worked together. When they could talk, man to man.

Now all he could think was that he wished the colonel would go away. Leave him to his misery.

"Just wanted to stop and make sure you and Donna would be coming to Thanksgiving dinner next week."

Thanksgiving? Had it only been a few weeks since he'd first laid eyes on Donna? Impossible. It felt as though he'd known her forever.

"Jack?" the colonel prompted.

He shook himself from his thoughts and focused

on the here and now. With no graceful way out of the invitation, he finally snapped, "Yes, Sir. Thank you, Sir."

Tom Candello's eyes narrowed slightly as he looked at him, and Jack found himself grateful the other man couldn't read minds.

"If I'm out of line here," the colonel said at last, "feel free to say so. This isn't between a commanding officer and his first sergeant. This is between a father-in-law and his daughter's husband."

Jack braced himself.

"Is everything all right between you two?"

"Sir?"

"Would it help if I invited myself to dinner? The three of us could spend some time together." He paused meaningfully. "Talk."

Jack shook his head. "I don't think so, Sir. Thanks, anyway."

"Jack," the colonel went on, "I think if you'll just—"

He cut him off, trusting the man had meant what he said about this not being about ranks. "Beg pardon, Sir, but this is between Donna and me. It'd be best if you back off."

Tom Candello's eyebrows lifted and he whistled softly, tunelessly. "That bad?"

Jack forced a shrug.

"Okay, Jack." Clearly reluctant to let it go, the colonel nodded. "You two work it out."

"There's nothing to work out, Sir. This was a temporary solution to a problem. That's all." The words sounded phony even to him.

Colonel Candello's features tightened slightly. "I'll butt out, for now. But don't you do anything stupid, Jack. Don't do or say something the two of you might come to regret."

"Sir." Neither an agreement nor a denial.

The colonel shook his head wearily. "I'll let you get back to work," he said, turning in the doorway.

Jack didn't answer. He didn't need to. The colonel was already gone.

That night the strained silence that had hovered between them over dinner, splintered suddenly.

Jack had been walking on eggshells around her, sure that one wrong word from him would send her racing to the airport, eager to get away and end this farce.

But, damn it, at the same time, he'd been torturing himself with thoughts of what might have been. He didn't know if he loved her or not—the way he was raised, he'd never been close enough to love to identify it, much less experience it firsthand.

But he did know that he looked forward to the

end of his shift now. He left his desk in a hurry every night, eager to return to this little house where Donna could be found. He liked fighting his way past her panty hose, drying on the rod, to take his morning shower. He liked the smell of her perfume as it seemed to hang in every corner of the house. He liked to watch her push her hair out of her eyes when it got in her way. And making love with her had filled all of the lonely, empty spots inside him.

Even with this terrible, uncomfortable tension between them, there was nowhere he'd rather be.

And he liked the way she hummed in her sleep.

But he couldn't live on the edge like this. Waiting for her to leave would kill him slowly. Much better to go out with a bomb blast and get it over with all at once.

"About Thanksgiving dinner at your father's house," he said.

"What about it?"

She kept her gaze locked on her dinner plate. The pot roast was good, but it wasn't *that* good. She simply couldn't look him in the eye, he thought.

"I just don't know if it's a good idea," he went on.

"Really?" She picked up her untouched plate and stood, turning for the sink.

The frosty tone in her voice sent shards of ice plunging like daggers into his heart. He steeled himself against the pain beginning to well inside. His gaze shot to where she stood at the counter, her back, stiff as a board, to him.

Odd, how hard this was, when he'd been expecting it all along. He'd known all his life that he wasn't worth loving. And he'd known from the first day of this supposed marriage that it would soon end. And he would have been all right with that, if he hadn't allowed himself to care.

"The holiday itself or the idea of us celebrating it?" she asked, drawing him back from the dark thoughts circling his mind.

Anger churned in the pit of his stomach. But the fury was directed at himself, not her. This was his fault. He never should have slept with her. He never should have become accustomed to having her around. To her voice. Her scent. He never should have awakened himself to possibilities that he hadn't considered before.

Jack inhaled sharply, deeply, and said, "Let's stop kidding ourselves, all right?"

"Kidding ourselves?"

She still hadn't turned to look at him. Maybe it was better that way. If he looked into those deep brown eyes of hers, he might falter. Might back away from the only conclusion possible, "What happened between us last night was—"

"What?" She challenged, her fingers curling around the edge of the counter. "A mistake?"

He released a breath he hadn't realized he'd been holding. There. She'd said it. Surprising, really, how much it hurt to know that she, too, considered those few, magical hours to be an error in judgment.

"Donna." He tried to keep his voice steady, even, so she wouldn't know just how much this was costing him. "There's no reason to pretend that last night was anything more than a case of raging hormones. We're both adults. Sex is—"

"Don't say it," she snapped, suddenly turning on him, her dark brown eyes blazing with indignation.

"Say what?" Prepared for her regrets, her anger caught him off guard. Instinctively, he rose to face her.

"'Sex is no big deal, Donna,'" she said in a deep, false voice. Obviously doing an impression of someone who had once thrown those words at her, she went on. "'It has nothing to do with love. Don't be so naive.'"

"I didn't say that."

She jerked him a nod, then shoved her hair out of her eyes. "You didn't have to." Tossing her hands high, she let them fall to slap at her sides. "Amazing. How do I find you guys? What? Am I some kind of creep magnet?"

Donna stomped out of the room, and Jack was no more than two paces behind her. Blast her, he was doing the right thing. Something that was tearing him open inside. He'd be damned before he'd let her lump him in with some jerk without so much as an explanation.

He grabbed her arm, spinning her around to face him. "What the hell are you talking about?"

"You know exactly what I'm talking about." Her eyes seemed to sizzle with sparks of fury. She jerked out of his hold and faced him, chin up defiantly.

Whoever this jerk from her past was, he'd hurt her badly. Old pain was evident in her battle stance.

"Tell me," he said flatly.

"Four years ago, I was engaged to be married."

He nodded. He did remember something about a wedding that didn't happen.

"We were saving ourselves for marriage," she went on, snorting a choked laugh at her own stupidity. "We wanted making love together for the first time to be something...sacred."

He couldn't help feeling a twinge of disappointment. She had been willing to wait for sacred with a different man. With him, she'd given in to her desires. How was he supposed to take that?

"But two nights before the wedding," she continued, her voice strangled with remembered humiliation, "I found him with my maid of honor."

Anger rustled inside him. Anger for the hurt

she'd suffered and because he hadn't been around to kick the man's ass for her.

She shook her head as if she still had a hard time believing it. "When I found them, he had the nerve to tell me that I was overreacting. That sex was no big deal and it didn't have a thing to do with his feelings for me."

"The bastard."

"Thank you," she said absently, and raced ahead. "I found out that he'd been *sacred* all over town." She started pacing wildly, her long, hurried steps carrying her back and forth across the tiny room in record time. "So I called off the wedding, made a fool of myself with my father's adjutant and then ran away."

Huh? What was that last part? he wondered. Then he shrugged it off. Wasn't important at the moment. Besides, she was still talking, the words tumbling from her mouth in a rush, and if he didn't pay attention, he'd be lost.

"Gone four years," she was saying. "And the day I get back, I do it again. Only this time the man actually married me before he says sex doesn't mean anything." She threw a wild look at the ceiling and heaven beyond. "Is this some kind of weird cosmic joke?" she demanded. "Because if it is, I don't get it."

"Donna," he interrupted, determined to at least

defend himself against being lumped together with a lousy ex-fiancé.

"No, Jack. I don't want to hear it." She shot him a look that should have frozen him in his tracks. But marines were made of sterner stuff.

"I am not that bastard who cheated on you and hurt you," he shouted as she walked away from him, headed for their bedroom.

She paused in the doorway and glanced back at him. The ice in her eyes sent a chill through him that ran bone deep. And when she spoke, he knew it was over.

"No, Jack. You're the man who married me for my own good, *then* hurt me."

Twelve

For the next week, they moved like strangers through the little house. No, not strangers, Donna told herself. Strangers at least give each other the courtesy of polite nods and disinterested glances. She and Jack were more like ghosts. Neither of them even seeing the other.

Nights were the worst. Lying in the same bed, where the distance between them was measured like the legend on a map—inches equaled miles.

From her seat on the couch, Donna stared out the window at banks of massed gray clouds, rushing in to cover the sky with the threat of rain. November had arrived suddenly, as it often did in California. Cool, sunny days had disappeared into early morning fogs drifting in off the ocean and cold, damp winds.

She sighed and threw a quick glance at the kitchen timer sitting on the coffee table. One more minute and she'd know for sure. One more minute and her world would change dramatically. Her stomach pitched and rolled briefly and she took several deep breaths in a vain attempt to settle it.

When the timer chirped like a hysterical bird, she jumped and reached for it, stabbing the Off button with her fingertip. Silence crowded around her. She heard her own heartbeat thundering in her ears and imagined she could even hear another, fainter heartbeat marching in time with hers.

Slowly, she set the timer down and picked up the white plastic wand that held the answers to her immediate future. Hesitating only slightly, she looked down at the test squares.

A plus sign.

She gulped in a breath.

Her fingers closed tight around the wand. She felt the sharp sting of tears behind her eyes as she turned her head back to the window. Appropriately enough, the rain had started, splashing polka dots on the glass panes.

Donna wiped a tear from her cheek and blinked the rest of them back into submission. She wouldn't cry. She couldn't afford to. She had to be stronger than that. One hand dropped to her flat abdomen where her child was already growing, counting on her to keep it safe. And loved.

She knew what she had to do. Still clutching the test stick, she stood and, to the accompanying patter of the rain, walked to her bedroom and started packing.

"You can't just leave," her father told her, "without so much as saying goodbye to the man."

"I can't say goodbye to Jack," Donna countered, and glanced at the closed door to her father's office before looking back at him. She knew damn well that if she tried to say goodbye, she'd never leave. And she had to go. For *all* their sakes.

"Donna," her father said, pushing himself out of his chair. Coming around the edge of the desk, he stopped directly in front of her and took both of her hands in his. "You're not thinking this through."

"Yes, I have," she told him, pulling free of him. If she gave in to the need for comfort now, she'd dissolve into a weeping, hysterical mess.

"What about the three months you agreed on?" he countered.

"Things have changed." To say the least.

"What things?"

She shook her head and blinked furiously, determined to keep the tears that were never far away, at bay awhile longer.

"You love him, Donna," he said softly, knowingly. "Even I can see that."

Pain tugged at her insides, poking, prodding.

"It doesn't matter."

"You're wrong," he said, and took the step that brought him right next to her. Laying both hands on her shoulders, he pulled her stiff form up against him and gave her a hug. "It's the only thing that *does* matter."

With his arms around her and her nose buried against his uniform blouse, Donna gave in briefly to the urge to be held. For most of her life her father had been there when she needed him. Ready to do battles on her behalf and right all the wrongs done to her.

She just wished he could fix this, too.

But he couldn't.

No one could.

"Daddy," she whispered, "you don't understand."

"I understand you're both being stubborn. And stupid."

She sniffed and confessed her secret. She had to tell *someone*. "I'm pregnant."

Taking her by the shoulders, he held her at arm's length, surprise etched on his features. "Are you sure?"

She nodded and silently cursed the solitary tear that had defied her to roll down her cheek.

"Does Jack know?"

"No," she said sharply and moved away from her father's gentle touch. "And he's not going to. Not for a while, anyway."

"You can't keep this from him, Donna," he said hotly. "A man has a right to know when he's going to be a father."

She knew all that. And she planned to tell him. In a few months maybe. Or after the baby was born. Just not now. At the moment they both needed time and distance to recover from the charade of their marriage before they tried to work together as single parents.

"I plan to tell him," she countered. "Sometime soon. A month or two maybe. Not now."

"Why the hell not?" Tom Candello's voice lifted in outrage. He stared at her as if he'd never seen her before. "You're walking out on the bargain you two made *and* keeping the fact of his child from him? What's come over you, Donna?"

She snapped. "What's come over me?" she repeated, staring her father square in the eye. "Pride."

He snorted as if to brush away an insignificant factor.

"And it's about damn time, too," she went on, warming to her theme. "After Kyle made a fool of me, I didn't have much pride left."

He tried to interrupt, but she sailed on.

"Then, after I scared your assistant all the way to Greenland, I sank even lower. Heck, I couldn't even face *you* for four years and I *knew* you loved me."

"Donna—"

"Then I make a mess of things again, and Jack rides to the rescue." She threw her hands up in the air and shook her head. "He doesn't want to be married, Dad. He was protecting *your* reputation. He was trying to be a good guy. Hell, all he was missing was the white charger and shining armor."

"Donna, Jack knew what he was doing. No one forced him to marry you."

"No, you're right." She nodded and turned her back on him, walking to a window where she could stare out at Camp Pendleton as the heavens dumped at least an inch of rain on it. Outside, marines in foul-weather gear marched in formation and went about their daily duties despite the steady downpour. Because it *was* their duty. Honor demanded it. Pride.

Still looking at the rain, she continued, her tone softer, less strident now.

"The only thing that prodded Jack into marrying me was his own sense of honor."

"And that's bad?" her father asked, dumbfounded.

He didn't understand, and she wasn't sure she

could explain it as clearly as she *felt* it. But, blast it, she knew she was right.

"Of course not," she said, and laid one hand on the cold, damp, rain-flecked windowpane. "His honor is part of who he is. It's so deeply ingrained in him, he never questions it and wouldn't be able to function without it."

"I don't see what you're getting at here," her father complained on a sigh.

She half turned to look at him. "Don't you get it, Dad? If Jack knew I was pregnant, he'd insist that we stay married. That we continue this charade that's only bringing both of us pain."

Tom Candello's features tightened.

"It's better this way," she assured him, trying not to sound as miserable as she felt. "I don't want a husband whose honor is the only thing keeping him with me."

She waited what seemed like a lifetime but was probably no more than a few eternity-filled seconds.

At last, her father nodded in resignation. "Where will you go?"

Donna wasn't sure if she was pleased or saddened that he had accepted the fact that her leaving was the right thing to do. Forcing a smile, she said, "For the moment, back to Maryland. I can stay with my old roommate for a while. And I'm pretty sure I can get my old job back if I grovel appropriately."

He gave her a wan smile, but nodded. "When are you leaving?"

"Now."

"Now?"

"I have a cab waiting outside," she told him. "My flight out of San Diego is in two hours. I'll just wait at the airport." The truth of the matter was, that she hadn't been able to stay another minute in the tiny house where she'd known such intense joy and misery. She much preferred the sterile, impersonal lounge of a busy airport.

"So soon," he said, then held his arms out toward her. "It feels like you've only been here a few minutes."

She went to him, allowing herself to luxuriate in the comfort of his bear hug for several long minutes. "I'm sorry I'll miss Thanksgiving dinner with you, but this way is better for me."

He smoothed one hand over the back of her head. "I know, kiddo. I just wish you weren't leaving."

Donna pulled back from his embrace and lifted her chin. "I'll be okay, Daddy. Don't worry."

He laughed dryly. "Trust me. I'll worry. And not just about you. But about my grandchild, too." Then he shook his head as if he still couldn't believe it. "A grandfather. Amazing."

Donna reached out and patted his arm. "I have faith in you. You'll be a great grandpa."

"Long distance," he complained.

"Dad…"

He held up both hands in mock surrender.

She picked up her purse from the edge of his desk and started for the door. As she grabbed the doorknob, she turned to say, "I'll call you when I get in."

"Okay."

"And, Dad…" she said, her voice steely. "Don't say a word about the baby to Jack."

He looked offended. "May I remind you, young lady," he said, "that I am a full colonel in the United States Marine Corps? We are trained to keep secrets."

She wasn't convinced. "I mean it."

"Donna, it's up to you to tell him about the baby. But speaking as a man—and a father—don't wait too long."

Donna nodded stiffly and opened the door. An instant later she was gone.

Colonel Tom Candello waited an extra minute, to make sure she was out of sight. Then he left his office to talk some sense into his son-in-law before it was too late.

The gray, rainy day perfectly complemented his mood, Jack thought grimly as he stared, unseeing, out the window. Even Tom had given up trying to talk to him and had run from the office, preferring

Mother Nature's rainstorm to Jack's black frame of mind.

When his office door opened and closed again quickly, he didn't even turn to look at the interloper. "Whoever you are, turn around and get out."

"I'll pretend you didn't say that," the colonel said flatly.

Startled, Jack jumped to his feet, shooting his desk chair backward where it crashed into the wall and bounced off a gray steel file cabinet. "Colonel, Sir," he said. "My apologies. I didn't know it was you, Sir."

"At ease, Jack," the colonel told him. "I'm here as Donna's father, not your commanding officer."

Jack's stance relaxed, but he turned a wary eye on the man crossing the room to stand opposite his desk. "No offense, Colonel, but I don't have anything to say to my father-in-law."

"Good," the other man snapped, leaning both hands on the edges of the desk and pinning him with a sharp, dark brown gaze amazingly like his daughter's. "Then I'll talk. You listen."

"Sir—"

"Donna just left my office," the colonel went on.

Donna? Here? Just a few steps away?

"She had a cab waiting," the other man was saying.

"A cab?" Jack asked. "Why didn't she use the

truck?" He'd been riding to work with one of the other sergeants so that Donna would have use of their only vehicle.

"Because she's on her way to the airport."

He felt as though someone had just delivered a solid blow to his midsection. Air left his lungs like a balloon had been popped.

"The airport, Sir?" he repeated, surprised he was able to speak at all past the sudden dryness in his throat.

"She's leaving, Jack. For good."

Stunned, he said only, "Maybe that's for the best, Sir." But inside, emotions tumbled through him, leaving him shaken. He stiffened his legs in response, to steady his stance. She hadn't even stayed the three months they'd agreed on in the beginning.

How could he feel so empty and still be breathing? he wondered. And how could his heart keep beating when it was laying shattered in his chest?

"Not this time, Jack."

His gaze snapped to the older man's furious eyes. "With all due respect, Sir," he said tightly, "this is none of your business."

"Don't be a fool, Jack. Fight for your wife. Your marriage."

"There's nothing to fight for," he muttered bleakly. "It's over."

"It's only over if you surrender or retreat," the colonel told him. "I've known you a long time, Jack, and I don't think I've seen you happier than you were with Donna. For a while, I thought it was going to work out."

So had he, Jack thought. In his dreams. His fantasies. It was only in reality that he lost her.

"If you *do* care for my daughter, fight for her," the colonel said, pushing up and away from the desk. "Don't make the same mistakes I did."

"Sir?"

"If I had been smarter," the colonel said, "I would have fought like hell to keep Donna's mother. If you love somebody enough, problems can be worked out."

"This isn't the same thing, Colonel," Jack said softly. "If Donna loved me or wanted to stay married, she wouldn't have left."

The colonel shook his head, clearly disgusted, then turned abruptly and stalked toward the door. He stopped and glanced back at Jack. "You tell yourself that, if it helps. And if I'm wrong and you don't love her, then stay here, First Sergeant, and let her go."

When he was alone again, Jack stared blankly at the closed door. Let her go? he thought, and felt a yawning emptiness open inside him. In his imagination, the years stretched out ahead of him.

Long, lonely years that he would spend alone, wondering where Donna was and what she was doing. His nights would be filled with torturous images of Donna, lying in another man's arms, having another man's children.

His hands fisted tightly as that emptiness inside him blossomed, swelling into proportions large enough to swallow him whole. He stared into the blackness that was his life and realized the one fact that he'd been trying to deny for weeks. He loved her. *Really* loved her. So much so, that without her, his life would be an endless succession of barren days and desolate nights.

But she was gone. Left without a word.

Still, he asked himself, if he had admitted his love for her sooner, if he had risked rejection and confessed his feelings, would she have left?

He didn't know. But, damn it, he was through retreating. He was going to make a grab at the chance offered him. The chance for what so many lucky people took for granted every day. Love. Acceptance. Belonging to a family.

Moving quickly, he raced across the floor and out the door, then marched double-time to the colonel's office just down the hall. He knocked perfunctorily and pushed the door open wide enough to poke his head inside.

"Permission to take a personal day, Sir?" he asked.

"Granted," the colonel shouted to be heard over the already closing door. Then Tom Candello leaned back in his chair and grinned at the ceiling.

After checking in at the ticket window, Donna gripped the strap of her carry-on bag tighter and started walking across the terminal toward her gate. Other travelers, most of them in a much better frame of mind than she, pushed past her with muttered apologies, eager to be on their way. The weekday, afternoon crowd of people surprised her, but other than that, she paid little attention to any of them.

Weaving her way in and out of the mob of people and luggage, she hardly noticed when someone else bumped into her from behind. But when that someone made a grab for her tote bag, she turned around quickly and stopped dead.

"Jack?"

God, he looked wonderful. Soaking wet, his short hair plastered to his skull, rivulets of rain water coursing down his body to puddle on the shiny linoleum floor. He wiped one hand across his face irritably, then took her elbow in a firm, insistent grip.

"What are you doing?" she demanded as he started dragging her toward the exit.

"Taking you home," he said shortly, his voice carrying over the noise of the crowd and the squish-squeak of his combat boots on the floor.

Donna tossed a wild look around her, but no one was paying the slightest attention to her and the determined marine carrying her off. She could scream, she told herself, then immediately pictured the sensation that would cause.

Instead she planted her tennis shoes firmly in place and jerked herself free of him.

Grumbling quietly to himself, Jack only snatched her carry-on bag and started walking off again.

"Hey!" she shouted, and sprinted after him, finally getting a good grip on the strap of the bag and dragging him to a halt. "Give me my bag," she demanded.

He tugged at the strap, hauling her closer. "I'm not letting you go, Donna."

One brief, brilliant flash of hope rose up in her chest before fizzling out. For a moment she'd actually allowed herself to believe that he'd come for her because he loved her and couldn't lose her.

But there was a much bigger chance that her father had shot off his mouth, telling Jack about the baby.

She yanked on the cloth strap. "Go back to the base, Jack," she said, and was proud of herself for keeping her voice free of the emotion strangling her. "It's better this way. In a couple of months you can file for divorce and we can both go on with our lives."

Jack looked at her long and hard. How had he

ever imagined that he would be able to live without her? All through that nightmare drive on a rain-slicked highway in a stolen—borrowed—Jeep, he'd rehearsed what he would say. Thought about how he should approach her.

Now that he was here, though, and faced with the most risky mission of his life, there was only one thing to do.

He let go of the bag and grabbed her in one smooth movement. Holding her tightly to his rain-soaked body, he coiled his arms around her. Her mouth opened in surprise and he lowered his head to take advantage of the possibilities.

The clamoring noise of the busy airport faded away. The bustling crowds of travelers dissolved into nothingness. His icy-cold, wet uniform held no discomfort anymore. There was only one reality in his universe and he was holding her.

Cupping the back of her head, he lay siege to her mouth, showing her without words that she was his breath, his heart...his life.

When at last he felt her go limp in his arms, he lifted his head, oblivious to the smiling faces of half the population of San Diego surrounding them.

Holding her face between his palms, his thumbs smoothed gently over her cheekbones and his gaze moved over her features hungrily. Then he said the words he'd thought he would never have the opportunity to say. "I love you."

She blinked and a solitary tear trickled from the corner of her eye. His right thumb caught it and wiped it away. He would spend the rest of his life seeing to it that she never had a reason to cry again.

As resolve filled him, he said the words again. "I *love* you, Donna." When she still didn't speak, he fought a frisson of panic and continued in his best, no-nonsense voice. "And you'd damn well better love me back. That's an order."

A long moment ticked by before she grinned. "Yes, First Sergeant," she snapped before throwing herself into his arms.

His heart started beating again as he buried his face in the crook of her neck, inhaling the sweetness of her perfume and reveling in the warmth of her love.

Then he reached down, grabbed up her bag and tossed the strap over his shoulder. When that was done, he swept her up into his arms and smiled like a idiot when she wrapped her arms around his neck.

And to the sounds of applause and hoots of approval from the crowd, he carried her back to the Jeep—and home.

As the rain pelted against the windows and the quiet gray light of a stormy afternoon filled their tiny bedroom, they lay exhausted in each other's arms.

"I love you," Jack whispered, and bent to trail a line of kisses down her throat.

"I love you." Donna sighed and tipped her head to one side, allowing him easier access. Her fingertips smoothed across his shoulders and she smiled, more happy than any one woman had a right to be.

Propping himself up on one elbow, Jack looked down at her, suddenly serious. As his right hand skimmed along her body, creating a ribbon of gooseflesh in its wake, he said, "I never thought that I would be saying those words to anyone."

She smiled up at him. "Get used to them, I'll want to hear them often."

"I love you," he whispered, and bent his head to kiss her. "You are everything I always wanted and never counted on having."

"Oh, Jack…" Tears stung the backs of her eyes, but she refused to cry. Not on the happiest day of her life.

He leaned over and planted a quick, hard kiss on her tummy. "I hope we just made a baby, Donna. I want to have children with you."

Her breath caught in her throat and those darn tears filled her eyes again.

He kissed her, a soft, swift kiss, then went on. "I want to build a family with you, Donna. The family I always wanted but never thought I'd find."

She reached up and dusted her palm along the side of his face. How could she ever have even

considered leaving this strong, gentle man? she
wondered, and then smiled at him proudly.

"You want babies?" she asked. "Well, Marine,
this is your lucky day. Have I got a surprise for
you."

* * * * *

SADIE JOLTED when Rick came up behind her. As hot as the July sun felt on her skin, his nearness made her temperature inch up just that much higher. There had never been another man in her life who had affected her like Rick Pruitt did. Not even her ex-husband-the-lying-cheating-weasel.

She took a breath, steadied herself, then looked up at him, trying not to fall into those dark brown eyes. It wasn't easy. He was tall and muscular and even in his jeans and T-shirt, Rick looked like a man used to giving orders and having them obeyed.

He was the quintessential Texas man. A wealthy rancher in his own right. Add the Marine Corps to that and you had an impossible-to-resist combination. As the quickening heat in her body could testify.

She'd always had a reputation for being prim and proper. The perfect Price heiress. Always doing and saying the proper thing. But that, she assured herself, was in another life. Just remembering the night she'd shared with Rick three years ago had her body stirring to life.

"Can you come in for a minute? There's something you need to see."

"Okay." He sounded intrigued but confused.

He wouldn't be for long.

She headed for the front door, let herself in and almost sighed with relief as the blissfully cool air-conditioned room welcomed her. A graying blonde woman in her fifties hurried over to her. "Miss Sadie, everything's fine upstairs. They're sleeping like angels."

"Thanks, Hannah," she said with a smile, not bothering to look back at Rick now. It was too late to back out. Her time had come. "I'll just go up and check on them."

The housekeeper gave Rick a long look, shifted her gaze to Sadie and smiled. "I'll be in the kitchen if you need anything."

Rick pulled his hat off and waited until Hannah was gone before he spoke. "Who's asleep? What's this about?"

"You'll see." She still didn't look at him, just walked across the marble floor toward the wide, sweeping staircase. "Come on upstairs."

If you liked this preview, pick up a copy of
ONE NIGHT, TWO HEIRS by Maureen Child
in July 2011 and don't miss a single installment
of this passionate new miniseries!

TEXAS CATTLEMAN'S CLUB: THE SHOWDOWN

They are rich and powerful, hot and wild.
For these Texans, it's showdown time!

Available from Harlequin® Desire® July–December 2011